A *Summer* TO REMEMBER

CAROLYN SWAN HILL

Inspiring Voices®
A Service of Guideposts

Inspiring Voices books may be ordered through booksellers or by contacting:

Inspiring Voices
1663 Liberty Drive
Bloomington, IN 47403
www.inspiringvoices.com
1-(866) 697-5313

ISBN: 978-1-4624-0543-5 (sc)
ISBN: 978-1-4624-0544-2 (e)

Library of Congress Control Number: 2013903233

Printed in the United States of America

Inspiring Voices rev. date: 2/25/2013

A Summer To Remember

This story is about a young woman's first extended vacation away from home, and how she coped and grew. Life took on many twists and turns changing her life, and she is forced to see things in a different light. Her heartache brings about many good changes, and she has to start a new beginning. Read about Nicole's journeys, and how she is off to a new adventure with lots of memories and hopeful for a wonderful future.

It was the first day of June, a day that would normally be warm, but it was chilly in Estes Park, Colorado. Nicole Thomas was wearing shorts and a T-shirt, but the cool wind had her seeking the warmth of the sun. Her long, below the shoulder length light-brown hair was tossing in the wind, whipping into her blue eyes, and her tall slender frame made it hard to keep her balance. She was visiting family friends at their cabin resort for two weeks, a gift from her parents, which would ultimately be stretched out for most of the summer. This was to be a most memorable summer, a summer she would never forget.

The mountain views were spectacularly breathtaking, and the sky was streaked with vivid shades of blue that were indescribably different from the sky in Ohio, where she lived. She was twenty and had just completed her sophomore year of college.

Catherine, a family friend, had picked her up at the airport and had stopped on the way back to the resort to let Nicole see the beautiful scenery of the foothills. After a few minutes Catherine called her back to reality, telling her they needed to get going. She assured Nicole that there would be more to come and more to see.

Catherine Maine was a six foot tall, muscular woman in her late forties. She had a full smile of straight white teeth, short wavy white hair and ice-blue eyes. She was an attractive lady, and Nicole was happy to see her again.

Catherine was the caretaker of the cabins, and Nicole offered to be her assistant while she stayed at the resort. After their chores were completed, and until the evening meal, they would be free to roam the foothills of Rocky Mountain National Park where Catherine could spot wildlife during the hours of daylight or darkness, and that talent proved to be quite interesting to Nicole. Catherine was good friends with all the local park rangers, and she wanted to introduce Nicole to a few of them.

After the plane ride, Nicole was tired, and wasn't up to meeting anyone else before going to the resort, and she and Catherine went directly to their cabin. Catherine lit a fire before the evening chill set in. In a short time it became cozy and warm, and Nicole began to nod off to sleep. Catherine awakened her, as they were to have dinner with their hosts at their cabin.

Virginia and Norman Parker had a lovely cabin with wide hardwood floors, area rugs and comfortable furnishings. As Nicole glanced around the room, she noticed framed photographs on the walls that Norman had taken over the years. The art captured the feel of the majestic mountains in the area, and she asked Norman if one particular photo included her father. He nodded and told her about the event. They sat around and talked, watching the flickering fire in the fireplace. It was so inviting to just sit awhile and listen to the stories. After dinner, they returned to the living room and sat near the crackling fire while the smell of cinnamon and spice filled the air. Virginia offered them a drink of the spiced cider she had made in the large pot hanging in the fireplace. It smelled so good and was soothingly warm.

Nicole knew from the moment she stepped into the Parker cabin that she was going to enjoy her vacation with them and Catherine. She felt at home, and she knew that she wasn't going to have time to miss her family or friends.

Catherine nudged her and asked, "Are you ready to hit the hay, little lady?" Nicole nodded, and then she hugged Norman and Virginia thanking them for the wonderful dinner and time together. Nicole and Catherine then headed for their cabin.

The night air was brisk, and the sweater Nicole wrapped around her shoulders didn't seem to keep her warm. When they stepped into their cabin, it was nice and warm from the fire Catherine had built earlier.

"Thank you, Catherine, for a wonderful first day," Nicole told her, "but if you don't mind, I am really tired and would like to go to bed."

Nicole headed for her bedroom, which was much larger than the bedroom she had at home.

This was to be her home in Colorado. It was especially nice to have her own bathroom that she didn't have to share with other girls in the college dorm. She decided to leave the unpacking until morning. Her full-sized bed was very comfortable, and when she snuggled under the layer of blankets and comforter, she wasn't awake for long.

It seemed that morning came very quickly. Catherine was already up and in her shower when Nicole awakened. She glanced at the clock and saw that it was only six thirty. Nicole thought to herself, "*Why are we getting up so early? There couldn't be any cabins to clean at this hour.*"

Catherine quietly opened Nicole's door and said, "Rise and shine. Breakfast is served at seven o'clock, and then our work begins."

Nicole was a working girl now, and she wanted to please Catherine. She was eager to start a new day in the mountains, so she got up and headed for the shower. After drying off, Nicole blow-dried her long hair as it would not dry quickly in the cool temperatures. It didn't take her long to get ready.

Catherine told her to dress warmer for the mornings and that a change of clothes would be necessary by mid-afternoon as the temperatures would be much warmer.

They went to the dining hall together where Catherine introduced Nicole to everyone in Norman and Virginia's employ. Charlie and Susan were the cooks; Jon was the grounds-keeper; Alberta and Evelyn were in charge of laundry; Judy, Anne and Mary Lou were the kitchen help; and Catherine and Nicole were the cabin maids. Nicole would learn very quickly that Charlie and Susan were very important people, as she would really work up an appetite working and touring in the higher altitudes.

Nicole and Catherine had some cabins to clean thoroughly, as several new families were on their way. They finished just in time for lunch. After eating, Catherine grinned from ear to ear and said, "I've got some friends I want you to meet."

They jumped into her jeep and drove up a mountain pass. As they drove, they noticed that it was snowing in the higher elevations above them, and Catherine stated, "We don't want to get caught up in that blizzard."

Nicole questioned, "But it's already June! Why should we be leery of a few snowflakes?"

Catherine laughed and said, "Don't you kid yourself, young lady. I've seen it snow even in July. It wasn't the bad stuff then, but it still snowed. You can't trust the snow storms in early June around here, but we don't have much further to go anyway." Just then she pulled off onto a narrow dirt road, and they drove up to a ranger's station. A very nice looking blonde-haired young man stood leaning against a post on the porch of the large cabin.

When Nicole and Catherine got out of the jeep, Catherine said, "Hello Scott. I want you to meet someone. This is Nicole Thomas, and she is my assistant for a few weeks at the lodge."

Scott quickly offered his hand as a welcome. While he still had her hand, he said to Nicole, "My name is Scott Thompson."

Nicole responded with a smile. He was very attractive, and she felt her hand getting warm. She didn't mean to stare, but she couldn't take her eyes off of him. He was tall with a tanned muscular build, big blue eyes, and a nice smile with deep inset dimples.

Just then, another tall man walked out onto the porch and introduced himself to her. "Hello. I am Todd Wheeler, and I am also a ranger here with my buddy, Scott. It's nice to meet you. Catherine has told us a little bit about you, and we have been looking forward to meeting and getting to know you during your stay here in the Rockies. Would you like a seat, young lady, and maybe something to drink? I would be happy to get you a soda or tea if you'd like."

Nicole heard herself stammer a little as she spoke to Todd, "I'm fine, thank you. I don't care for anything right now, but thank you for asking." She looked at Catherine, and Catherine quickly looked away from her. Nicole knew Catherine was up to something.

The two men spent some time telling Nicole and Catherine wildlife stories and showed them numerous photos of the different wildlife that had been spotted in the area. They also said they wanted to show Nicole places that were filled with herds of elk and deer.

She was interested in seeing all the wildlife they had talked about, but she wanted Catherine along until she got to know them better.

Catherine must have read her mind because she expressed a desire to go along.

Scott replied, "We always like to take Catherine along with us because she can spot a herd a mile away. We've taken her on a lot of hunts to help ear tag some wildlife. We tag them as a harmless way to mark them for future observation."

Nicole was really amazed at how interesting their jobs seemed to be, and how much they enjoyed Catherine being with them. She felt privileged and honored to be asked to ride with them on a few of their searches.

Scott was explaining to Nicole that the elk and deer would feed at dawn and dusk, and dusk was usually the best time to locate them.

Catherine pointed to the right side of the jeep, and said softly, "A small herd of deer is over in the brush."

Evening was drawing near and Nicole couldn't see a thing in the dim light, but Todd shone a small spotlight in that direction, and sure enough there were five deer staring into the beam of light. They weren't moving at all as though they were mesmerized by the light.

Nicole felt a rush of warmth flow through her, and she gasped. It was exciting to see her first spotting.

Scott asked if she was all right, as he heard her gasp.

She whispered, "They are such amazing animals. The buck looks so kingly with his large rack of antlers stretching high above his head." She was overwhelmed with the sight. She felt such a peace come over her just thinking about being near such magnificent animals. She thanked Catherine more than once that evening for taking her to the ranger's station.

As Nicole and Catherine were leaving, Catherine smiled and said, "You are most welcome, young lady. I'm glad you like the outdoors and appreciate the animals too. We seem to have a lot in common when it comes to recognizing God's beauty on this earth, and it is especially beautiful out here. By the way, tomorrow is Sunday. Would you like to go with me to the little country church down the road from the resort?"

"I think I would really enjoy that," Nicole replied.

"It is nothing fancy, but very picturesque with the mountains as a backdrop. The music is beautiful, and the sermons are always good. I haven't really found anything to complain about where that little church is concerned. I am glad you'll be going with us. Norman and Virginia will be going too, and I know they will be happy that you want to go along. After church and dinner, we'll do some cleaning, and if we have time we'll go back to see Scott and Todd. I'll ask them to show you the films of the wildlife that have been found in this area, so you'll know what to look for when we go on the tagging searches. It's really quite interesting, plus that will give them more time to get to know you."

Sunday morning was a beautiful day. The sun was bright and warm, and puffy white clouds were few and far between. It was a beautiful day.

The church was made of gray stone, and the steeple was very high. It was a lovely old church that showed history in its making. Each stone was hand carved and set. Catherine must have known what Nicole was thinking because she brought her a brochure on the church and its history. Nicole laughed out loud while they were in the foyer. "Catherine, you can read my mind, can't you?"

The service was starting, so they walked inside and sat with Norman and Virginia. It was a wonderful service, and the music was pleasant to her ears. She loved to hear those old hymns, and every one they sang, she knew almost all the words by heart.

After church was over, Catherine and Nicole were standing on the sidewalk waiting for Norman and Virginia who were talking with Scott. She hadn't seen him in the service, but Catherine said she had. He looked even nicer than he had yesterday, because today he was not in uniform. His golden hair was neatly combed, and it shimmered in the sunlight. She caught herself staring at him, and then he looked at her and smiled.

Virginia asked Scott to have dinner with all of them at the resort. Scott looked at Nicole and smiled again. "That would be lovely Virginia, and thank you for asking me."

Nicole saw Scott looking at her. She felt a lump in her throat, and knew she couldn't speak.

Scott asked if she would like to ride back to the resort with him. She looked at Catherine who smiled and nodded. All of a sudden she felt as though she was the clumsiest person in the world because she was all feet, and was constantly tripping over them. It was embarrassing to her, but Scott didn't let on that he even noticed.

When they arrived back at The Haven Resort, he jumped out of his jeep and came around the jeep to open her door. He was so charming. With a smile he gently grabbed her hand and gave it a little squeeze as he helped her out. She gave him a quick smile and shyly mused, "Thank you for not letting on that I am very nervous and clumsy."

He didn't let go of her hand but gently pulled it to his lips and pressed a soft kiss on the back of it.

She could have melted on the spot, but she remained somewhat composed. Nicole knew she was turning red because she felt warm. He had to know that she was beginning to like him and was hoping that she wasn't reading too much into his attention. He walked with her into the dining hall where they sat down beside one other on a bench.

Catherine and Virginia stared at them with sheepish grins. Nicole felt embarrassed again, but Scott broke the ice by talking to Norman about business and the weather.

Scott asked, "Catherine, Will you and Nicole be coming to the station this afternoon? I would really like to show Nicole some of the films we have on the wildlife in this area."

"I already told her we would visit with you after we finish our duties here. Is three o'clock too late?"

"That will be fine. Virginia and Norman, would you like to come along too?" Scott questioned.

Virginia replied, "No, but thank you for asking. We have six new guests coming in this afternoon, and they will be staying for ten days, so we must welcome them upon their arrival. Todd may be interested in their oldest daughter. From what I understand she is quite a beauty, and is a senior in college. Maybe for fun and a chance to meet you both, she could come along with Nicole and Catherine sometime."

Scott nodded as he finished his meal. He was getting up from the table when he looked at Nicole. "I will see you this afternoon young lady, and thank you Norman, Virginia and Catherine so much for the delicious meal and lovely company." Then he headed for the door.

Nicole never thought they would get all the beds made and the cabins cleaned for the new vacationers, but she and Catherine worked at top speed to finish. Before the family of six arrived, they were in Catherine's jeep headed for the ranger's station.

When they arrived, Nicole noticed right away that Scott's jeep was not there. Todd greeted them at the steps and said, "Scott had to go check on some cages, but he should be back shortly. We have a new ranger with us now, and I would like both of you to meet him. This is Bill Martin, and he is originally from Ohio."

Bill, like Todd and Scott, was a tall and attractive man. He was very tan with dark brown hair and brown eyes, and was very muscular. Nicole, being five feet and eight inches, had to look up to him, even when he was standing on the ground.

Catherine began to tell Todd and Bill about the new family that would be arriving that day. She told them what Virginia had said about the oldest daughter being in college and is believed to be quite attractive.

Todd raised his eyebrows and looked over at Bill, "Are you ready for a challenge Bill?"

Nicole didn't particularly like that response, because people do not need to fight for the attention of another person. Liking someone should never become a contest.

Todd explained that Scott may be out for some time since he wasn't back already, and maybe they should start watching the films he had wanted Nicole to see. Catherine told her they could wait a while longer, so they might as well watch the films to pass the time until Scott came back. The films were two hours long, and when they were finished there was still no sight of Scott.

Nicole asked, "Is Scott doing something dangerous?" She was beginning to get a little anxious. Todd and Bill grinned.

Todd answered, "No, it's nothing dangerous. He just had to check on some cages we put out to catch some critters to tag. If you have to go back, I'll tell him you were concerned, and maybe he will call you. Okay?"

She nodded and was embarrassed that she had let them know she might be interested in Scott.

Catherine looked at her and chuckled, "We'd better go on back to the resort and see what Charlie and Susan have fixed for supper. When you don't have to prepare the meals, you like to eat while the food is still warm."

Nicole answered, "I am getting pretty hungry." To the men she said, "Hey thanks fellows for the movies. They were very enlightening. See you tomorrow maybe."

Bill felt sorry for her. "Nicole, it was nice meeting you and Catherine. I'll make sure Scott calls you when he gets back."

"Thank you Bill."

They got into Catherine's jeep and in silence drove back to the resort. When they arrived, Catherine softly touched Nicole's arm and said, "He'll be just as disappointed as you are that he didn't get to spend some time with you. I bet he'll call. You'll see."

When they went into the dining hall to eat, Virginia and Norman were waiting on them to introduce the Simmons family. Virginia said, "Ladies, this is Mr. James Simmons, his lovely wife, Barbara, daughters, Emily and Sharon, and their young sons, Steve and Timothy. Emily is the beautiful college girl I was telling you about, and I hope that the two of you will include both the girls in some of your festivities."

Nicole politely went over to Emily and said, "It's very nice to meet you, and I hope we can become good friends while you are here."

Emily responded. "Thank you."

Catherine said her hellos to the whole family, and they all sat down together and ate dinner. Emily asked what there was to do around the resort for entertainment.

Catherine answered, "We go hiking, ride bikes, go on sightseeing tours, visit the ranger's station to watch films, play cards, play bingo, swim in the pool, go to town occasionally, or anything else that is within reason."

Emily stated under her breath, "How boring!"

Nicole heard her and responded, "From what Catherine has told me, I don't believe there is anything boring around here. I plan on having a great time."

"I'll believe it when I see it," Emily said under her breath.

There was no more conversation between Emily, Catherine and Nicole for the rest of the meal. They only listened to Norman, Virginia, Mr. and Mrs. Simmons, Sharon and their boys.

When they all finished eating, Virginia said, "I hope you will all enjoy your stay here with us, and if there is anything we can do to make you more comfortable, please let us know."

Emily piped up, "I know I don't have enough blankets on my bed. That open room you have me in is so cold, and since I have to share a room with my sister, at least I want to be comfortable."

Virginia stated, "Catherine and Nicole will get right on that for you."

When Catherine got up she nudged Nicole for her to come along. When they reached the outside, Catherine stopped and looked at her. "I don't think we are going to have a very good time with Miss Emily."

"She sounds a little spoiled to me," Nicole said out loud.

"Oh well, let's get the little princess a few more blankets and see if we can get the room a little warmer for her."

When they went to the Simmons' cabin and went to the loft where Emily and Sandy were staying, Emily came out of the bathroom. "Don't touch any of my things while you are cleaning up."

Catherine answered, "All right."

Emily looked at Nicole and sneered, "You could be really pretty if you wore some makeup and different clothes. Are you poor or something?"

"No, I am not poor, and I don't like to wear a lot of makeup, as I like to look my natural self. And as for my clothes, I am here to work and play, not go to a ball."

Emily turned quickly to go back into her bathroom.

"Emily, if you want it to be warmer in here, you're going to have to keep the windows shut," Catherine stated.

Emily retorted, "I have to have my windows open when I sleep. Heat rises you know, and I need plenty of fresh air. It's better for my complexion and lungs."

Catherine restated, "Well, it will stay warmer in here if you only open one window just a crack instead of all the way."

Nicole could tell that Catherine was getting a little upset and was ready to leave.

As they were walking back to the cabin, Catherine snapped, "I bet that pretty young lady has never been taught how to be gracious to anyone, but she sure does need to learn it. I can see right now that we are not going to have a lovely next ten days with her tagging along."

Nicole nodded and laughed a little.

When they reached the doorway of their cabin the phone was ringing. Nicole ran to pick it up, but it stopped. She wondered if it was Scott. She wanted to call the ranger's station to see if it was him, but she didn't want to appear anxious. Bill or Todd might answer the phone and say that Scott wasn't back yet.

Just as she was settling in for the night the phone rang, and she sprang from her bed to answer it. It wasn't Scott. It was her parents. She was glad to hear from them, but was disappointed at the same time. They told her they had tried to reach her earlier, but no one answered, so she knew Scott had not called. After a short conversation with both her mom and dad, she slipped back into bed and pulled the covers up around her neck. She couldn't fall asleep because she was thinking about Scott. She wondered if he was all right, if he might have a girlfriend that no one was telling her about, or if he might think she was already becoming infatuated over him when he might not feel the same way. She looked over at the clock, and it was one o'clock in the morning. She couldn't think about him anymore because six thirty would come early, and she didn't want anyone to see her with bags under her eyes, especially him.

When the alarm went off, Nicole wanted to put the clock under her pillow. She didn't want to hear it anymore, but she realized she had to get up. She took a quick cool shower to help awaken her. She put on her clothes, dried and combed her hair, brushed her teeth, put on a little makeup and ran out of her room to meet Catherine.

They walked to the dining hall and Catherine said, "I heard you talking to your parents last night, and I'm sorry Scott didn't call you. Maybe the guys forgot to tell him. Anyway, I know you probably had a hard time sleeping, but don't you worry your pretty little head about Mr. Scott. I know he likes you. I can sometimes tell about these things, and I'm a pretty good judge of character."

Nicole answered, "Thanks Catherine for being so kind, and for knowing me well enough to give me words of encouragement."

They went through the line choosing their breakfast, said their hellos to everyone in the kitchen, and then sat by themselves at one of the smaller tables. They had almost finished when Scott appeared.

He came over to their table, sat down beside Nicole and told her how sorry he was for not being at the ranger's station when she was there. "Todd left a note to have me call you, but I didn't call because I got back so late, and I knew you would probably be in bed.

"When I went out to look at the cages, one had been ripped off at the stake and was badly bent, so I had to throw it away. I found a very large bear print on the ground near the cage. It looked like it belonged to a grizzly, and they usually aren't seen this far down in the foothills. I also found a dead deer that was torn to shreds and was partially buried under some brush and leaves. It had been half eaten, so I looked at some other cages, and talked to some campers without trying to scare them. I needed to warn them at the same time. It was a little scary to think that a grizzly is roaming free in this area. When they are hungry, nothing stops them but a bullet, and we don't want to think about going that route unless it is necessary. We don't want anyone to get hurt or killed by it either."

"Scott, how do you warn the campers, and what do you tell them to do?" Nicole asked.

Scott replied, "Well, first we try not to alarm them to the point they run for their lives. Then we tell them not to keep food out of any kind, to keep a campfire burning day and night, and to never go anywhere alone. A grizzly will stock a person. If he is really hungry, he won't care how many are in the group, but he will usually stock only one at a time, then he'll wait until he can corner you. He'll swat you so hard with his claws, that if you are not dead, you will wish you were. Then he will drag you off somewhere so he can feast on his kill. Then he will bury the remains for a later feeding. Sometimes people are never found. So please, don't go anywhere without one of us or Catherine. Okay?"

Nicole nodded.

When Scott finished telling them of his find and explaining his whereabouts yesterday, Emily walked in and came over to their table asking, "Now who is this handsome man? Have you been holding out on me ladies?"

Catherine cleared her throat in disgust and said, "Oh, yes! Scott, this is Emily Simmons, a guest of ours for the next ten days. Scott is one of our rangers for this area."

"Oh, Scott," Emily said sheepishly, "Are you the one who is interested in Nicole? What do you see in such a plain girl? How old are you anyway? About twenty-five? I am twenty-two, and I'm a college senior. I probably have more in common with you than her, we are much closer in age."

Scott politely acknowledged her presence but continued to look at Nicole and asked, "Will you be coming out to the station today? I'd really like to make up for our lost time yesterday. I'd like to take you around a little and show you some of the scenery on our routes."

Before Nicole could open her mouth to reply, Emily blurted out, "Well, what about me? Don't I get a tour? After all I am a guest here at this resort, and she's just hired help."

"You are more than welcome to come to the station. I am quite sure Todd or Bill would be more than happy to show you around, but I have plans with Nicole."

Emily was beginning to show her true spoiled self by whimpering. "Well, what if I don't like Todd or Bill, and I want you to show me around? I've never met this Bill or Todd. I might not find them attractive like I do you."

Nicole began to feel angry, and Catherine noticed. She lightly touched one of Nicole's arms, patted it gently, and whispered softly, "She's not worth you getting all upset over. He won't be interested in her. She's too pushy."

Nicole smiled and turned to Scott, "I'd be happy to come over when we get our chores done. That is if Catherine will bring me. What time do you think we'll get done Catherine?"

Catherine nodded, "Is three o'clock or so a good time?"

Scott smiled. "Sure, that would be great. We'll see you then."

Emily glared at Catherine and blurted out, "I'll be ready by then."

Catherine and Nicole had never seen such a mess as Emily's family cabin. The girls' clothes were thrown everywhere. Sharon was embarrassed and was trying to pick things up when Emily walked in. She looked at Sharon, then Catherine and Nicole and said, "It's their job to clean up after the guests, so quit picking up the dirty laundry."

Sharon replied, "No it's not their job to clean up our clothes. They only clean the cabin, give us fresh towels and stuff. You need to quit being so mean and stupid."

Emily screamed, "Don't call me stupid, Sharon! You are the stupid one in here picking up things when they should be doing it. They're the hired help, not us."

Then in a demanding voice Emily told Catherine and Nicole, "And you two better hurry up because I want to take a nice bubble bath and get into something nice for our three o'clock appointment with Scott. And don't worry, Nicole, I'll have him let you down easy. You can probably have one of the other fellows. I like what I saw in Scott, and I usually get what I want, so you be a nice little girl and stay out of my way. Okay?"

Nicole wanted to haul off and slap her, but she knew that would not accomplish anything. It would only cause more trouble.

Catherine winked at her and whispered, "Let's hurry up and get out of here."

When they finished, they practically ran out of the cabin and went quickly to their own.

"I can't believe the nerve of that girl, can you?" Nicole asked.

"No, she will get what is coming to her in the end. They always do, and I bet Scott will put her in her place when we get there," Catherine replied.

Nicole said, "I wish we could just leave without her."

Catherine stated, "That would be nice, but we'd never hear the end of it. Maybe she will be different when we get her alone with us."

Catherine tried to make Nicole feel better, but she didn't feel good about Emily tagging along. She just knew there was going to be trouble with her being so spoiled.

It was almost three o'clock, and Nicole was hoping that Emily was still taking her bubble bath so that she and Catherine could wait another five minutes and then leave without her. At five minutes after three, out walked Emily dressed in her tight faded jeans with a tight, short midriff top. She was also exposing a diamond stud in her navel. She had on the wrong type of shoes for hiking mountain paths. She was on the hunt, but not for wildlife. She was out to find a ranger, and his name was Scott Thompson.

When they arrived at the ranger's station Todd was the first one to greet everyone. He was really falling all over himself to meet Emily, but she wasn't the least bit interested in him. She had already made up her mind about Todd. He was too easy for her. She wanted a challenge, and that was Scott. She knew he liked someone else, and she wanted that to change in her favor.

She was introduced to Bill, and he acted as though he wasn't all that impressed. He came over to Nicole and asked how she was, and if Scott had ever called her. She said, "No, but he came over this morning to tell me what happened. Thank you for asking."

"I told him you were concerned and wanted to make sure he was all right," Bill responded.

Emily butted right in and looked at Bill. "You are a tall, good looking ranger, now aren't you? I might just like to get to know you better."

Bill looked straight at Emily and said, "Well Emily, I think Todd is more your type."

Just then Scott came from around the back of the station. Emily ran to meet him and put her arm inside of his, walking in front of everyone. Scott released her from his arm. "I see you've met everyone, and I have asked Todd to show you around today."

Emily snapped, "I don't want Todd to show me around. I want you to do that. I am the guest, remember?"

Scott explained, "Well, Nicole is also a guest here today, and she is my guest, and I will be showing her around. So, if you want the tour, you will have to let either Todd or Bill be your guide, or we will have to take you back to the resort. I am not available to show you around today."

Nicole was so delighted that Scott had put Emily in her place, and Catherine was grinning from ear to ear.

Emily chose Bill to escort her, but Bill didn't seem very excited about this turn of events. He took Scott aside, and told him he would take Nicole if he felt there would be a problem with Emily.

Scott replied, "Thanks Bill, but Nicole is mine, and Emily will just have to find herself someone else to latch on to. It's not going to be me."

Bill took Emily in his jeep to the sight they were going to look for wildlife, and Scott drove Nicole and Catherine in his vehicle.

When they arrived at the south pasture, they noticed that a herd of deer were spooked at the sound of their jeeps. "Something must have scared them, as they don't normally run when they see or hear us coming. They are use to the sound of our jeeps," Scott said out loud.

All of a sudden they all heard something, and Nicole asked, "What was that?"

Scott replied, "It sounded like a big bear. Maybe it's the grizzly. I saw bear tracks again yesterday when I was rechecking the cages. It is a very large bear. A male grizzly bear can sometimes get as tall as eight to nine feet, and this one has to be every bit of eight feet anyway. Don't be frightened. It can't outrun the jeeps. Bears can run fast, up to thirty-five miles per hour, but not for long distances. They give out after a while.

Nicole nervously said, "It doesn't make me feel any safer knowing a grizzly is on the loose."

Scott smiled and jokingly quipped, "Why Nicole, don't you trust me with your life? I will protect you and Catherine. Doesn't that make you feel safe?"

She blushed. "I am grateful that you will protect us, but I don't like wild bears any better than I do snakes, and I don't like them at all."

Scott patted her hand. "Nicole, we have snakes out here too, but don't you worry. I will make sure you never have to see a bear or a snake as long as you are with me."

Catherine smiled and commented, "Scott, that's a tall order to fill, don't you think?

They cautiously got out of the jeep and walked up to Bill's vehicle where Emily was still sulking in her seat with her arms crossed. Scott took Bill aside and talked with him for a little while. Nicole went over to Emily and tried to make conversation with her.

Emily huffed, "Don't even talk to me. You are not being very nice to a guest of your hosts, and they will hear about this."

Catherine answered, "Emily, you can tell Norman and Virginia all you want, because in actuality, Nicole is their guest also. She just offered to help out while she is staying with us. Her parents are good friends of mine and the Parker's, and they gave her this trip."

Emily retorted, "Nicole, you are just barely out of high school, and Scott is paying attention to you? I'm a senior in college. Does he know you are just a child?"

Nicole politely looked at Emily and said, "Yes, he does know that I will be a junior in college this fall, and it doesn't seem to matter to him that I will be twenty-one next month. Does that answer your question?"

Emily turned around searching for Scott and Bill. They had left them at the jeeps to check out the noise they had heard in the brush. When they returned, they told the women to please hurry and get in the jeeps. Without an explanation they drove back towards the ranger's station.

Catherine looked at Scott in the rear view mirror and asked, "You spotted it, didn't you?"

"Yes," Scott answered. "It was eating a deer it had killed. It was not hungry enough to chase after us, but it was too close for comfort, and we will have to do something about it.

Nicole questioned. "Can you sedate it and take it back where it should be? I've seen that on television where they sedate and haul animals off to another place where they won't be a danger to anyone."

Scott answered, "That's very possible, Nicole We don't want to harm it unless it starts picking out people to be its prey. I don't like to kill any creature unless it becomes necessary. I want both of you ladies to lay low until we figure out what to do with it. Don't come out here alone, and Catherine, please make sure your jeep is always full of fuel at all times. Okay?"

"Sure thing Scott," Catherine answered.

Nicole was getting a little nervous about the rangers chasing down a grizzly bear, especially where Scott was concerned. He must have felt her apprehensiveness as he gently squeezed her hand and smiled at her. Then he said, "I'll be all right, Nicole. I am very cautious around all the wildlife, but especially the bears. You don't have to worry about me, and I truly appreciate you wanting me to be careful."

When they returned to the station, he got out of the jeep and walked around to the passenger side helping Catherine from the front seat. Then he lifted Nicole from the back seat and embraced her in his arms.

While Scott was hugging Nicole, Bill returned with Emily in his jeep. Bill heard Emily say, "Yuck! That makes me sick! I can tell you have feelings for Nicole, so why don't you go after her, and I'll take care of Scott?"

Bill replied, "Nicole doesn't have feelings for me, and Scott really likes her. I would not even want to try to come between them, and you would be better off if you just forgot about Scott. Todd thinks you are a goddess, and he's a good looking guy, so why don't you settle for him? I know he'd really like to see you."

"Get real!" Emily retorted. "I don't even like Todd. He's too much of a pushover. I like a challenge in a man. You wait and see. I'll have Scott before my ten days are up, and I'll give you Miss Nicole on a platter."

Bill shook his head and walked up the steps into the ranger's station without saying another word to her.

Emily was disturbed that Scott was still paying attention to Nicole. They seemed to be in another world that did not include her, and she didn't like that. She kept clearing her throat to get their attention, but they either didn't hear her or were pretending not to.

Catherine finally stepped up and said to Emily, "Why don't you just go on up to the station? Better yet, I'll help you."

Emily snapped, "Let go of my arm! I'll go in when I'm darn good and ready, and I'm not ready yet."

Catherine continued to hold her arm and said, "Oh, yes you are." She pulled her up the steps and into the station.

Emily let the screen door slam in hopes that Scott would hear her dismay and stop the public affection with Nicole.

Scott and Nicole talked more than a few minutes before they walked into the station. They both had big smiles on their faces. Then Scott went over to talk with Bill and Todd about the bear problem.

Catherine decided it was time for the ladies to head back to the resort.

Bill turned around in his chair and said, "Goodbye Catherine and Nicole. Be careful, and I hope to see you again real soon."

Emily commented, "Hey Bill, you know I'm leaving too, and Scott will you walk me to the jeep?" Bill nodded and replied, "Oh yeah, good-bye, Emily."

Scott looked at Emily and said, "I'll be walking all of you to Catherine's jeep." Emily put her arm in his, and Scott dropped his arm and walked away from her. He put his arm around Nicole's shoulder and they talked all the way to the jeep. When Emily sat in the front seat beside Catherine, Scott lifted Nicole into the back and kissed her good-bye.

"Nicole, I will definitely see you tomorrow. Okay? I'll call or surprise you."

Emily looked sternly at Scott and then at Catherine and snapped, "Can we get out of here, now?"

They returned to The Haven. Virginia and Norman were outside walking. They stopped Catherine and asked, "Did you young ladies have a good time at the ranger's station?"

Nicole answered, "Yes we did, thank you."

Emily piped up and said, "Speak for yourself, Nicole. I didn't have a good time at all. It seems your hired help doesn't know what it means to show the vacationers a good time."

Virginia replied, "Oh! Well, Catherine has never had any complaints from our other visitors. You are the very first one to complain, and I am truly sorry. Maybe tomorrow will be a better day for you."

Virginia winked at Catherine as she drove off towards Emily's cabin. Emily jumped out with a huff, and walked toward the cabin, not saying a word.

When Nicole and Catherine were getting out of the jeep, Catherine looked at Nicole and said, "Don't go too fast Nicole. I know you and Scott like one another a great deal, but don't hurry the relationship along. Remember you will only be here for a short time."

"I know," replied Nicole.

Catherine suggested, "If you were to stay until we close up for the season, we could arrange that you ride back with me. The roads get so bad here even in the early Fall, so we close the resort right after Labor Day. I don't live that far from your home in Springfield, Ohio, and I'd really enjoy having the company for the long ride home. Would you like me to say something to Virginia and Norman?"

Nicole answered, "I would really like that. I would enjoy spending more time here and then riding back with you. I enjoy working and being with you Catherine. You are already like a big sister to me, and I'll do everything I can to help you."

They went to the dining hall and ate their dinners. While eating, their conversation was about the bear situation. As they finished taking their dishes back to the kitchen, they said their goodnights to everyone and headed for their cabin. Once inside Nicole told Catherine that she was really tired and wanted to lie down for awhile. She took a quick hot shower, dried off and slid under the covers. She tried to remember everything that had happened that afternoon with Scott, and wanted to return to him in her dreams.

Nicole suddenly realized that her nap had turned into a full night of sleep. She was so refreshed when she got up. She was singing while putting on her makeup and fixing her hair in a ponytail. Scott had never seen her wear her hair that way, and she wanted him to see her look a little different today.

Catherine laughed to herself watching Nicole primping with her makeup and hair.

They walked into the dining hall where Virginia and Norman were seated at a table by themselves. Virginia motioned Catherine and Nicole to come eat with them. She noted that Nicole looked radiant and said, "Nicole, you look so beautiful this morning. What have you done that is so different?"

Nicole smiled and answered, "I'm just wearing my hair differently along with a little bit of makeup. Do you like it?"

Virginia replied, "Yes, I do. Doesn't she look just beautiful this morning, Norman?" Norman was reading his paper, but he pulled down one corner, smiled, nodded, and then went back to reading.

Catherine asked Nicole to go ahead and pick out her breakfast while she needed to discuss something with Virginia.

Virginia asked, "Is anything wrong?"

Catherine said, "Oh, no! I asked Nicole if she would like to ride back to Ohio with me to keep me company on the long drive back after we close the resort. She doesn't have to report to college until the second week in September, so she'll still have plenty of time to get ready for school. What do you think?"

Virginia looked at Norman, and Norman not even putting his paper down said, "I think that would be a lovely idea. How's it going with Nicole and Scott?"

Catherine replied, "They are doing just fine. It's Emily I worry about. She wants Scott for herself, and I think she is going to be trouble for the both of them, and us. She's a royal pain in the behind, but I can take care of her. Scott paid a lot of attention to Nicole last night, and I thought Emily was going to have a first-class fit.

"Scott and Bill found the grizzly bear last night while we were there. It was feeding on a deer at that moment, but they don't want to take any chances, so they are trying to come up with some type of plan to save it, plus everyone else in the valley."

Virginia said, "That sounds dangerous to me. You ladies be very careful out there. I wouldn't want anything to happen to either of you. And I will call the Thomas' this afternoon and ask if Nicole could stay and ride back with you when we close the resort."

Just then Nicole came back with her breakfast. Before she started to eat, she waited for Catherine to return. She smiled looking at Catherine and said, "It's your turn to say grace." Catherine smiled back and gave thanks to God for all His many blessings.

They were almost finished eating when Scott came in. He came over to their table and sat down beside Nicole. He put his arm around her and asked, "How's my favorite lady in the State of Colorado?"

Catherine didn't give Nicole a chance to answer, but said to Scott, "Oh! Do you have other ladies elsewhere in the United States?"

Scott stammered, "Well, well, no, I don't. That was just a figure of speech." They all laughed, but Nicole was blushing. Scott lifted her face with his hand saying, "Don't blush pretty lady. I didn't mean to embarrass you. Isn't she beautiful, Virginia and Norman?"

Norman put his paper down, and with a big smile said, "She's a mighty pretty lady, and you better watch yourself, Mr. Scott Thompson. She has a lot of us looking after her, and we don't want anything to happen to her while she's staying with us."

"You have nothing to worry about with me Norman. I have only her best interests at heart, but I want you all to know that I really care for her. Now Nicole, I said it in front of everyone so you don't ever have to worry about me with anyone else. I only have eyes for you, and you don't have to worry about Emily because she's not my type of girl. Okay?

"I came to see if you could go to Fort Collins with me today. I'll have you back right after lunch. I need to pick up some supplies and some new cages. It seems that grizzly bear likes to tear up the cages we had out. We're not going to put anymore out until we capture it, but we need to have a supply on hand. Would you like to go along?"

Nicole could hardly stand the thought of not being able to go with him, but she looked at Catherine and then to Scott, and said, "I'd love to go, but I have a job to do with Catherine, and she really needs my help."

Catherine laughed in reply, "Not today my dear! Today is your day off, so go and enjoy the whole day with Scott, if you would like."

Nicole beamed and said, "Thank you Catherine."

While they were in Fort Collins, they decided to see a matinee at the movie theater. Neither one knew anything about the movie that was showing, but they weren't really concerned about the content. The movie was over, and they were pleasantly surprised that it was good.

Scott reminded her that he needed to get some supplies and run them back to the station. They drove to the hardware store and picked up the new cages and the rest of the supplies. They jumped back in the jeep and headed for the station. It was such a beautiful ride in the open jeep with the wind blowing back her hair. Nicole couldn't imagine a more perfect day.

Scott looked over at her, smiled and asked, "Are you having a good time?"

Nicole replied, "Yes. It's a perfect day."

Scott headed a different way back to the ranger's station so Nicole could see some different scenery. He drove up to a bluff where he stopped the jeep. They both got out and looked at the valley below. It was such a gorgeous sight with the sun rays beaming down on the valley. It was so beautiful that it almost took her breath away.

He put his arms around her and kissed her neck. He held her head in his hands and told her, "Nicole, I know this is happening very quickly. I have come to realize that I have very deep feelings for you, and I am hoping you feel the same way about me."

She looked at him and said, "Scott, I have had feelings for you ever since I first met you at the ranger's station."

He lifted her up off the ground and whirled her around in a circle. "I know that I don't want to lose you when it's time for you to return to Ohio. I like you being in my life, and I want us to continue to be together. I know you told me that your education has already been paid for by your parents, so I would not want to interfere with that. You told me that your parents worked very hard to make sure you could complete your education, but I still wish you could be closer to me. I know you don't want to disappoint them either, so I'll just have to call you, send you text messages, e-mail you, and come to see you whenever I can get away."

"Scott, Virginia and Norman will be talking with my parents about my staying for the rest of the summer, and I have yet to hear their opinion. Let's see if the rest of the summer is okay with my folks before we do any major planning."

Scott was elated about that possibility.

When they arrived at the station, Todd and Bill came out to help carry in the supplies.

Todd asked, "Did Larry have everything in stock that we needed?"

Scott nodded "Yes. Nicole and I got everything on the list and then some. She thought we needed to have some popcorn and sodas to have in case we wanted to show a movie up here. We could invite some of the campers, and even some of the resort visitors. So what do you think?"

"I think that's a wonderful idea," Todd said. "What about you Bill?"

Bill looked at them and responded, "That's a darn good idea. That will enable us to let the campers and those at the resort know who we are. They might feel more comfortable with us, and be able to call on us anytime they need help. Good idea, Nicole! You are not only beautiful but intelligent too. I like it!"

Nicole answered, "Thank you. Now that that is all settled, when would you want to have your first party? We will need some preparation time."

"First of all, we need to look at the scheduling calendar and then set a date," Todd reminded them.

Bill voiced his opinion, "I like the idea a lot, but I want one thing understood. I am not going to be with that Emily chick! She and I are like oil and water, and I don't want to be stuck with her anymore. How about you, Todd? You seem to like her don't you?"

"It's not me she's after, it's Scott."

Scott smiled looking at Nicole and replied, "I've got my hands full with this little filly, and I'm not looking to be tamed or lassoed by anyone else. Emily is open game for either of you, just not me. I'm taken."

Bill laughed and said, "You've got it bad, old man. Nicole's too sophisticated and beautiful for you."

She put her hand on Scott's arm, and then grabbed his hand.

He gently squeezed her hand, and said, "Well, I've got to get my lady back to the resort before it gets dark, so I'll see you guys later. Nothing happened today on my day off, did it?"

Todd replied, "No it was quiet all day, and that's eerie."

As Scott drove Nicole to The Haven, they heard a loud roar echoing through the mountains, and they both knew the grizzly was letting everyone know he was out there somewhere. She scooted as close to Scott as she could possibly get.

He tried to reassure her that the bear was a long way off, and she would be safe with him.

When they arrived at the resort, Catherine was walking to the dining hall. She looked up and said, "You're both in time for supper. Have you two eaten anything today?"

Nicole laughed and said, "We had popcorn."

Catherine looked sternly at Scott and scolded him, "You can't live on love and popcorn alone, young man."

He looked embarrassed and apologetically blurted, "I'm so sorry, Nicole. I didn't even realize I forgot to buy you lunch. Time just slipped away. Again, I am so sorry. Will you forgive me?"

Nicole smiled and replied, "Lunch was the last thing on my mind, so you don't need to apologize. Will you have time to have dinner with us?"

Scott answered, "I would like to stay, but I need to get back to the station. With that bear on the loose, I need to hear it again so I can estimate how far away it is tonight. Thank you anyway, and Nicole, I will hopefully see you tomorrow. I will call you. Okay?"

Nicole followed him to the jeep and they talked for a few moments until he hugged her goodbye.

Suddenly they heard someone clearing her throat. Emily had just returned from a trip with her family and was on her way to the dining hall when she saw them hugging. "Do you two know how to do anything else?" she snapped. "Can't you see he's just playing with you? You're too young for him."

Scott looked only at Nicole, gave her one more hug, hopped into his jeep. He reached out and took her hand and said, "Until tomorrow, my sweet lady. Sweet dreams. You definitely will be in mine tonight." He started up his jeep and drove off.

She felt as though her feet weren't even touching the ground.

Emily brought her back to reality. "You know, you two are sickening!" She walked off, leaving Nicole standing there alone.

Nicole suddenly realized that she was very hungry, so she hurried to the dining hall, picked out her food and sat at the table with Catherine.

Catherine smiled a sheepish grin but said nothing.

Nicole broke the silent moment by saying, "I had a lovely time today, Catherine. Thank you for letting me enjoy some time with Scott. I think he is the one for me, but I'll follow your advice and take it slow."

Catherine smiled and continued to eat.

Just then Virginia walked over to their table and looked at the two of them and said, "Catherine, do you remember that sweet, sweet boy, Mike Fuller, who came here last summer to do his apprenticeship for Hotel Management?" He goes to a college somewhere in Oklahoma. I can't seem to remember the name of that school. Anyway, Norman got a letter from him today asking if he could come here again this summer to get more hours of experience towards his degree, and Norman willingly agreed. Well, to make a long story short, we just got a call from him, and he will be here tomorrow. Isn't that exciting? And Nicole, you are just going to love Mike. He is such a nice looking man and a real sweet one too. I know you will just adore him. Catherine, do we have a one bedroom cabin available for him, or do we need to bunk him in ours?"

Catherine thought for a moment and then responded, "We won't have a one bedroom available for two more weeks, so I guess he will have to bunk with you and Norman for awhile."

Virginia began to turn as she was speaking, "Well, I need to let Norman know right away so he will clean up that spare room in the back. See you later."

Catherine made a low groaning noise, and then looked at Nicole. "They think he is such a nice young man, but I had plenty of complaints from some of the young female guests last summer. They said he was overly aggressive, and one girl slapped him so hard it left red marks on his face for a couple of days. He has a hard time keeping his hands to himself."

Nicole mumbled, "That's too bad." After a moment of thought, she blurted out, "Hey Catherine, I know the perfect match for him, Emily! I think she could handle a grizzly bear, and this Mike might be right up her alley, and besides she won't be here that much longer, so she'll be able to tolerate him. What do you think?"

Catherine nodded her head, smiled a big smile, and said, "I think you've got something there, my dear."

A good night's rest in her warm comfortable bed seemed like a dream, but Nicole didn't want to let go of the memories of that day. When she turned over to look at the clock it was late, and she had to be up at six. She knew it was going to be a long day because she and Scott had not made any definite plans. It seemed that she had no more than closed her eyes when her alarm went off, and she had to get up, take her shower and get ready for the day ahead of her. Since she had been gone the whole day before, she knew she would have a lot of extra work to do.

Catherine met her at the cabin door, and they walked together to breakfast laughing and chatting all the way. They were so busy talking that they hadn't noticed that they were both trying to get through the doorway at the same time, and they almost got stuck. A huge banter of laughter came from the kitchen help, and Catherine and Nicole laughed even harder.

They took their breakfast to a table when suddenly Norman and Virginia walked in with a tall, blonde haired man in his early twenties. He was attractive, but he carried himself as though he was arrogant, and Nicole knew she probably wasn't going to like him very much.

Norman introduced Mike to everyone. Virginia, Norman and Mike got their breakfasts and came to Catherine and Nicole's table where Mike was reintroduced to Catherine, and then to Nicole.

Mike looked at Nicole and said, "Where have you been all my life?" She smiled at him but didn't give him an answer. She immediately looked at Catherine and Catherine winked at her. Within a moment of meeting Nicole, Mike put his arm around her and stated, "We are going to enjoy this summer, aren't we, Sugar?"

Catherine spoke up, telling Mike, "Well, you'll have to stand in line, because Scott Thompson has swept her off her feet, and vice versa."

Mike replied, "Oh, I don't think I have anything to worry about with Ranger Scott. He's just not in my league."

Nicole had all she could stand from this forward person, and she retorted, "Well, after just meeting you I think you should find yourself another girl to pick as your partner, because I'm not available to you or anyone else other than Scott, thank you."

Mike looked at her, smiled and said, "Oh! She has spunk, and that really turns me on."

Norman could see that Nicole was feeling a bit uncomfortable, so he told Mike, "Lay off it with our Nicole. She's a very dear friend of our family, and we don't want you causing any problems where she is concerned. Understand?"

Catherine spoke up, "Well, Mike, we do have a beautiful young lady available for you. She's a real good looker, and she's closer to your age. Her name is Emily, and she's sitting right over there all alone. Why don't you go and introduce yourself. I know she will find you irresistible."

Mike turned around and took a good look at her and said, "Now she's one beautiful woman. I don't mind that she's not as gorgeous as Nicole, but since I've been told that she is off limits, Emily looks better all the time." He picked up his tray and walked over to introduce himself to her. He sat down beside her and used the same forward approach.

Virginia looked startled and asked Catherine, "Was he like this last year?"

Catherine replied, "I think he was a little quieter last year, but he hasn't changed a whole lot, other than he now seems to have more confidence in himself."

Virginia couldn't believe what she heard, and with a look of dismay, she excused herself from the table and went back to her cabin.

Nicole actually felt sorry for Emily, but Emily was eating up all the attention, and she was sitting so close to Mike that they almost looked connected at the hip.

Catherine looked at Nicole and smirked, and then commented, "Good luck ole girl, Emily. You have met your match."

After breakfast, Catherine and Nicole finished all their cleaning chores, and now they had free time for themselves.

Nicole chose to go back to their cabin and take a short nap. She was tired and her bed felt comfortable. She was almost asleep when the phone rang, and she jumped out of bed to answer it.

It was her father calling. "Nicole, are you having a good time? Virginia and Norman called and said that you wanted to spend the rest of the summer there? What have you been doing with yourself? Are you eating?"

"Dad," she interrupted, "Please let me have a chance to answer you back. I'm having a marvelous time, and I am spending the rest of the summer here. I'm eating well, working hard, and really enjoying myself. Are you both all right? I do miss you. Norman, Virginia, and especially Catherine have made me feel like one of the family, and I really enjoy their company. Catherine and I are sharing a cabin, and it is very homey and warm. I hope you are not offended by my telling them that I will stay until after Labor Day."

Her father said, "Well, we haven't heard from you, and we just wanted to make sure you are all right and that you really wanted to stay until Labor Day."

"Dad, I'm just fine. I have met a young man. He is one of the forest rangers in this area. His name is Scott Thompson, and we have been seeing one another for a little while. Most of the time Catherine goes along, but yesterday afternoon I went with him to Fort Collins to pick up supplies and to see a movie. I really like him, Dad."

Her father replied, "Well, just don't get to liking this young fellow too much, as you'll be leaving to go back to college in a couple of months."

Nicole smiled when she even talked about Scott, and then she said to her father, "Bye, Dad. You and Mom take care of yourselves. I miss you, and I love you both. I'll call you next week, okay?"

The conversation ended and Nicole hung up the phone. She had hoped it was Scott, but she was glad to hear from her father again.

She could no longer nap because she was wide awake. She decided to read a book. She went into the living room, nestled up in a big chair, and began to read a book she found on the shelf. Most of the gold lettering had come off the cover, and it was faded. The inside pages were discolored and the print was so small it was hard to read. It was from 1932. After reading a few pages she couldn't get interested in it, so she put it down on the table and just stared into space. Then she decided to put on her bathing suit and go for a swim at the pool.

Catherine walked in when Nicole was almost ready to leave for the pool. She said, "Hey, that swimsuit really looks good on you. If you wait a few minutes, I'll put on my suit and we can go there together. Mike is there, and of course Emily is hanging all over him, but that's good."

Nicole responded, "Thank you Catherine for looking out for me where that Casanova is concerned. I don't really want to be alone around him. I don't trust him, and beside that, I don't like him very much."

"I know." Catherine answered. "He can be a real jerk sometimes, and this year he seems to be worse. Mike is over-compensating for having such a horrible upbringing. His parents abandoned him and took him to his elderly grandparents when he was very young, and they both died when he became a teenager. His parents were on drugs and had no money to take care of him, so he was in and out of foster homes until he was almost seventeen. No one seemed to want to take on a teenage boy, so he tried to raise himself. I think that is why he became so overbearing. He had only himself to depend on. He has been putting himself through college, and his grade point average is tremendous for a young man carrying such a past on his shoulders. I also think his being over confident is a mask to hide the fact that he's scared to death of being rejected, and being left alone again. He's never been in trouble with the law or the schools he attended, so his grandparents did teach him how to be a decent young man. You have to give him credit for that. He's one tough kid to have been through all that turmoil, and I think he looks at Norman and Virginia as substitute grandparents. That is probably why he likes to come here every summer."

Nicole responded, "Thanks for telling me about him, Catherine. I guess that will help me to not judge him. I shouldn't judge him anyway, but he was so obnoxious when we first met. At least now I will try to be civil to him."

When they arrived at the pool, Emily and Mike were sharing a lounge chair. Mike looked up when he saw Catherine and Nicole come through the gate, and he immediately stood up leaving Emily alone. He walked over to the two ladies. With a sexy voice Mike said, "Hey, come lay your lovely bodies next to ours, and Nicole, you look delicious."

She looked at Mike and replied, "I don't think that would be a good idea, as you already have the company of a beautiful young woman. Haven't you ever heard that three or more are a crowd? And you don't want us to distract you from your wooing, do you?"

Mike lightly touched Nicole's elbow and said, "I'm not wooing her, it's just that she finds me attractive, and she is very beautiful, but she's not my type."

"And what type would that be, Michael?" Nicole asked.

Mike said, "She's too much into herself."

"And you're not?" Nicole questioned.

Mike replied, "I guess I've given you the wrong impression of me, Nicole. I like class and elegance in a woman, one that likes the quiet and finer things in life. I don't want someone who is always worried about a hair being out of place, or who always has to check her makeup, or tan lines. Emily is a beautiful and lovely young woman, but she's a show piece, and nothing more. I know I started off on the wrong foot with you, but I am a nice guy once you get to know me."

Nicole answered, "Well, you're right. You did start off on the wrong foot with me, and I thought you were very much into yourself. I promise I will try to give you a chance to start over again, but if I hear or see you acting like a conceited jerk, that's it. Just be the person you really want to be, and we will get along fine. I also want you to know that I like Scott very much, and I would appreciate it if you would respect that relationship. Okay?"

Mike nodded then went over to the other side of the pool to be with Emily while Nicole and Catherine tried to catch some sun rays and relax.

Emily was watching the entire time and asked Mike, "Are they too good to sit over here with us?"

"No, they wanted to give us some privacy."

Emily stated, "You know I really want Scott for myself, so if you really like Nicole, maybe we could work something out. We could get you to be with her and make him jealous, and he'll drop her like a hot potato. What do you think about that proposition?"

Mike responded, "Let's take things slowly for right now, and we'll see how things progress on their own."

Emily snapped back, "I haven't got a lot of time left to take things slowly. I want to be with Scott before I have to leave, and that is only seven days away. Being slow is not the way I work. So, when I want something, I go after it. They have become very close, and I really don't like that. Are you going to help me or not?"

Mike stared at Nicole from across the pool and said, "I don't know."

Virginia and Norman came over to check the temperature and the chlorine in the pool when they stopped to talk with Nicole and Catherine. Virginia told Catherine and Nicole, "The phone was ringing in your cabin when we came by, but we didn't go in to answer it."

Nicole looked saddened as she knew it had to be Scott calling.

Catherine looked over at her and said, "Sweetheart, you can't just sit by the phone and wait for it to ring, you know?"

Nicole said, "I know, but I just wanted to hear his voice." She had her hand up across her forehead to shade her eyes to see Catherine while she was talking to her. Then she noticed a young man walking through the gate. She sat up because she recognized him, and it was Scott.

He walked over to them and said his hellos to everyone. She stood up to greet him, and she noticed him eyeing her in her bathing suit. He raised his eyebrows and smiled, responding, "You look great in that suit, Nicole. What a sight after a long day's work. Bill, Todd and I have been chasing that grizzly all day, and we think he has left the area, but we'll know if our chase was effective within the next few days."

"Virginia and Norman, would you mind if I take a swim while I'm here?"

Norman said, "Sure thing. Do you need some swimming trunks? If you don't have a pair with you I'm quite sure Mike left some extras in the men's dressing room."

Scott said, "I always carry a pair in my jeep. I'm all set, but thank you, Norman. Speaking of Mike, is he coming back this year?"

Norman pointed across the pool and said, "He's already here. He got here yesterday, and he'll be here the rest of the summer. He's putting in more hours for his hotel management degree. I know he'll be anxious to see you, and say hello." Norman no more than got the words out of his mouth when Mike came over to greet Scott.

"Hey! My man! How are you? It's been a long time. You look about ten pounds heavier and a lot more muscular than I last remember. Are you still a ranger at the park?" Mike asked.

Scott shook his hand and replied, "Yes, I'm still a ranger at the park, and I have put on a little weight. We have a weight room at the station now, and we work out as much as time allows. You look good Mike. You look like you've grown another foot."

Mike replied, "I grew another four inches this last year, but I think I've finally topped off at six-four. We'll have to get together this summer while I'm here. I've always enjoyed our talks and tagging hunts. Well, I guess I better get back to my friend over there. You know Emily, don't you?"

Scott answered, "Yes, I do, and I'm glad she has latched onto you instead of me." He put his arm around Nicole's shoulder, smiled and said, "I've got my lady right here, and I don't want anyone else."

Mike smiled and responded, "She's a fine looking young woman with a lot of class, and you're a lucky guy to have her."

"Thanks Mike. I know I'm a very lucky guy."

Scott left to go to the men's dressing room to change into his swimming trunks. When he came back to Nicole, he immediately pushed her into the pool.

Nicole hadn't planned on getting totally wet, but it was fun to be playful with him. She had missed him even though it had only been a day since she last saw him. They were splashing when some water reached Catherine.

She was drying herself off when Scott looked up at Catherine and apologized for getting her wet.

Catherine looked at them and said, "Well, we don't normally come to the pool to stay dry. You two have fun. I'm going to the cabin and get cleaned up and maybe even take a nap. Are you going to stay for dinner tonight, Scott?"

"Do you think it would all right if I do?

Catherine grinned and nodded while she was walking out of the pool area.

Scott looked at Nicole and asked, "Would you like me to stay and have dinner with you?"

Nicole responded with a hug, and he immediately knew her answer. They swam a few laps, got out of the pool and walked to their lounge chair to relax and talk. They were facing one another holding each other's hands. They were oblivious to anyone else at the pool, and they seemed to have a lot to talk about.

Emily noticed them and said to Mike, "I think I'm going to be sick watching those two lovebirds. Why can't that be me with him instead of her? What does he see in her anyway? I want him."

Mike took her hand and patted it saying, "You don't know do you? He sees a classy and sweet lady. She's not overbearing, but quiet and laid back, radiant and reserved."

Emily questioned, "Hey Mike! Are you saying that I don't have those qualities? It sounds like you've got deep feelings for her. Do you?"

Mike answered, "Let's just say that I would like to have a chance with her sometime, but for right now, I am no competition with him. I'll have to play my cards right, and play the waiting game. I know you don't have time for that, but you will have to work that out for yourself."

With a disgusting look on her face, Emily got up from her lounge chair and went to the changing room.

Mike lingered on until he saw Scott and Nicole get up and leave. He followed them from a distance and then went to his room to clean up and change into something appropriate for dinner. He intentionally wanted to be in the dining room at the same time they would be. He wanted to sit at the same table with them. He was intent on watching to see where Nicole was vulnerable with Scott, and then plan his action from there.

Mike was already in the dining room when Scott and Nicole walked in. He asked, "Would it be all right for Emily and me to sit at the table with you?"

Nicole answered, "It will be fine as long as Emily doesn't try to start something."

"She'll be good, I promise. If she acts up I'll take her to another table."

Just then Catherine walked in with Norman and Virginia, and Emily was right behind them. Mike motioned for all of them to come to their table. After they all filled their plates, they came to the table and sat down. There was much laughter throughout the entire meal. Emily behaved nicely, but she continued to stare at Scott most of the evening. Nicole noticed, but said nothing. Scott also noticed.

After they finished eating Scott kept his arm around Nicole. Catherine was watching all of them but saying little.

Finally, Scott told Nicole he had to get back to the station. They both excused themselves from the table and left the room. She walked with him to his jeep. There was a big, full white moon overhead, and he put his arm around her as they leaned up against the jeep. He pulled her to him and whispered in her ear, "Sweet dreams, and I'll do the same."

She held on to his hand until he started to drive away, and then they let loose of one another. She had tears in her eyes, and was happy to have those giddy feelings.

When Nicole walked to the cabin, she hadn't realized she was so tired. She fell asleep as soon as she laid her head on the pillow. Her thoughts were only of Scott, and she wanted to dream about him all night long. She didn't hear when Catherine came in.

The early morning was still a little dark and chilly, but Nicole didn't care because today was going to be special. She knew she would see Scott again after she and Catherine got all their chores done. Before she got dressed the phone rang, and it was Scott.

"Hello Sunshine. How's my favorite girl this morning? I just called to get my day started off on the right foot. When I hear your voice, I have a smile on my face. I hope you slept well last night. I slept like a rock, and I must have had some pretty nice dreams about you. Todd and Bill told me I had a smile on my face when I went to bed last night, and when I got up this morning, it was still there. See what you do to me? I can't wait to see you again, so tell me when it would be a good time for me to come over?"

Nicole was blushing. "I should be available late this afternoon. It will probably be after five o'clock. We have a lot of guests pulling out today so Catherine and I have our work cut out for us. The cleaning is a lot more extensive when the guests leave. Sometimes we even have to shampoo the carpets."

Scott asked, "Why would you have to shampoo the carpets? Isn't that a little overkill?"

Nicole replied, "Some people spill all kinds of things, and some bring their pets, which makes it imperative that the carpets get shampooed. It's not that bad, but it does take extra time."

Scott said, "I didn't realize you have so much work to do, but I want to take you out to dinner tonight in Fort Collins. I will be there to pick you at six o'clock if you think you'll be ready by then. Just wear something casual. Don't dress up, because the place I want to take you is not very fancy, but the food and atmosphere are terrific. I want you all to myself tonight. Would that be all right with you?"

"Yes, I would really like that very much," Nicole answered.

Catherine and Nicole had four units to completely clean and take inventory. When Nicole looked at her watch it was four o'clock. She needed to finish up quickly so she would still have time to take a shower, fix her hair, dress, and put on a little makeup. She wanted to look especially nice tonight. She wanted Scott to really know how much she cared for him, and she was looking forward to having a nice peaceful and quiet time with him alone.

Catherine noticed Nicole looking at her watch and asked, "You have a date with Scott tonight, don't you?"

"Yes, I do. How did you know?" Nicole asked.

Catherine answered, "I saw you looking at your watch, and then checking outside. Are you and Scott doing something special tonight?"

Nicole replied, "Oh Catherine, he is taking me out to a restaurant in Fort Collins. He wants a peaceful and quiet dinner with just the two of us. Almost all the other times we're together there are a lot more people around. He said the restaurant he's taking me to is not fancy. So I can dress casually, which suits me fine. He'll be here at six o'clock if that's all right? If we are not close to being finished I can call him and make our date a little later."

Catherine responded, "We are almost finished, so you go ahead and get yourself ready. I can finish the little bit that is left to do. This is the last cabin, and all I need to do is take inventory." Catherine hesitated, and added, "If you don't mind me talking to you like a big sister, I would like to say something to you. I know how much you care for and think about Scott, and he is a wonderful person, but don't go too fast. You have your whole life ahead of you, and you have your own plans for your future. Don't let anything happen that would enable you to not pursue your own dreams. If he is to be the one, and even if he may not be that Mr. Right, you need to remember your dreams. Just think about what you'll feel and think about him, and yourself, in the morning. Don't rush into anything, but go slow and remember what I've been trying to tell you. I don't want you to get hurt. When the time is right, you'll know, I promise, but I'm positive now is not the right time."

"Catherine, Scott and I both respect one another too much for that. I will be going away to school, and I don't want to ruin my future plans by doing something I might regret. We are only trying to get to know and enjoy one another's company right now. I really appreciate you caring enough about us, and I don't think you are overstepping your boundaries with me."

Nicole had tears welling in her eyes just thinking about how much she loved Catherine, not just as her friend, but much like an older sister. She truly respected her wisdom and her love. "Catherine, I love you, and I thank you for caring enough about me to tell me what's on your heart."

Catherine smiled. "You are done, so go get yourself ready for your date. I want you to have a wonderful time with your special guy. Please just remember what we talked about and don't ever let your emotions take over any situation. Okay?"

"Okay, Catherine." Nicole gave her a hug and a kiss on the cheek before she ran to their cabin to take a shower and get ready.

After showering and drying her hair, Nicole selected a pale yellow sundress from her closet. She had been saving it for a special occasion, and this was the right time. The dress looked so nice against her tanned skin, and her hair looked perfect. She was so pleased with the way she looked. She was dancing and twirling in her dress in front of the mirror when Catherine came in.

"Oh! You look so beautiful in that dress, but it needs a little something that I think will touch it up just a bit," Catherine said.

Catherine went into her bedroom and came back with a heart shaped gold locket on a gold chain and a white shawl to wrap around Nicole's shoulders.

Nicole gasped at the intricate design of the shawl and the necklace, and said, "Catherine, I can't wear these. What if I would do something, like break the chain on the necklace or get a stain on the shawl? Both are so beautiful."

Catherine replied, "Now you listen to me, young lady. The shawl belonged to my mother, and I can't think of anyone I trust more than you to wear it. If it gets a stain on it, we'll get it out. The necklace was given to me by a fellow I was almost engaged to. He gave it to me before he left to go to war, but he was killed in action. I once had our picture in it, but I took it out. You can't live in the past, and I know it would mean a lot to me to see you wear it tonight."

"Catherine, you are so sweet, and I can't thank you enough for all you do, and for all you mean to me." Nicole hugged her and gave her a kiss on the cheek. As Catherine was fastening the necklace around Nicole's neck, Nicole became teary eyed.

"Do you have a slight scent of perfume to wear?" Catherine asked.

"Oh, yes. I would have forgotten to put some on. What would I do without you, Catherine? Thank you. How is this scent? Do you think he will like it?" Nicole asked.

"If he doesn't then his nose isn't working, because you smell so good." Catherine responded.

No more had they finished commenting on the fragrance of Nicole's cologne when there was a knock at the door. Nicole knew it was Scott. She tried to walk unhurriedly, as she didn't want him to think she was overly anxious, even though she was. When she opened the door he looked at her, and his mouth turned into a huge smile. He brought a bouquet of yellow roses from behind his back and gave them to her. The colors of the roses matched her dress perfectly. She invited him into the cabin while she found a vase to put them in.

Catherine came out to say hello when Nicole walked back into the room with the flowers in a large crystal vase. She commented, "They are such beautiful flowers, Scott. How nice of you to bring them to me, and then she laughed."

Nicole laughed to herself as she smelled them and put the vase on the coffee table.

Scott had not yet said a word because of what Catherine had said, but then he realized she was only joking with him. He was mesmerized by the sight of this young woman standing in front of him.

Catherine looked at Scott and said, "Earth to Scott, earth to Scott."

Scott looked over at Catherine and stammered, "Oh, I'm sorry Catherine. I haven't been able to take my eyes off of Nicole. She looks stunning."

Catherine looked at Scott and whispered, "Why don't you tell her that?"

"Oh! Sure," he said.

"Nicole, you look amazing and breathtaking at the same time. You are so beautiful, that I'm almost speechless." After a moment's pause he asked, "Are you ready to go?"

Nicole was feeling so good about herself, that she looked at him and answered, "Yes." As they walked out the door, she looked around at Catherine, smiled a big grin and winked. Catherine remained at the door until they were out of sight.

When Scott walked Nicole to the jeep, he asked her to wait a moment while he laid a soft blanket over the seat. He didn't want her dress to get dirty. He lifted her into her seat and then quickly ran to the other side. He turned to her, put her left hand in his, and gently kissed the back of her hand. His voice was cracking a little when he said, "Nicole, you do look stunning, and I am one lucky guy. I can't stop looking at you, but I guess we won't get anywhere if I don't start the jeep. I promise to drive slowly so the wind won't mess up your hair."

As they were leaving the resort, Norman and Mike were working in the flower garden near the entrance. Norman waved for them to stop. He came over to the jeep and said, "I just wanted to see my girl all decked out. Nicole, you look more beautiful than ever. Mike, do you see our Nicole?

Mike said, "I'd have to be blind to miss her. Nicole, you look stunning. I hope you have a wonderful time, and Scott, you better behave yourself."

He looked away from Norman and smiled at Mike. "I definitely know how to treat a lady, especially this one."

Norman backed away from the jeep. "You drive carefully." He waved as they drove out of the resort and onto the highway.

The drive to town was warm and the air smelled so fresh. She was glancing at her handsome man when he pulled the jeep over to a grassy area, leaned over toward her and gave her a kiss on the lips. He smiled and said, "I have very deep feelings for you, Nicole. I hope you feel the same way about me. Every day we are together I know you are the one for me. That is the reason I wanted to stop here now, because I want to give you a small gift." He put his hand in his jacket pocket and pulled out a small white box. He handed it to her, and as she opened it, she was so surprised to find a beautiful gold locket necklace.

When Nicole was finally able to speak, she looked at him. "Scott, this is the most beautiful necklace I have ever seen." He took the necklace from the box and opened the locket to show her a picture of the two of them together. He placed it around her neck over the top of Catherine's necklace. He lifted her hand and kissed it.

Nicole asked, "Where did you get a picture of us together?"

Scott replied, "I had Bill take the photo at the station the last time you were there." He quickly looked at his watch. "We need to get going or we'll lose our reservation."

As he was driving off the grassy area, Nicole looked at him thinking, he is so handsome, and a good person. He is rugged, but very gentle and tender at the same time. He has a deep passion for things he believes in, and is committed to whatever he sets his mind to do. But most of all, she had fallen for him, and he with her.

When they arrived at the restaurant Scott found a parking place very close to the front entrance. He walked around to Nicole's side and lifted her from the jeep. He took her hand, and after opening the door, he touched the small of her back while gently nudging her into the restaurant. It was a rustic looking place with log beams, and on the walls were scenic pictures of nature from the area. It was quiet, and she liked the atmosphere.

"Scott, I want to thank you for bringing me to this place." Before she could finish what she wanted to say, the waiter came to take them to their table, and she noticed he was leading them to a very secluded area with a large picture window overlooking a lake with mountains in the background. It was a fantastic view. She looked at Scott and smiled, touched his hand and said, "Thank you for this special night, for the beautiful gift, and for us having some time to ourselves. I hope you realize that I also have feelings for you. I know you keep telling me about your feelings for me, and I want to let you know that my feelings for you are mutual."

Scott took her left hand in his and pointed to her ring finger. "I hope the next piece of jewelry I purchase for you will belong on that finger. Would that be something you might like?"

Nicole smiled. "Scott, we barely know one another, and I think we need some time together before we even think about an engagement. Don't you?"

Scott stated, "Nicole, you are so levelheaded. I don't want to rush you into anything yet, but I do know how I feel about you, and I want to pursue those feelings. We need to take it slowly, but you won't be here after your classes start. I don't have a lot of time left to be with you."

Nicole answered, "I have another two years of college left before I can even think of a long term relationship with anyone. I know how I feel and what I want to tell you at this moment, but I don't know if I believe in the old saying that 'distance makes the heart grow fonder.' Do you really think you will be able to wait for two more years? My parents have saved for years for my education, and I need to honor them by completing it. I am, I guess, a very practical person, and I realize that a lot can happen in two years. Do you feel you can really make a commitment to me with us being together only occasionally, or not seeing one another for another two years?"

He thought for a moment. "I can certainly try. I have fallen for you Nicole, and I know what I want, and that is you. We can call one another, send e-mails, letters, text messages, photos, and maybe I can even come and visit you once in a while. You might even be here again next summer, so we would be able to carry on where we left off. Could I be right?"

Nicole looked at him with tears in her eyes. "I want to love you with all my heart, but I won't do that to you or to myself right now. Two years is a long time, and I know I won't be able to afford to get on a plane every time I want to be with you."

The waiter came to take their order, and while they were talking a small band was playing soft music that was easy to dance to. Scott took Nicole's hand and asked her to dance with him. He was a good dancer, and she was enjoying the closeness she was experiencing with him. They continued to dance until the waiter brought their dinners to their table. They sat down, and Scott blessed their food. He prayed, "Dear Lord, please bless this food to the nourishment of our bodies, and our bodies to your service. Amen."

Nicole was pleased to hear him pray.

Scott said as they continued eating, "I know we are both too young to get married right now, but I want us both to think about it even if it takes us two more years. I would like to have a family while I am young. My father was a lot older than my mother, and I missed being able to do some of the things my friends got to do with their fathers. We never went camping. He had crippling arthritis. He couldn't play catch with me, and he couldn't come to my ball games because he couldn't sit in the stands for very long, nor stand up for long periods of time. Even though I knew he couldn't help it, I had some animosity towards him. I truly want to be an active part of my children's life. I want to grow old with them. I knew my dad loved me, but he never attended anything I was in at school, which caused even more hard feelings. My friend's fathers had to stand up for me as my parent. My mother attended as much as she could, but she had to work two jobs to provide for our family. I knew it was beyond his control, but I wanted my dad to be there for me, and he wasn't. He has since passed, but I needed him. That's why I want to enjoy my children while I'm young. I want to be a big part of their lives."

Nicole put her hand on his hand. "I am so sorry you had to endure that. I can't really imagine the heartache you went through because my parents have always been very active in my life. I can't remember them not ever attending anything I was in, but I was their only child. I don't know if that really made a difference, because I had friends who had other brothers and sisters, and yet their parents seemed to always be in attendance for most of their activities. In this day and age, young people are waiting a lot longer before they have children because, for one thing, it costs more to raise them, and it is smarter to have a home and the costs involved with owning and furnishing it already paid for, or set in a budget. I don't want to raise a child in an apartment or high rise building. I dream of living in a home with a backyard where children can play. Those are my dreams, and I realize that in today's world I need an education in order to help provide those things for my family. I know a lot of young people today who jump right into marriage without having a solid foundation to build upon. As the hymn says, 'On Christ the solid rock I stand, all other ground is sinking sand.' We all need a solid foundation for everything we do."

Scott looked at Nicole and said, "You are so smart and wise, and I know you are right. I know I will miss you terribly, and I guess I just wanted some assurance of us having a future together."

Nicole whispered, "Let's just enjoy this evening and not worry about tomorrow or the next day. I want to enjoy the time we have right now. Okay?"

Scott nodded and smiled his approval. After enjoying steaks and dancing together, they decided it was time to leave.

When they got into the jeep, Scott started the engine and drove back onto the highway. He was taking her home, she thought, but instead he took her to a very secluded area on a mountain pass. He stopped the jeep, came over to her side and helped her get out. He embraced her in his arms and then walked with her over to a bluff that overlooked the valley below. The full moon glistened through the trees, making it look as though it was dusk. It was so peaceful and quiet until they heard a loud roar close beside them. Scott picked Nicole up and ran for the jeep. He hurriedly placed her in her seat, ran around to his side and started the engine. He immediately put it in gear and sped onto the road. He looked in his rear view mirror only to see that the bear was standing where they had just been. Luckily it was not chasing after them. He drove without saying a word, but he pulled off the side of the road near the resort, put his head against the steering wheel and sighed a breath of relief. "That was a very close call. Are you all right?"

Nicole answered, "I'm okay. I was really frightened, and I'm still shaking a little. Was that really a close call for us?"

Scott responded, "Yes, that bear was on the prowl, checking things out. Luckily he wasn't hungry because he didn't chase us. If he had been hungry, he would have lashed out at one or both of us. He was that close. I will have to report this sighting to Todd and Bill and then notify the campers and resorts to be on the lookout to inform us of where and when he reappears."

When Scott drove her back to the resort, she was still shaking and a little anxious. He asked if she was cold, and she shook her head, no. He pulled into the resort and drove to her cabin. When he stopped the jeep, he, put her hand in his and said, "My sweet Nicole, you mean so much to me, and grizzly bear or not, I love the mere thought of you. You were brave back there and stayed calm."

Trembling, Nicole said, "That's because I was so frightened, I didn't know what else to do. I couldn't scream because nothing would have come out. Thank you for getting us out of there. I really didn't want to have a big bear feeding on me, nor on you!"

Scott laughed a little to relieve the tension. "As for the conversation we were having at the restaurant, I understand, Nicole. I will wait for you, but I may have a possible solution. Why don't I try to get a job where you will be going to school? That way we can be together. I just can't stand the thought of being away from you. I know I need you in my life every day, and any time away from you won't change that."

Nicole answered, "Scott, I don't want to discuss anything right now. I just want to take a hot bath to get myself calmed down."

Scott embraced her and kissed her lips. "Nicole, please go take your hot bath and get into bed. I'll come by tomorrow to see how you are doing." She didn't return his kiss, but ran up the steps and went inside.

Catherine was watching television when Nicole walked in the door. She looked at her and saw that she was white as a sheet and asked, "Hey, are you all right?" Nicole started to cry, and Catherine walked over to her and grabbed her arms. "Did Scott do something to you?"

"No, Scott was fine. It was the grizzly bear that scared us both to death."

Catherine raised her voice and asked, "What grizzly bear and where?"

Nicole, still shaking stated, "We were out on a mountain pass not more than ten miles from here, looking down in the valley, enjoying the scenery and each other's company, when we heard a loud roar very close to where we were standing. Scott grabbed me and put me in the jeep. He quickly started the engine and raced out of there. When we looked in the rear view mirror, we saw the grizzly was standing where we had been. We hadn't heard anything until it roared. It was so big, Catherine. I am still shaking from what I saw. Scott tried to comfort me, but I couldn't stop shaking. I told him I just wanted to take a hot bath and go to bed. He said he would come by and check on me tomorrow."

Nicole looked at Catherine and said, "I think that's exactly what I want to do. If you'll excuse me, I'll go start my bath water."

Catherine responded, "Let me start it for you. I've got a bottle of soothing bath oil, and I'll get everything ready. You just relax if you can until it's ready, okay?"

Nicole said, "Thank you, Catherine, and oh, here is the necklace and shawl you loaned me. They both accented my dress, and thank you for letting me borrow them. Scott surprised me with my own locket and chain. It has our pictures in it. He gave it to me before we arrived at the restaurant. Thank you again, Catherine, for loaning me your things. Tomorrow, after I have been able to calm down, I would like to show you the locket Scott gave me along with the photo inside."

"You're quite welcome," Catherine said. "I will put the necklace in my jewelry box, and the shawl will go back in my closet. If you ever need to borrow the shawl, I'll be glad to get it for you."

Catherine had Nicole's bath ready in a few minutes, and Nicole wanted to be alone with her thoughts of all the things that had happened that evening. She stepped into the hot bath, and it felt wonderful. She soaked and replayed the evening in her mind for what seemed to be hours, but it was only fifteen minutes. The water was still warm but it was beginning to cool. She was tired and wanted to go to bed. She stepped out of the bathtub, dried off, put on her pajamas, and slid under the covers. She was almost asleep when the phone rang beside her bed.

Nicole said, "Hello."

"Nicole, this is Scott. I just called to make sure you are all right. I was worried about you."

"Scott, I'm fine, just tired. I took a hot bath, and I do feel much better. I just crawled into bed, and I'm warm, relaxed and almost ready to go to sleep. I really want to thank you for a wonderful evening. You are so sweet to call and make sure I am all right. I also want to thank you for the beautiful locket. I will wear it knowing that you will always be close to me."

"Nicole, I love you," Scott said. "I will try to get over to see you in the morning. Sweet dreams, my sweet lady. Goodnight."

Scott was saddened about the scare of their evening. It was not the perfect ending he had planned. Now he had to talk with Bill and Todd about the closeness of the grizzly in their territory, and the threat it would be to the campers and nearby resorts.

The next morning was Sunday. Virginia, Norman, Catherine and Nicole were readying themselves for church. Catherine was going to drive them there, except for Mike, and he was going to stay behind to handle the resort.

Catherine said to Mike, "You will take care of everything here won't you? I know you have feelings for Emily, but the rest of the camp needs to run smoothly, and Virginia and Norman don't need to worry. Okay?"

Mike answered, "I will take care of everything. I promise, and you needn't worry about Miss Emily. She and her family are going on an outing today, but I will tell you something she told me. She is trying to convince her parents on letting her stay here until we close, as she, like Nicole, doesn't have to return to her campus until mid September. I don't know if you need to inform Nicole of that. I don't know if Emily's father will be agreeing to her desire. What I do know is that she normally gets what she wants. She has that pretty well mastered."

The concerned look on Catherine's face told Mike everything he needed to know. They both knew Emily would be putting herself between Nicole and Scott, and they didn't need that this early in their relationship.

Scott was a little late getting to church, but he spotted Catherine and Nicole right away. He made his way down the aisle and excused himself as he stepped over both of them. Nicole smiled, showing him that she was wearing the necklace and locket he gave her. Then she put her arm around his. He gently squeezed her hand and held it for the rest of the service.

After the service was over, Scott walked out with Nicole and said his hellos to the pastor, Virginia and Norman. Virginia asked if he was going to have lunch with them, and he told her that he would very much like to do that. Nicole rode back to the resort in his jeep. He seemed quiet, and she asked him if everything was all right. He nodded, but she knew something was really bothering him.

After they all sat down and thanked the Lord for their food, Catherine noticed that he seemed troubled. She asked him, "What's eating at you, Scott?"

Scott looked at Catherine, Norman and Virginia and stated, "The grizzly bear that has been roaming around the mountains is getting more aggressive, and we have to call in reinforcements to capture it. It broke into a campsite last night and tore up the entire camp. Luckily, no one was there, but it was searching for food, and if it smells a human scent, then it will come after humans for its meal. A grizzly will stock you, then attack, and sometimes you don't even know it is happening until it is too late. I don't know if Nicole told you or not, but we saw it last night, and it was within ten miles from this resort. We need all of you to be prepared. Norman, do you have a high powered rifle at your place?"

Norman was frightened but said, "Yes, I have a high powered rifle in the closet. If I need to use it, will that be enough to bring it down?"

Scott replied, "It should be enough, but if you do see it at close range, pump a few shells into it. Okay?"

Norman nodded his head and then took Virginia's hand. He asked her, "What should we do about the vacationers here at the resort?"

Scott interrupted Norman. "We don't want to alarm them first of all, but you need to tell Mike, and let him handle some of your concerns. He might want to call a meeting to inform them that a big bear is on the prowl, and that the local rangers and wildlife personnel are tracking it down to remove it from the area. We don't want to frighten anyone away. We just need to be cautious and safe. I will be in constant contact with you regarding this. If you have any questions or concerns, please do not hesitate to ask me. Norman, you need to let Mike know about your rifle and see if he knows how to use it."

Nicole had seen the large bear standing on its hind legs, and she knew it was very big and tall. All this talk about the bear frightened her again. She was worried about Scott's safety. It would be a difficult ordeal to drug the bear, and then having to relocate it would be even worse. Scott sensed her tension, took her hand under the table, and squeezed it gently. He looked at her and said, "Don't you worry your pretty little head about me, as I have backup and then some. I will be all right."

After Scott finished his lunch, he asked Nicole to walk with him to his jeep. "I have to leave now as Todd, Bill and I have to discuss our plans with the wildlife deputies. I promise I will call you later to let you know we are all right. We have to track Mr. Grizzly down before dark. We have to search in pairs so that none of us are alone to be stalked. I won't be able to call you until after dark. Okay?"

Nicole hugged Scott. "Please don't get hurt. I will worry about you until I hear from you. I love you, Scott."

Scott hugged her back and gently kissed her. She wanted to hold him and not let go, but he released her and jumped into the jeep. After he started the engine, he threw her a kiss and yelled, "I love you my sweet Nicole. I'll talk to you later."

The day wore on, and Catherine and Nicole cleaned up a few cabins and did some laundry of their own. They went back to their cabin and watched a little television, but Nicole was very restless and couldn't get interested in a program. She went to her room and tried to read a book. She couldn't get interested in that either. She decided to lie down and rest, but her mind was constantly thinking. She was worried about Scott. She couldn't do anything but think about the danger he was going to be in.

Scott, Todd and Bill, along with six wildlife deputies got together and discussed their plan to capture the grizzly. If and when they caught it, they would tranquilize it, bag it and call for a standby helicopter to carry it off to another area. If it couldn't be done in the length of time they were allotted before the tranquilizer wore off, they would have to kill it. None of them wanted to do that, but because it already knew the smell of humans, it might prove to be very dangerous.

As they all paired up with one another, Scott was with Jerry, a new wildlife deputy. Jerry had not been on the force for very long, and he was frightened and nervous about them possibly being the ones to find the bear. Scott assured him he knew the procedures, and all Jerry needed to do was follow his lead. Jerry seemed a little less nervous after Scott explained their tactics.

The phone was ringing at the ranger's station, and Bill answered it. He was writing something down on a pad of paper when they heard him say, "Thank you for the information. We will certainly be looking into this situation and see what we can do to eliminate the problem."

After he hung up the phone, Bill said, "Well boys, we just got a report on the whereabouts of our grizzly. It was spotted on a bluff on the west side of the canyon. Some hikers saw him. They were very frightened to see a grizzly. They ran to their car and drove off.

Todd asked, "Are we ready to go? We have radios that will reach anywhere in these mountains. Don't forget to take it with you. Keep it close to you." Todd instructed. "If anything should happen to your radio and you are in trouble, shoot three shots in a row so we can hear where you might be. We'll try to find you and come to your rescue. Most of all, remember your partner at all times, and don't under any circumstances leave him to be on his own. Everyone understand that command?" Everyone nodded their heads and then checked their rifles and their supply of ammunition. "Everyone have enough ammo?"

Scott let Jerry carry the radio and the ammo pack so he would feel more secure. They hiked toward the bluff and Jerry seemed to step on every twig he could find, leaving a noisy trail for a bear to hear. All of a sudden the bear appeared in front of them. Jerry froze and forgot all the training from the briefing. For a short moment the grizzly just stared at them but suddenly came down off his hind legs and started running toward Jerry. Jerry threw the radio in the air and ran as fast as he could, leaving his gun on the ground. Scott wanted to find the radio, but he didn't see where Jerry threw it. He needed to find Jerry and the radio. He held his rifle in the air and shot three times in the air in hopes to scare the grizzly from the area, and to also alarm the others for help. He was fearful that the bear would come back to attack him. The gun shots did not frighten the bear at all, and he came back to attack Scott. Scott didn't want to shoot it, but he had no choice. He took aim and shot the bear, but the bear kept on coming. A set of right front claws swiped Scott's lower left leg, and blood was streaming down his torn pants. The bear was still coming after him, and he knew if he didn't do something, the grizzly would tear him to pieces and have him for a meal. He still had the rifle in his hands. He quickly took the butt of it and hit the bear between the eyes. It stunned the grizzly, but Scott knew that it wouldn't be dazed for long. He had enough time to reload his rifle and turned only to find the bear ready to attack him again. He shot at it a second time and it went down. He wasn't sure it was dead so he shot it a third time. It didn't move. Scott knew he had killed the grizzly.

He needed to find the radio that Jerry had thrown to call for help. It was dusk, and he knew he had to find it soon. His leg was still bleeding and he couldn't physically make it down the bluff by himself, especially in the dark. He took off his belt to use as a tourniquet, but his leg was still bleeding. He pulled it tighter, but the pain was so intense he passed out. When he regained consciousness he managed to double the belt around his upper leg and fasten it. Then he took his rifle to act as a crutch, but the pain was too severe for him to bare any weight on it. He sat back down against the tree, took his rifle and again shot three shots in the air to let someone know he needed help. He continually yelled for Jerry, but he didn't answer. There was nothing more he could do but wait for help to come.

As dusk was turning into darkness, the other teams all returned to their jeeps. Scott and Jerry were not back yet.

Bill asked, "Did any of you see or hear the bear, or see Scott and Jerry?" They all shook their heads, no. "Scott knows to be down here by dark, so one of you go ahead and radio him." There was no reply, but within a few minutes Scott yelled out as loud as he could and shot his rifle three more times. Bill asked the other men, "Did any of you hear someone shooting a rifle?"

Todd said, "I think I heard something from up on the bluff right above us. There are so many trees and boulders, so it could have been an echo, but I do think I heard something."

Bill motioned for the others to follow and span out a short distance from one another. "I will yell frequently, and all of you listen for a response."

As they all walked further and closer to the bluff where Scott was, Bill yelled, "Scott!" They all heard a reply.

Scott yelled as loud as possible. He was going in and out of consciousness, and he hoped that he was not dreaming. He had lost a lot of blood and was growing weaker with every minute passing.

Bill yelled, "Scott!" They all heard a weak reply. Again Bill yelled, "Scott! Yell if you are able so we can hear you!" He told the men to stay close. He was sure Scott was very near.

Scott yelled again and said, "I am up on the bluff, right up from the jeeps."

Todd responded, "Are you all right?"

Scott didn't answer. All of a sudden he saw a flashlight and heard men talking. Scott starting yelling with what voice he had left. Suddenly they found him sitting, propped up against a tree.

Bill bent down and saw that his left calf was partially missing, and he was losing a lot of blood. The tourniquet was helping so he wouldn't bleed out. If they had been much later in finding him, he might not have been alive.

Scott grabbed Bill's arm and said, "I can't feel my left leg, and I know I can't walk. I am so glad you found me. I was attacked by the bear, but I killed it. Didn't you hear my shots? I am now out of ammo, so I couldn't shoot anymore to let you know where I was."

Bill questioned, "Where is Jerry?"

Scott replied, "I don't know where he is. He ran when the bear first went after him, and he threw the radio, so I don't know where the radio is either.

Bill asked the deputies, "Have any of you seen or heard from Jerry?" They all answered, "No."

Todd told Scott that he was going to the jeep to get a cot to carry him down, and he would return.

Bill told Todd to also make sure to bring the medical kit.

Bill instructed the deputies to search for Jerry and the radio. "Just keep calling his name. Shoot your rifles in the air so he will know we are looking for him."

Scott told Bill that he had no more ammo because Jerry was carrying the whole box with him. "I only had five rounds in my pocket, and I used them all."

One of the deputies had everyone else turn off their radios so he could try and locate the tossed one. They found it in some brush not too far from where Scott believed Jerry ran from the bear.

As Bill and Todd were readying Scott for the cot, one of the deputies looked at the bear and noticed that it had flesh in its mouth along with a piece of uniform. One of the deputies asked Scott, "Did you hear Jerry scream for help?

Scott said, "No, Jerry ran so fast I don't think the bear could have caught up with him."

The deputy said, "We'd better look around to see if we can find him. How long was the bear gone before he turned back on you?"

Scott replied, "Not more than a few minutes. I started shooting in the air as soon as Jerry ran. I was trying to scare the bear off, but I obviously attracted it in my direction."

A few of the deputies left the area with their flashlights shining on the ground, and before Bill and Todd had Scott secured on the cot, the deputies came back with Jerry slumped over one of their shoulders. His back had been ripped open, and a chunk of his right shoulder was missing. Jerry had bled to death.

Scott was emotional at the sight of Jerry. "I told him not to run, but he panicked and ran anyway. I didn't hear the bear attack him at all. I hate that the grizzly took him down, and I am so sorry for your loss."

Bill told the deputies that they were taking Scott to the hospital in Fort Collins, and if they wanted to take Jerry there, the hospital would clean him up and ready him for his family to have an undertaker take him home.

One of the deputies that knew Jerry well said that he only had his father remaining. He had no siblings, and his mother died several years ago. The deputies all agreed with Bill's suggestion and followed Todd and Bill to the hospital.

Todd drove Scott's jeep with Scott as his passenger lying across the back seat.

Scott asked Todd, "What will you do with the bear?"

Todd replied, "We'll have him picked up. Please don't worry about anything. Our first obligation is to get you patched up. Just lay there so you don't bleed out on me before I can get you to the hospital. I want you to set your mind on healing. Okay?"

When they arrived at the hospital Scott was immediately taken to the Emergency Room. Scott's leg wound seemed to be pretty deep.

Todd wanted to call Nicole, but decided to wait until they were told something from the ER doctor on duty.

As Bill and Todd waited, Dr. Williams came out of the Emergency Room and told them that Scott needed immediate surgery. After a couple of hours the surgeon came out to talk with them.

"Ranger Thompson lost a lot of blood and had to have several transfusions. The muscle was ripped almost to the bone in his calf area, but the surgery went well. We sewed up the tear, but we couldn't save all the muscle that was shredded. He needs time to heal and recuperate while it mends. Luckily he is healthy and in good shape, which will help in the healing process. You need to prepare yourselves, as he may have a lengthy recovery time that requires plenty of rest and rehab. Right now he needs to remain in this hospital for at least two or three weeks. We will keep a constant watch on his wound to try and prevent any type of infection. I ask that anyone who visits him be healthy and not get close to his face or wound area. After a month or more, he will need to start physical therapy at another facility. Have him come see me in my office two weeks after he is discharged. The nurse on duty will schedule it for him."

Bill asked, "We would like to stay here with him for a while if that's all right."

Dr. Williams nodded and said, "He will not be responsive for quite a while, but you are more than welcome to keep him company."

"Thank you, Dr. Williams."

Scott's nurse had just given him a sedative to help him sleep and not feel any pain.

Todd looked at Bill. "I think I'd better call Nicole. Scott told me that he needed to call her as soon as we got back from capturing the grizzly. I hate that she is going to be so upset, but she needs to know."

When Todd called Nicole, she answered the phone on the first ring, and she promptly started asking, "Scott, are you all right? Did you capture the bear? I've been so worried about all of you out there with that big bear."

Todd interrupted her and stammered a little which made Nicole very nervous. She quickly asked, "Todd? Is Scott all right?" Todd swallowed and then told her the story about the bear attacking him, and that it killed one of the rangers.

Nicole quickly asked, "Where is he?"

Todd explained that Scott is in the hospital in Fort Collins. "He's going to be all right. He had surgery on his left leg, and he'll have to stay in the hospital for a while to recuperate and keep any infection from setting in. Then he'll have to spend some time in physical therapy."

Nicole questioned, "Can I see him?"

He told her in a calming way that Scott was sleeping from a sedative the nurse had given him after his surgery, and he wouldn't even know she was there. "He'll be home as soon as he gets through with his physical therapy, which will begin after the hospital releases him in two or three weeks. Right now he needs plenty of rest. I will be happy to take you to see him tomorrow. Will that be okay?"

"I will be ready," she cried. "Thank you Todd for calling to let me know."

Nicole went into Catherine's room crying.

Catherine was startled and asked, "Nicole what is wrong?"

Nicole told her the story that Todd had relayed to her about Scott being attacked by the grizzly bear, and that one of the deputies was killed. Catherine quickly went to Nicole and put her arms around her, allowing her to cry into her shoulder.

"Scott is in the hospital in Fort Collins, and I cannot see him until tomorrow. All I know is that he had surgery on his left leg, and he has to stay there for several weeks. He'll have physical therapy after that, and Todd doesn't know how long that will take," she whimpered.

Catherine asked, "Would you like for me to sit with you for awhile until you can calm down enough to go back to sleep?"

Nicole nodded and said, "Yes, please." After an hour or so Nicole told Catherine she was ready to go back to bed. Catherine walked her back to her room and waited until Nicole went to sleep.

Catherine whispered to Nicole, "Tomorrow is a new day, and God will make things better for both you and Scott. You'll see."

Nicole was up earlier than Catherine. She had already showered and was out doing cabin cleanup details from vacationers that had left early that morning. She wanted to be ready for Todd to take her in the hospital. She carried her new cell phone with her just in case he called.

Catherine found Nicole after she had already finished cleaning two cabins. She tapped her on the shoulder. "Nicole, you are done for the day. Now go and see that young man of yours."

Nicole responded, "I can't Catherine. I'm waiting for Todd to take me to see him, and he hasn't called me yet to tell me when he's picking me up."

Catherine said, "I didn't check your room before I rushed to Virginia and Norman to tell them about Scott. I was hoping you would get a little more sleep. Mike was there too, and he overheard my conversation with them. I told them you were still asleep, and that's when Mike told me he saw you cleaning a cabin awhile ago. Now, I'm here to tell you to stop cleaning, as you have the rest of the day off."

Nicole pleaded, "I need to keep busy Catherine. If I think too much, I might go stir crazy just thinking about not being able to be with him. I really need to keep busy until Todd picks me up."

Nicole had no more than finished her conversation with Catherine when Nicole's cell phone rang. "Hello Todd. I'll be ready in just a few minutes. Could you pick me up at our cabin? Catherine has given me the day off so I can spend the rest of the day with Scott, if that's all right?"

Todd was there in ten minutes. Nicole was too nervous to do any talking. She rode in silence with just her thoughts about Scott and how he is doing.

When they arrived at the hospital, Todd told her, "I will take you right to his room and then I need to check with the admitting staff about his insurance, and anything else they may need. Please do not get near his face or his wound. He doesn't need an infection on top of everything else. Okay?"

"Thanks Todd," Nicole said. "I really appreciate you bringing me here and for being so thoughtful".

When they reached Scott's room, he was not alone. To Nicole and Todd's surprise, there sat Emily sitting in a chair right next to Scott's face. When Scott saw Nicole, he asked Emily, "Would you mind moving to another chair so I can see my girl?"

Emily did not respond, so Nicole went to the other side of the bed and sat in the other chair as close as she could get to him. Scott motioned her to come closer to his face, but Nicole said, "We were told to stay away from your face and wound area because of the possibility of infection."

Emily snapped, "Are you two going to start that mush stuff again in front of everybody?"

Nicole asked, "Emily, what are you doing here?"

"Well, Mike told me that Scott was in the hospital, and I wanted to see him. So, what's wrong with that?"

Nicole politely said, "Emily, nothing is wrong with you wanting to visit Scott, but I know that is not your only motive. You want Scott for yourself, and if I can help it, that's not going to happen."

Emily replied, "We'll see!"

"Emily?" Scott asked. "Could you please excuse us for a little while? I would really appreciate it? Maybe I'll see you the next time I'm visiting Nicole at the resort."

Emily retorted, "I'm not going anywhere. I came to visit with you, and I'm not leaving until I'm done. Besides, I will be staying at the resort with my mother and sister until the lodge closes in early September. I don't have to be back at school until the twenty-first, so I'm not leaving until we get the chance to know one another better."

"Emily, you can attribute my bluntness to my being on pain medication, but I don't want to get to know you any better. I have asked Nicole to marry me, and she said she would. Therefore, I don't have room in my life for anyone else, but I do appreciate you coming to see me. I would really like for you to leave. I need to spend time with Nicole."

Emily did not like his tone of voice, and she started to cry.

Todd came in and said, "What happened?"

Scott answered, "Todd, could you escort Emily back to the resort?"

Todd stammered and said, "I, I can't. She drove herself."

Emily composed herself and said, "Scott, you will be sorry you have treated me this way. Nicole is not right for you. She's too young, and you need a real woman in your life. I am what you need, and you'll find that out before this season is over. Just remember I'll be watching and waiting for you to come to me."

Emily decided it was best to let him ponder what she had said. She left and drove back to the resort.

Nicole was dumbfounded on how Scott had reacted to Emily. She looked at him and asked, "Don't you think you were a little harsh with her? And why did you tell her you proposed to me, and that I accepted? We haven't really discussed our future together?"

I know, I shouldn't have said what I did, but it was somewhat of the truth, and I want her to leave us alone. I have no place in my life for her, and besides, I don't really like her. She's too pushy, plus she's stuck on herself. I don't like that type of girl. I never have, and I never will."

Nicole answered, "Scott, I have never seen you be so brash, and in a 'tell it like it is' mood. I really don't want to compete with her for you. I'm glad you told her though, but don't you think you might have told in a little softer way? You really hurt her feelings." Scott pulled her to him and said, "Kiss me, my wife to be. I've missed you."

Nicole smiled, but didn't kiss him. "I'm not allowed to get near your face. Remember? I'm glad you are feeling better, but how exactly is your leg?"

Scott told Nicole and Todd, "The bandages will be changed this afternoon. The nurse will let you look at it, but you can't touch it, and you'll have to wear a mask.

Todd told Scott, "There is a high possibility that you could get an infection. The doctor told us that a bear's mouth is usually full of infectious germs. He also said that those germs can cause problems for a deep wound like yours."

They spent the rest of the morning and mid-afternoon talking and planning his activities once he would return home. Scott's lunch was delivered to his room, and both of them stayed until he finished. The nurse came in to take his tray. She told Scott she would be right back to give him a bath and change his dressings.

Nicole and Todd left to go to the cafeteria to get something to eat.

When they finished eating they returned to find Scott sleeping. The nurse was taking his vital signs, and she told them, "I have given him another sedative to help him get some rest. He needs as much rest as possible to help him heal more quickly and ward off infections. He will probably be asleep for up to four hours, so if you want to leave and then come back, it would probably be better for him."

"Nicole, would you like to see some of Fort Collins while we're waiting?" Todd asked.

Nicole questioned, "Do you need to relieve Bill at the station?"

Todd replied, "No, Bill is filling out paperwork about the accident and the destroying of the grizzly. If he needs me, he'll call my cell phone. I have the whole day off. Now, if I have answered your questions, would you like to see a movie or window shop, or do whatever suits our fancy?"

Nicole replied, "I would enjoy your company in seeing what Fort Collins has to offer for four or five hours."

Todd touched her elbow and said, "Well then pretty lady, let's go see what we can find to do."

Todd and Nicole toured Fort Collins. They went to a historical museum to see how Fort Collins got its name. It was originally a fort built in 1865 to house military Calvary to oversee the Overland Trail for the pioneers coming through on their way to settle further west. It was also a post for the United States mail delivery by the Pony Express. After touring the historical sight, they sat through a movie at the theater.

Four hours had passed and Nicole looked at the time on her cell phone. "Todd, I would really like to go back to the hospital to see Scott."

Todd complied with Nicole's wishes, and they returned to the hospital to see how Scott was doing.

When they entered Scott's room he had just awakened. He was a little groggy, but he recognized Nicole and Todd. He pushed the button to raise his bed to a semi-sitting position, and he held out his hand to Nicole. She instantly placed her hand in his and he pulled her to him.

She kissed him on the forehead and said, "Now, I hope that makes you feel much better."

Todd asked, "How are you feeling buddy?"

"When the pain medicine wears off I hurt, and I know I couldn't begin to walk. The swelling is making my leg feel tight and it throbs, but I'll make it. As long as I have my girl nearby, I'll be just fine. What did you two do while I was napping?"

Nicole replied, "We went to the historical museum and then to a movie. The museum was very interesting, and the pictures of the area were simply beautiful, but the movie wasn't the best, but it helped pass the time until we could come back to be with you."

Scott looked at Todd. "Did you behave yourself with my girl?"

Todd answered, "I was a perfect gentleman. Just ask Nicole."

Nicole looked at Scott and laughed, "You have nothing to worry about with us spending time together. Todd and I are friends, and we were passing time until we could come back to be with you."

With that answer Scott looked at both of them and smiled. "I trust you Todd, with not only my girl, but with my life. If it weren't for you and Bill I wouldn't be here, and I am so grateful for both of you guys carrying me down the bluff and bringing me here. I know I will heal and be fine, but in the meantime, I need you to make sure my girl is okay."

Todd nodded his head and said, "No problem, my friend."

Nicole and Todd stayed until it was dusk, and then it was time for Scott to eat his dinner and take his pain medication. Not more than twenty minutes after he ate, he was groggy again, so Nicole kissed him on the forehead, ran her fingers through his hair, and whispered in his ear that she loved him. Todd patted Scott on the shoulder, and they said their goodbyes.

Nicole turned around to Scott and said, "Until tomorrow. Sweet dreams." Scott mumbled something but they couldn't understand what he was saying, so they left to go back to the resort.

When they got into the jeep, Todd looked over at Nicole and said, "Thank you for today. I really enjoyed the time we spent together."

Nicole smiled. "It was fun, and thank you for showing me around Fort Collins."

Todd started the jeep and they rode back to the resort in silence. When they pulled into the entrance, Mike and Emily were talking in front of Norman and Virginia's cabin. Todd slowed down to acknowledge them, and Emily commented to Todd, "Oh, I see you're stepping into Scott's shoes while he's not able to take care of his little girlfriend. Maybe that's a break for me, as I am going to drive to Denver tomorrow morning, and I plan to spend the entire day with him."

Nicole said nothing, and Todd drove away from Emily, taking Nicole to her cabin.

"Would you like to eat something before you go back to the station?"

Todd shook his head in embarrassment because he had forgotten to offer her dinner before they left Fort Collins. Neither of them had eaten since an early lunch. "I'm so sorry I didn't offer you something to eat before we left the hospital. My mind was on Scott. Thank you for the offer, Nicole, but I need to get back to the station."

Nicole responded, "Todd you need to eat something, and I know there is good food waiting for us in the dining hall. I would like it if you would eat with me."

Todd replied, "Well, if you insist. I'll let you twist my arm this time. I am hungry, and I know you must be too." He left his jeep parked by Nicole's cabin and they walked to the dining hall.

Once they filled their plates, they went to a table in the corner. All of a sudden Emily and Mike walked in, and Emily started antagonizing Nicole and Todd. She asked, "Does Scott really know about the two of you?"

Todd looked at her and said "Scott knows that I will be taking Nicole to and from the hospital, so what's your problem?"

Emily gave Todd and Nicole a devilish look and replied, "It's going to be a big deal when I tell him what I see happening with his princess and his best friend. He'll get rid of you, little Miss Nicole, when I get through telling him what I see going on. Then he will realize what a catch I am for him. Your days are numbered, little princess!"

Before they could say anything else, Emily left the building. Nicole and Todd just laughed, but Nicole was a little worried about how far Emily would go to take Scott away from her.

Todd put his hand on Nicole's arm and noted, "Miss Emily will not get Scott, because he will be able to see right through her, and her actions. I'm a man, and I don't like her deceitful ways. She may have the looks, but she's not beautiful on the inside like you are. You have a wonderful personality to go along with your good looks. And before I do any more damage with my mouth, I need to get back to the station. I hope you have a wonderful, restful evening, and I'll call you in the morning to see when you can get away to go back to the hospital. Maybe Catherine would like to come along too."

Nicole wished that Scott had a phone in his room, but he didn't. She wanted to call him to see how he was feeling, and to let him know about Emily's intentions to distort their relationship. She would just have to let Scott take care of whatever Emily would say. It had been a long day, and she was very tired. She decided to turn in for the night.

Catherine stopped her in the living room and asked if Nicole was all right.

Nicole answered, "I'm okay. I'm just very tired. Sitting in a hospital room for even a few hours seems to have drained all the energy out of me, and then this problem with Emily doesn't make me feel any better."

Catherine questioned, "What is she up to now?"

Nicole responded, "Emily is going to try to make Scott jealous by inferring that Todd and I are starting a relationship. Because Scott's not available right now, she said she would make sure that Scott dumps me. She will be going to the hospital in the morning and will be staying all day with him. Todd told me that Scott won't want anything to do with her, but I don't want her putting any doubts in his head right now, especially when he needs to focus on healing. He shouldn't be worrying and thinking that I might be cheating on him."

"Oh, Nicole, he'll see right through her, and you don't need to lose sleep over Emily, and what she thinks she's going to accomplish. You just need to get some sleep, and everything will look better in the morning. After we get done cleaning you can go to see your guy," Catherine told her.

Nicole added, "By the way, Todd told me to tell you that you are welcome to come along if you'd like. I know I would certainly like for you to go with us."

"We'll see," Catherine replied.

Nicole got ready for bed and was under the covers in a short time. She had Scott on her mind when she finally dozed off. She started dreaming about how his leg wasn't healing, and it looked like he would not be able to walk properly, which would cause him to lose his job as a ranger. Then she dreamed that Emily had taken Scott away from her, and she woke up sobbing. Once she realized it was only a dream she decided to clear her mind, and just get some sleep.

When she awakened the next morning she found that Catherine had let her sleep in. It was already eight o'clock, and she smelled food in the other room.

Catherine had gone to the kitchen and had Charlie make Nicole something special for breakfast, and it was ready for her to eat. There was a note on top of the foil covering the plate, and it read, "Take your time this morning. There were only two cabins to clean, and I've already cleaned them both. You'll have plenty of time to eat something, and get ready to go see your Scott. If Todd is too busy this morning I will drive you to the hospital. I need to see that young man of yours. I can also see what Emily is up to and try to convince her to come back to the resort and spend the day with Mike."

Nicole wanted to thank Catherine for being so thoughtful in letting her sleep in, getting her breakfast and for cleaning without her help. She finished her breakfast, and then she took a warm shower. After she dried her hair, she dressed for the day. She was happy that Catherine wanted to take her to see Scott. She didn't want any trouble, but she was hoping that Catherine would convince Emily to return to the resort. She wanted to spend the day with Scott without interference from Emily.

Nicole picked up the phone and called Todd. He answered after the second ring. "Hello. I was getting ready to call you, but I didn't think you would be done with your cleaning jobs yet."

"Catherine let me sleep in this morning, and she told me that we are all done for the day. She would like to take me to see Scott, if that's all right with you? She wants to see him too," Nicole relayed.

Todd answered, "That will work out great for me because I have some work to do until this afternoon. If you would like me to bring you home this evening, I will. I doubt that Catherine will want to spend all day with Scott, do you?

Nicole answered, "No, I wouldn't think so.

Todd responded, "Then I'll meet you there."

When she hung up, Nicole took her dishes back to the dining hall and thanked Charlie for the special breakfast. "Charlie, it was delicious!" After a few minutes of conversation with him, Catherine walked in and asked if she was ready to go.

"You bet!" Nicole replied.

Catherine was motioning to the door, "Well, let's get going!"

The two of them went back to their cabin and grabbed a couple of sweaters. Catherine started her jeep and they drove out of the resort.

Nicole told Catherine, "I contacted Todd this morning, and he said that if you didn't want to stay all day at the hospital, he could bring me back.

Catherine smiled. "You don't have feelings for Todd, do you?"

Nicole replied, "No, Catherine! I only have feelings for Scott, and you don't need to worry about that. Todd is very nice to me, but there is nothing romantic going on between us. Do you think I would give up Scott and start seeing someone else? I wouldn't do that, nor give Emily that privilege. She wants a war, and now she's got one."

When they arrived at the hospital, Emily was with Scott rubbing his hand and arm. Immediately the hair rose on the back of Nicole's neck. She was jealous. With a controlled voice she went to the other side of the bed, leaned over Scott and gave him a very sweet kiss on the forehead.

Emily stopped rubbing and said to Nicole, "Hey, I'm right here, you know? I was here first, and I'm not leaving. All your kisses will not force me to leave!

"Oh! That's all right Emily. I know Scott doesn't mind sharing our time with you. It is so nice of you to visit with him. I know he must be bored just lying in bed having no one to talk with."

Emily retorted, "What's that got to do with anything? I'm still not leaving!"

Catherine decided it was time for her to say something. "Scott, I hope you don't mind all this company. I just wanted to see for myself that you are all right and getting better every day."

"Catherine, I'm doing okay, but I'm not healing as quickly as the doctor would like. I'm so tired of lying in this bed. I'm really happy to see all of you. I get so bored watching television and having no other contact except for the nursing staff."

Nicole reached over and touched his lips with her fingers, and she noticed that his lips were very warm. She touched his forehead, and it too was warm. His eyes looked dull, so she knew he wasn't feeling well. She asked, "When did the doctor say he would be coming in to see you, Scott?"

Scott replied, "The nurse said he would be in sometime this morning."

Nicole took it upon herself to go to the nurse's station and ask if one of them could come check Scott for a fever. "He seems very warm to me, and he normally doesn't have that dull look in his eyes. I would appreciate it if one of you would please check on him right away."

A nurse came immediately to check his vital signs. She put a thermometer under his tongue, checked it, and then told Nicole that she would contact the doctor.

After an hour of visiting with Scott, the doctor walked in. He asked the three ladies to please leave the room while he examined him. When the doctor finished his examination he came to them and said, "Scott's infection is getting worse. We cannot seem to get rid of it, and we are transporting him to the hospital in Denver. They will hopefully be able to rid him of the infection that is spreading. We have done all we can do here. Scott is not responding to our treatments like we thought he would. An ambulance will be taking him within the hour. I suggest you all say your good-byes in order for us to get him ready for the ambulance."

Nicole and Emily both went into his room and started to hug him at the same time. Scott looked at Emily and asked if she would mind him saying his good-byes to Nicole alone.

Emily stared at Scott and said, "What about me? Aren't you going to say good-bye to me?"

Scott nodded and replied, "Give me a hug, Emily." She hugged and kissed his neck and wouldn't let go.

Scott reacted, "Please! Let me have some time with Nicole." She left the room without saying a word, but she was still in the hallway.

Nicole leaned over and kissed Scott on the forehead. She didn't want to get near his mouth in fear of passing germs that might enhance his infection.

Scott held her tightly and asked, "Will you be able to come see me in Denver?"

Nicole responded, "I will make every effort to see you as often as I can. Maybe Todd can bring me whenever he makes the trip. Todd was planning to come see you this afternoon, so I will call him and tell him you are being transported to a hospital in Denver. You know

I love you, and I will be with you as often as I am able. Please take care of yourself, and get rid of this infection. Okay?"

"I will try very hard," Scott answered.

The nurse came in and asked them all to leave.

Catherine waved and said to Scott, "You are in my prayers. Heal quickly so this young lady won't worry herself to death."

Nicole wanted to stay until they put Scott in the ambulance, and Catherine nodded.

Emily declared, "Well, I'm going to drive to Denver every day to see him, but you won't be riding with me."

Nicole just ignored her. It was difficult having Emily hanging around, but she kept her thoughts on Scott knowing how much she would miss being with him.

When Scott was being put in the ambulance, Emily was already outside, and she was there to watch and say her goodbyes to Scott. When she saw Nicole and Catherine coming, she was disgusted and walked away toward the parking lot.

Nicole thought to herself, knowing Emily, she'll probably follow the ambulance to Denver. She couldn't understand why Emily was fighting so hard to make Scott love her. She knew he didn't love her, yet she just wouldn't give up. The question was would her persistence pay off? Would Scott find her attention loving and caring? Would he cave in to her persistence and fall in love with her? "I can't think this way," she stated out loud.

"What way are you talking about?" Catherine asked.

Nicole admitted, "Catherine, I'm just thinking out loud and wondering if Emily's persistence will cause Scott to fall out of love with me, and turn to her? If she does go see him every day, he could very well feel that she loves him more than I do, and I don't want that to happen. I love Scott so much, and I would never want to lose him to someone else." Nicole started to cry and Catherine hugged her tightly.

Catherine answered, "Don't worry yourself about losing Scott. I've seen the way he looks at you. He is deeply devoted and in love with you. Don't give up on the love you both have for one another. Emily is pushing herself on him, and men don't really like pushy women. It makes a man feel out of control. Just continue to be the same sweet and loving young lady that he loves. We'll try to get you to Denver as often as we can, but you must realize that it will only be once or twice a week at the most. It's an hour drive with the new detour, and then back again, and with a resort full of guests, we can't leave for long periods of time. Maybe Todd can take you there more often than I could. He's always going there to pick up supplies that they can't get in Fort Collins. We'll make sure you get there as often as possible. I know Todd and Bill will want to visit with him too, so don't worry. Scott Thompson will see his sweet Nicole. Since the ambulance has already taken him, we might as well head back to the resort."

Nicole responded, "Yes, I am ready to go. Thank you Catherine for helping me visualize the better side of this situation. I don't know what I would do without you."

When Scott was settled in his room in the Denver hospital, the sedation was wearing off, and he was starting to feel uncomfortable. His nurse on duty hooked up an IV and gave him medication that would ease the pain. Her name was Helen, and she asked Scott if he would like something to eat, and he said, "Yes."

After he ate lunch, Helen came back and took his tray away. On her return she sedated him so he would sleep through the afternoon. She asked, "Scott would you like some extra pillows and a warmer blanket?" He nodded, yes.

Helen came back with two more pillows but he was already asleep, so she propped up his leg under the blanket, put another pillow behind his head, turned off the light and let him rest.

When Scott awakened, it was morning. The sun was shining in his room. He pushed the button for someone to come, and Helen had been replaced by a morning nurse. Her name was Janice. She was an older, robust woman who didn't look like she would take anything off anyone, but her appearance did not match her personality at all. She was so sweet and kind. Janice brought Scott some breakfast, and he was very appreciative for her knowing that he was really hungry.

Janice stated, "After you finish your breakfast, I will come and give you a sponge bath. After the doctor has a chance to see your wound and decides what procedure he needs to do, I'll change the dressings. Does that sound like a good deal to you?"

Scott looked up from his eggs and said, "I guess so. I'm willing to do anything to get this thing healed up so I can get back to my job and my girl."

While Janice was bathing him the doctor came in, and said he would come back when they were finished. She told the doctor she would only need a few more minutes.

Within five minutes Dr. Graham came back and looked at Scott's leg. "You had quite a chunk of your calf taken out, young man. Can you tell me what happened? I have your records from the hospital in Fort Collins, but I always like the patient to tell me from his point of view."

Scott told both the doctor and Janice that he is a Rocky Mountain Ranger, and a grizzly bear had attacked him and clawed a piece of his calf off during their encounter.

The doctor said, "Well, we are going to take you to surgery in the morning, so nothing to eat after nine o'clock tonight. Okay?"

"Yes sir," Scott replied.

Dr. Graham began to tell Scott what his team would do in surgery so he would not be surprised or apprehensive about the procedures. After all the questions and discussions between them, Scott was all right with the upcoming surgery.

After Dr. Graham left the room, Scott asked Janice if he could call his girl to let her know what is going on. Since the hospital policy was not to allow long distance calls on the hospital phones, Janice let him borrow her cell phone. He immediately called Nicole.

Nicole was on her way to eat breakfast with Catherine when they both heard her cell phone ringing. She ran back to the cabin to answer it, and she screamed with delight to know that Scott was all right. "I have been so worried about you that I could hardly sleep last night. Are you okay?"

Scott told her how much he missed her, and then proceeded to tell her about his upcoming surgery in the morning.

Nicole was full of questions. "Are you okay? Are you frightened about the surgery? What time is it scheduled? Is it a nice hospital? Is your bed comfortable? Do you need anything?"

Scott interrupted her. "Nicole! Nicole! I am doing fine. Everything is nice and clean and fresh, and I am getting treated like a king. The doctor explained everything he could about what is going to take place tomorrow, and I am okay with it."

Nicole sighed and asked, "Did he tell you what time your surgery will be? I wish I were there with you. Maybe Todd or Bill will bring me to the hospital. If possible I can be there when you wake up, if not before."

Scott answered, "I think he said it will be around nine in the morning, but I'm not sure. They really keep me sedated, and it's hard for me to remember everything. I would really like for you to be here, before I go into surgery. I'll call the guys at the station when I get off the phone with you, and have one of them call you." Scott was quiet for a moment, and then he said, "Nicole, I love you!"

Nicole smiled and answered back, "I love you more." Just then she heard a familiar voice through the phone. It was Emily. "Scott, what is she doing there?"

Scott replied, "I don't know, and I didn't ask her to be here either."

Janice came into the room and told Scott that she was in need of her phone. He said his good-byes and hung up.

Nicole was left with a sinking feeling in her stomach, and she walked over to the dining hall to tell Catherine what was going on.

Catherine looked at her, placed her hands on her shoulders, and said, "Mike just told me that Emily, her mother and sister, had checked out early this morning and were going to continue their vacation in Denver.

Nicole informed Catherine that Emily came into Scott's room while she was talking with him on the phone. Nicole started to cry. "There is nothing I can do. I am going to call Todd and see if he or Bill might be driving to Denver to be with Scott before his surgery at nine o'clock in the morning. Catherine, I know there is a lot of work to be done here, but I really want to be there for Scott if that is possible."

Catherine smiled and put a finger under Nicole's chin saying, "You do whatever you feel you need to do. These cabins are not your responsibility anyway. You are here to have a vacation, not to be working yourself silly. Before you know it, your summer will be over, so I can handle the cabin cleaning for a few days. I wish I was able to take you myself, but I can't leave right now, and I know how important it is for you to be with Scott. We'll get you there somehow."

Nicole left without eating breakfast and ran back to the cabin to call Todd and Bill. The phone rang a few times, and Bill answered.

Nicole told Bill all about Scott's upcoming surgery, and asked, "Have either of you heard from Scott today?"

Bill replied, "No, we haven't heard from him, and we had no idea what was happening. One of us will have to be at the hospital in the morning to give them Scott's insurance and personal information. If you want to ride with one of us, it will be fine. We will have to leave around six-thirty to get there before his surgery, and allow us some time to be with him before they sedate him."

Nicole replied, "I'll be ready and waiting at the cabin door. Thank you, Bill."

In the morning Todd was there at six-thirty to pick her up, and Nicole was happy to see him. She was glad he was taking her to see Scott. They got along well with one another, and it would be easy to talk with him on the hour ride.

Todd was such a gentleman. He got out of the jeep to help Nicole get in. He looked at her, and with a pause, he questioned, "Are you ready for what's ahead?"

Nicole answered with her head down, "I think so."

Todd placed his hand on her hands and gently squeezed them. He started the jeep, and they waved at Catherine as they were leaving.

The ride was going to take longer due to the detour, but they didn't care. Nicole shared with Todd about Emily walking into his room at the hospital while Scott was on the phone telling her about the time of his surgery. He told her that he didn't know Emily was coming, and he really didn't want her there, but there she was.

"I really don't know how to react to Emily's insistence of pushing herself on Scott." Nicole said.

Todd suggested to Nicole, "Why don't we let him see that we are there for him, and that we can also be compassionate with Emily. It isn't Scott's fault that she is so intrusive and thoughtless of others. She seems to be a spoiled young woman who has her eye on the prize, and she isn't willing to not get her way, regardless of who she hurts in the process."

They made excellent time and were there a little before eight o'clock. Todd went to the registration station and gave the clerk

Scott's information. They were told his room number, and they hurriedly left to find him before he was sedated.

When they reached the room, the nurse was preparing the IV for his medication drip. Scott saw the two of them and was elated that they were there before his surgery.

Scott excitedly exclaimed, "I am so glad to see both of you. Thank you for making it before I am too groggy to know anything. Thank you again for coming. Nicole, I am so glad to see you. Come here so I can hug you my sweet girl. I missed you all night long. All I have been thinking about is that I wanted to see both of you before my surgery, and here you are. I will be so happy to get rid of this infection, and hopefully the surgeon can help me with that. He's already told me that my antibiotics will be heavy doses, but whatever helps me get back on my feet again is all right with me."

Nicole was hugging Scott and telling him that she missed being with him too. "I know we just saw one another yesterday, but it seems like such a long time ago to me."

Just then Emily walked into the room and gasped at the scene of Scott hugging Nicole, and she said rather loudly, "What are you doing here?"

Nicole answered, "I should ask you the same thing. If you must know, I am here to see my Scott before his surgery." Nicole remembered what Todd had said, and she decided to take a different approach with Emily. "How are you, Emily?"

"What do you care, Nicole? I am here to see Scott, and that is all. You two can leave now that I am here."

Todd looked at Emily and said, "We are not going anywhere, as we are here until after his surgery, so it's going to be a long wait for the three of us, so you might as well get use to it. Now, if we can remember that Scott is being prepared to go into surgery, we all need to be cordial and upbeat for him. He shouldn't have to worry about us. He needs our support, not our unpleasantness."

Scott asked, "Emily, are you going to be nice while I'm asleep? You know how important Nicole and Todd are to me, and if you are going to stay, I want you to be nice to them. Okay?"

Emily gave Scott a loud sigh and said, "Okay."

Emily went over to Scott's bed and asked Nicole to please move, as she wanted to say something to him before they gave him the sedation. Nicole moved, and Emily sat right beside him on the bed. She leaned over and gave him a long kiss near his lips and said, "I love you Scott, and I'll be here waiting for you."

Nicole was shocked at her aggressiveness, but she held her temper and smiled.

Todd squeezed her hand and slightly shook his head. Nicole and Todd looked at one another and almost burst out laughing, but they held their composure.

Scott reached his hand out for Nicole but Emily grabbed it and wouldn't let go. As a nurse and attendants were preparing to wheel Scott to the operating room, they had to tell Emily that she could go no further, so she would have to release his hand. When she finally released it, Scott blew a kiss to Nicole and winked at her.

Todd and Nicole sat side by side in adjoining chairs in the waiting area while Emily sat on the opposite side of the room and stared at both of them. Nicole and Todd talked about the ordeal with the grizzly bear and how it would have been shot regardless. It already had the taste of human blood and flesh, and therefore it was a danger to people. Nicole had many questions about the bear, and their conversation continued for quite some time.

Emily dropped a magazine and looked at them almost shouting, "How can you two sit there and talk about a stupid bear while Scott is in surgery and may lose his leg or his life because of that animal? Do you not have any remorse about you? Scott risked his life for all of us, and you are sitting there talking about blood and guts from a stupid bear. You both are sick!"

Todd looked at Emily and said, "We are just as concerned about Scott as you are, and probably even more than you, because we have known him longer, and we love him, not just as someone we can capture or control, but someone we feel is a brother to me and a future husband to Nicole."

Nicole also answered, "I know you care about Scott, and I know he appreciates your attentiveness during this time, but he's my guy, and I'm his girl, and I'm not going to let him go for you or anyone else. We are making marriage plans Emily, and I would appreciate you not stirring up the pot with your lies and sore intentions."

Emily was in the process of telling them both off when Dr. Graham walked in to talk with them about Scott's condition and recovery treatment.

He said, "With time and proper treatment Scott should be up in a few more weeks to start some light physical therapy, but we need to be careful that no more infection sets in. He will have a permanent scar and some loss of muscle from the bite area, but he should be as good as expected in five or six months. He will need to attend additional physical therapy after he leaves the hospital, and then I want to see him in my office for a final examination and give him his release papers to allow him to go back to work. One more thing, I want everyone to be concerned about your own health. If any of you have a cold or any type of illness, please refrain from visiting him. He does not need to be fighting an illness as well as the infection. No kissing his lips or breathing into his face. I would rather all of you stay away from his facial area. Do you have any questions?"

Immediately Emily asked if she could see him. The doctor told her that Scott was still in recovery, and because of the medication he was given, he will probably sleep the rest of the day. He preferred that he get total rest and no visitors until tomorrow. He asked if they had any other questions, and Nicole asked, "Is the infection gone?" Dr. Graham answered, "We hope we got all of it, and the treatments we will be giving him in his IV will treat whatever we couldn't get through surgery. He is very lucky to still have his lower left leg."

Todd and Nicole both said at the same time, "Thank you, Dr. Graham."

Without so much as a good-bye, Emily left them standing there, and neither of them knew where she was going, but they were certainly happy to see her leave. Even though they knew Emily might be gone for now, she would surely be back bright and early in the morning.

Todd looked at Nicole and said, "We need to find a hotel to stay in tonight. Would you like to call Catherine and let her know what is going on?"

Nicole answered, "Yes, I do need to call her. She had no idea I would not be back this evening, and neither did I."

"I saw a hotel when we were driving here that is not far from the hospital. I'll make arrangements for the both of us."

Nicole agreed but told him that she would pay for her own room.

Todd smiled and questioned, "Did you think I was going to try and take advantage of you?"

She blushed and smiled, which made them both laugh.

When they were registering for their rooms, they looked up and saw Emily standing on the steps staring at them with her hands on her hips. She came toward them and started yelling, "You are not staying here! I was here first, and I don't want to be in the same building with the two of you."

Todd gave her a stern look and told her to calm down. "We have every right to be here, just as much as you do."

Emily stalked off but then turned around and said, "Wait until Scott hears that the two of you are sharing a room together."

Todd replied, "Check the register and you'll find that we have separate rooms on different floors."

Emily questioned, "What's to stop you from slipping into her room tonight?"

In a soft voice Todd answered, "I respect Nicole too much for that, and I know she belongs to my best friend, Scott. I wouldn't do that to her or to him. You have an evil mind, Emily."

"Look who's talking," Emily lashed back as she walked away.

Nicole told Todd that she was ready for a hot shower and a good night's sleep.

Todd asked, "Are you hungry?"

Nicole replied, "I had forgotten we haven't eaten much today, so yes, I would like something to eat before going to bed."

He noticed that the hotel had a nice restaurant, so they ventured off for a good dinner. As they were eating and conversing with one another he told Nicole a funny joke, and they both laughed.

Nicole said, "I needed that." It had been a long day, and she thanked him for lightening things up a little. He nodded in compliance.

After dinner Todd walked her to her room then left to go up the elevator.

She was very tired, but she knew she'd feel better if she took a warm shower before retiring. She called Catherine to let her know what was going on, and that she was spending the night at a hotel near the hospital. She told her about Scott's surgery, and that Emily was at the hospital hovering over him, and that she was also staying in the same hotel. Todd was in a room several floors above her, so she was alone and very tired.

"Catherine, I'll call you to let you know when we'll be back. We want to see Scott for awhile tomorrow, but he will be heavily sedated, and we won't know if he'll even be awake long enough to know that we are there. I'll call you tomorrow to let you know what is going on. I am so tired, and I just want to go to sleep. Goodnight Catherine. I'll see you tomorrow." Nicole said.

She laundered her under garments with shampoo and hung them over the shower curtain to dry and then got under the covers. The bed was very comfortable and she dozed off almost immediately.

Todd had already taken his shower and was lying on his bed thinking about Nicole and how much he really liked her. She was smart, levelheaded, witty and very attractive. He could envision why Scott loved her so much. He had to be careful, because he was beginning to have deeper feelings for her, and she was his best friend's girl. If Emily could pick up on his feelings toward Nicole, he knew Scott would also. He had to be very careful to hide those feelings from everyone, especially Scott and Nicole.

The next morning Todd called Nicole in her room to see if she was ready for the continental breakfast that was being served.

"I'm almost ready. I'll meet you there in a few minutes." She really didn't like wearing the same clothes again, but since neither of them came prepared to stay overnight, they didn't have a choice.

After breakfast they drove to the hospital, and as they had expected, Emily was already in Scott's room talking to him. Scott was so thrilled to see Nicole that he asked Emily to let her sit next to him. Emily was not at all happy with Scott just throwing her to the side. She moved but told him, "Did you know that they slept together last night."

Scott looked at them and asked, "What's going on?"

Todd said, "We were in separate rooms on separate floors, and we would never do that to you. Emily is just trying to cause trouble as usual."

Emily retorted, "I saw him follow her to her room."

Todd explained, "I walked her to her room to make sure she got there safely, and left immediately. I didn't go into her room. You know me better than that."

Nicole retorted, "Emily, You are such a liar, and Scott will never believe anything you have to say!"

Emily was almost yelling, "Then why are you so sensitive about what I said, Nicole?"

Finally, Scott had all he could take. "Emily, I would like for you to leave, now!"

She started to say something else, but he interrupted her. "I don't want to hear another word you have to say, and by the way, I don't want you to visit me anymore. I don't like, nor want to put up with a liar."

Emily was crying. "You can't mean that! I'm always here for you. Don't you know that I love you? I love you more than anyone could ever love you, including her. You'll be sorry Scott, that you've been so mean to me." As she was walking out of the room she cried out in between sobs, "I will still be here for you. I'm not leaving Denver. You'll be calling me when little Miss Nicole messes up, and that will be sooner than you think."

Nicole and Todd looked a little alarmed at how unsympathetic Scott had been with Emily. Neither of them minded that she would not be around, but she got her heart broken by the one person she wanted to love her, even though it didn't seem to be reciprocated.

Scott looked at them and asked, "Was I really that hard on her? She has tried and tried to turn me against you Nicole, and she would go to any lengths to accomplish her task. I am finally tired of it. She will never be any more than a friend to me. Now I hope she won't even be that. Do you understand?"

Nicole replied, "Yes, I do understand, but you are going to be here in the hospital for a while longer, and I won't be able to see you as often as I would like. I have to depend on Catherine, Todd or Bill to bring me here. Maybe if you explained to Emily that all you can be is a friend to her, and nothing more, maybe she can keep you company when I can't be with you. Whenever Todd or Bill has a need to come to Denver, I will be here. I just want you to realize that as much as I want to see you, I can't be here every day. I will try to work it out to be here at least once or hopefully twice a week. That's probably the best I'll be able to do."

Nicole continued, "You can call me every day now, and I will do the same. I do realize your physical therapy will be hard at first as you are scheduled to have it twice a day. You may be too tired to have company or talk on the phone until you can build up your stamina. You have not been able to move around much since the accident, and you are going to be hurting once the therapist has you in physical therapy."

"Nicole, I want to see and hear from you every day. I can't imagine you not being with me but only once or twice a week, and not hearing your voice will be horrible. Since I will be stuck in this hospital for awhile, that will be harder on me than the physical therapy. You can't imagine how much I miss you." Scott answered.

Nicole added, "Scott, this will be good training for us because I will be leaving soon to go back to college. We definitely won't be able to be together on a regular basis then. Maybe this will be a good time for us to adjust and endure being absent from one another. You can call me anytime, and I can call you back. By the way, where is your cell phone?"

"I don't know. I can't find it, and I don't remember what I did with it. I don't even want to think about it." Scott replied.

Todd responded, "Hey buddy, let's think about the positives here. You will be out of here in a short time as long as you work hard to accomplish that goal. Then you will be able to see Nicole every day until she has to leave for school. Doesn't that make you want to work harder?"

Scott lowered his eyes and answered, "You're right. I can do this, and I will work as hard as I can to get back to my job and to both of you. I have a lot to be thankful for, and I'm sorry I have been such a grouch. I will have a better attitude. I promise."

"I will look into what might have happened to your cell phone, and if it can't be located, I will make sure you have another one. We want you to be able to keep in contact with all of us. First I'll try calling your phone to see if we can hear it ring." Todd dialed Scott's number from his own cell phone, but there was no ringing anywhere in his room. "I will report it missing." He tried to call it again to make sure he dialed the right number, and it rang twice and someone answered. It was Emily.

Todd asked, "What are you doing with Scott's cell phone?"

Emily answered, "He gave it to me to hold onto when he was first brought to the hospital. Why? What's it to you anyway?"

Todd replied, "Emily, you need to bring it back to Scott in the morning. He needs his phone to keep in contact with us."

"Why would I want to let him have contact with the likes of you two?" Emily asked.

Todd responded, "He still has to keep in contact with his employer, and he wants it to contact his friends. He doesn't know that you have it, but he will need it back."

Emily retaliated, "I don't know if I will do that. Maybe I don't want him to contact the two of you."

Todd reacted, "That's not up to you to decide. I can report it stolen, but better yet, I'll just get him a new phone with a new number, and he won't need the phone you won't return. There's always a way around you, Emily."

"I will bring it back tomorrow morning, but I'll make sure he doesn't have either of your numbers on it." Emily said.

Todd replied, "Whatever Emily!"

After Todd and Nicole had visited for several hours, Helen, Scott's favorite nurse, brought his lunch and some medication to allow him to eat and not get sick to his stomach.

Helen said, "I'll be back after you eat to give you more medication in your IV. When it takes effect, I'll have to ask your friends to leave.

Helen looked at Scott and Nicole and said, "He really needs some sound sleep to allow his body to relax and promote the healing process. His chart showed that he had a very restless night. The more sound sleep he gets the sooner he will start to heal. I know you have traveled from Estes Park, and it's a long drive, but it would probably be a good idea to come back tomorrow."

Todd looked at Scott and held his hand. "Take care, buddy. We'll either talk or try to come back tomorrow." Todd left the room to give Nicole and Scott some private time.

Nicole kissed Scott on the top of his head. She had tears in her eyes as she laid her head on his chest. She didn't want to leave him, but she knew she had to for his sake.

Scott hugged her tightly and kissed the top of her head. "I love you, Nicole. Don't be too long. I need you more than ever right now."

Nicole kissed Scott's hand and left the room.

Tears were streaming down Nicole's cheeks, and Todd took his handkerchief and gently wiped her tears. He put his arm around her as they walked out of the hospital. He wanted to pull her into his arms and console her, but he knew he should not do that. He had very deep feelings for her at that moment. He knew she only thought of him as a good friend to both her and Scott, but he had wanted a moment like this for a long time.

When they got to the jeep, Todd held Nicole and let her cry into his shoulder. When she had calmed down, he helped her get settled in her seat. He came around to the driver's side, hopped into his seat and sat there for a few minutes thinking. He knew it was the wrong time to say anything about his feelings for her. He knew he would have to wait for the right time.

As they drove back to the resort, they didn't talk very much. The silence was almost too much for him. He knew how she felt about Scott, and if he confessed his feelings he might ruin any relationship the three of them might have.

When they arrived at the resort, she asked him to have dinner with her and Catherine.

"Yes, I would really like to do that, but I need to call Bill first and let him know where I am, and when I'll be back at the station."

Catherine was so glad to see them both. She noticed that Nicole had been crying and she looked at both of them. Todd noticed her looking at them, and he slightly shook his head, and nodded to let Catherine know that he would clue her in at a later time.

Virginia, Norman and Mike came in and sat with them, and they talked about Scott's progress.

Nicole had tears in her eyes, but she remained reserved as they discussed the additional length of time he would have to remain in the hospital.

Norman told Nicole that she could use their car anytime she wanted to go see him. He informed her that their plans were to close the resort the day after Labor Day, so she would still have a little more time to visit with him.

Nicole appreciated the offer, but told Norman, "I don't really feel secure enough to drive to Denver by myself."

Norman said, "I won't be able to leave the resort now, but Catherine could use our car if it is needed."

Catherine said, "Thanks Norman, but I have my own car."

They all laughed.

"I'll take you, if you would like me to." Mike offered.

Todd grinned. "I don't think Scott would appreciate that very much. I think you are thought of as competition for him with Nicole."

Mike laughed. "Well, you can't say I didn't try."

Everyone laughed again, and Nicole and Todd felt a sense of relief from the lightness and laughter at their table.

After dinner, Nicole and Catherine returned to their cabin. Todd followed in order to talk with Catherine while Nicole took her shower.

He told Catherine all about Emily and Scott, and everything that had happened. "Nicole was heartbroken about not being able to see Scott on a daily basis, and just knowing that Emily will be returning to try to turn Scott against her was another thing. Even though Nicole encouraged Scott to continue to let Emily visit with him, it was with much concern, but a wonderful gesture on her part. We had to defend ourselves to Scott against Emily's lies, and that is when Scott forced her to leave. Nicole is afraid that Emily will continue to make up lies and Scott will eventually believe them. With Nicole not being in his presence on a regular basis, plus their relationship from such a long distance after the resort is closed, it would be a strain on both of them, and with Emily's input it may not survive."

Nicole's shower relieved all the tightness she had in her body. Now she was ready for a good night's rest. She put on some sweat pants and a baggy sweatshirt and came out to the living area to say good night to Catherine and Todd.

Todd told them all good night. He needed to get back to the station.

Nicole walked him to his jeep, and he hugged her, and held her close for a few seconds. He smiled and kissed her on the forehead, and said, "Good night Princess."

She didn't know whether to smile at him or not. The kiss on the forehead left her a little confused, but she felt something for Todd. She just didn't know what it was.

After he left, she went back into the cabin and shared with Catherine the happenings of her day.

Catherine listened intently to how she was telling her story. "Nicole, you need some sleep and let all the turmoil of the day be released from your thoughts. Pray before you fall asleep. It always helps me."

Nicole gave Catherine a goodnight kiss on the cheek and went to her bedroom.

Before she went to sleep she decided to call her parents. "Hello Mom! How are you and Dad? I miss you too, but I'll be home soon. Norman told us tonight that the resort will be closing the day after Labor Day. After we clean and close up all the cabins, Catherine and I will be heading home. I have so much to tell you about my wonderful summer in Colorado. Tell Dad I love him too, and I'll see you both soon. Yes, I'll be careful. I'll call you before we leave to come home. Okay? I love you too. Bye Mom."

When she hung up the phone, she crawled into bed and nestled in for a good night's rest. She was tired and drained from all the day's events. She prayed for Scott and his fellow rangers, and everyone who worked at the resort, especially Catherine. Tomorrow would come soon, and she decided to let her body and mind relax to enjoy some sleep.

The sun was shining in Nicole's windows, and the warmth of it awakened her. She had a good night's sleep, and she felt refreshed and well rested. She turned over and looked at the clock on her night stand. It was eight-thirty. Catherine had let her sleep in again. She jumped out of bed and rushed into the bathroom to get ready for the day. After she got dressed and made her bed, she ran to the dining hall. She was out of breath when she saw Catherine, Norman and Virginia sitting at a table.

"May I join you?" Nicole asked.

They each nodded and replied, "Sure, we've been waiting on you."

She picked out her breakfast and went back to the table. "I'm sorry I slept in this morning. I didn't realize I was so tired," Nicole responded.

Catherine said, "I know you had a lot on your mind, so I wanted to make sure you got a good night's sleep. I hope you did? When I came in to check on you this morning, you were sound asleep."

Nicole replied, "I know I dreamed a lot, but I don't remember anything. I am truly refreshed this beautiful morning and ready to go."

Virginia added, "Don't you just hate when that happens, especially when you think your dreams were really good ones?"

Everyone laughed.

Mike came in to see if there was anything left for breakfast. He asked if he could join them, and Virginia patted the bench beside her. After he filled his plate and came back to the table, he asked Nicole, "How is Scott doing?"

Nicole answered, "He is doing much better. Thank you for asking. Todd and I had to leave earlier than we had anticipated because his nurse gave him a shot to help him rest, and she told us we should come back tomorrow. He had a few restless nights before and after the surgery, and that his recovery will require him getting a lot of rest. He is to start his physical therapy in a few weeks, and he'll need to build up his stamina to be able to walk and do the other exercises. After he received his shot, he nodded off within a few minutes, so Todd and I left because he went into a deep sleep. I will call him later on. He won't be too happy that Todd nor I will be able to see him today, but I know he will understand. Any of us driving to Denver every day is simply out of the question, and he knows that. Emily will probably visit with him in our place."

Mike said, "I can take you to Denver every other day. I'm taking a class now at the University, and it's only for two more weeks, so I could take you and drop you off. My class starts at nine o'clock and ends at three. He wouldn't have to know that I was driving you back and forth."

"I really appreciate the offer Mike, but I have duties here, and I feel badly that Catherine has to pick up the slack for the work I am supposed to be doing." Nicole answered.

Mike replied, "Well, if you change your mind just let me know. It won't be a problem for me. The hospital is just a block or two from the university."

Catherine knew that Mike probably had other motives in mind, but she kept her thoughts to herself. It was a nice gesture though. Maybe the ole boy was changing into a nice guy after all, but she doubted it. He always had an ulterior motive.

Nicole asked, "Now that I've eaten a delicious breakfast, and I'm wide awake, what can I do to help you, Catherine? I know you probably have almost everything done by now, but I do want to help."

"Nothing, as I got everything done early this morning. We are free to relax. How about a swim at the pool and some time to talk? By the way, your parents called while you were in Denver. I told them you would call them back when you got a chance." Catherine said.

Nicole responded, "I called them last night before I went to bed. Mom didn't mention that they had called earlier, but they are doing fine and are anxious for me to come home before I have to leave for school. I do miss them. I spent very little time with them before I came out here because I got on a plane one day after my finals. It was nice to talk with my mother. I don't remember where she said that Dad was, so I didn't get to talk with him, but all seems to be well in Springfield."

While they were sitting at the pool, Nicole's cell phone rang. It was Bill. "Hello Bill. How are you today?"

He answered, "I'm fine thank you. I just called to tell you that I have to be in Denver tomorrow morning for a meeting, and I don't exactly know how long it will be, but I thought maybe you would like to spend some of the day with Scott?"

Nicole said, "I would love to spend some time with him. Catherine is right here with me at the pool. May I call you back after I ask her if she would mind me being gone tomorrow? Hold on Bill, she's walking toward me now. She said I'm not needed, so thank you for thinking of me. What time do you need to leave?

Bill answered, "I'll be there at seven thirty. I'll pick you up at your cabin. Okay?"

"Thanks again Bill. I'll be ready and waiting," Nicole said.

Nicole asked, "Catherine, are you sure you won't need me to help you?

Catherine replied, "We are low on visitors right now, and we won't have any more people coming until the weekend, so it's very slow, and I want you to go visit your young man while you have the chance. We'll start having more visitors beginning next week, and in mid-August before school starts. Our long term visitors will be leaving before all that rush comes. Then, I'll need your help. Until then, I want you to see Scott as much as you can. Just give him our love, and tell him we are all praying for his quick recovery."

Nicole and Catherine were at the pool splashing one another and laughing so hard they were both crying. For Nicole it was such a release of all the worry and stress.

Catherine could see it on Nicole's face and her slumped shoulders. "I know it's hard when you know Emily is just around the corner waiting for you to slip up, and for Scott to be tired of you not being there for him, but as you already know, Emily has slipped up a few too many times, and he knows that. So don't you worry yourself into a stupor. Everything is going to work out just fine. Say, let's have some fun and not think of all this serious stuff. I am going to challenge you to a lap race."

They both jumped in and swam the length of the pool six laps until Nicole was expended of all her energy.

"Wow Catherine! You are so fit. I couldn't do another lap if I tried, and you are ready to swim more laps. I guess I'm getting flabby at my age, and I need more physical exercise," Nicole exclaimed.

Catherine acknowledged, "I know. That's why I wanted us to race. Just sitting in a hospital talking and waiting is not very healthy for your body. Since there is no one here right now to swim, I wanted us to do some laps. You'll be sitting tomorrow, and Scott will be lying in a bed, so you won't be doing any exercise at all."

Nicole laughed and said, "I think, I thank you, but I'm not sure. My muscles ache right now, and I hope they calm down by tomorrow."

Catherine added, "If they cramp, you'll have to get up and walk around a little. Then you'll have some exercise even if it's just walking in circles."

After each of them showered and dried their hair, they changed into some comfortable clothes. Catherine suggested they go visit the ranger's station.

Nicole thought that was a great idea.

When they arrived Todd was working on the grounds, and he walked over to see who was there. "Oh! It's my two favorite ladies. Hello Catherine, hello Nicole."

Catherine answered, "We just wanted to find out if Scott had talked with either of you, and secondly we just needed to get away from the resort for a little while.

Todd looked at Nicole, smiled and told her that they just got off the phone with him. "Scott was wondering if we had seen or talked with you, and I told him that Bill will be bringing you tomorrow morning to spend the day. He seemed really excited with that news."

Nicole asked, "Did Emily give him back his cell phone, or did you have to get him a new one?"

Todd replied, "Emily did relinquish it freely to Scott because I threatened her. I told her I was going to tell him that she took it, but she told him before I could."

Nicole smiled and took out her cell phone and dialed Scott's number. He answered on the second ring.

Scott answered, "Hello, My sweet girl. I was hoping you would call me because I know Emily took your number along with Todd's and Bill's off of my phone so I couldn't call you. When it rang I knew it was you."

"How are you feeling today, Scott? Have you started physical therapy yet?" Nicole asked.

Scott responded, "I have some progression, but I'm still a long way from being somewhat normal. I feel so much better today, but now I feel terrific because I'm talking with you. Yes, I have started a light physical therapy. It's tough, but I'll work hard at it. I heard you are coming to see me tomorrow. Todd told me that Bill is bringing you. I can't wait to see you. I don't have to be on such heavy medication now that the infection is pretty much gone, so I won't be such a sleepy head."

"Is Emily still coming to see you?" Nicole asked.

Scott replied, "Yes, she came today, but I told her I didn't want her here tomorrow, at all."

Nicole questioned, "Do you think she will listen to you? If she knows I'm going to be there, she will be there for sure. She doesn't want me near you."

Scott said, "I don't care what she wants. If she shows up, I will ask her to leave. Okay? My therapy is at nine-thirty in the morning, but it sometimes changes depending on the therapist. I have it again at three o'clock, and you will be allowed to help me with that one. That is if you want to?"

Nicole answered, "I don't know how long Bill's meeting will be, so I can't tell you how long I'll be able to visit with you. If I am still there for your three o'clock session, I would love to help you. I can't wait to see you Scott!"

Scott said with excitement, "I can't wait to see you either. If you should try to call me and I don't answer, it's because I'm in therapy, and they won't allow us to bring cell phones in there. So don't ever think I don't want to talk with you because I do. I hide my phone in my cabinet so Emily won't take it. If she answers it, just hang up on her."

Todd looked at Catherine and said, "Nicole's got it bad, doesn't she?"

Catherine just nodded her head and then said, "She does have it bad for that young man." To change the subject, "Is Emily still in the picture?"

Todd nodded his head. "She won't give up even though Scott told her to never come back. He says she's always there in the morning until dark, and won't listen to him telling her, I don't want you here, Emily! I know Scott is very sincere with his feelings toward Nicole, and I feel Nicole is just as sincere. I just hope she doesn't get hurt by all this."

Catherine nodded in agreement with Todd. Then she laughed and said, "Well ranger boys, it's time for us to head on down the road.

On the ride home Nicole wore a huge smile, and Catherine smiled too.

When they drove into the resort, Virginia came to the car and told them that a skunk had walked into their cabin, and neither she nor Norman were too anxious to chase it out. "We left all the doors open so it could find its way out, but we don't think it has taken the hint."

Catherine and Nicole burst out laughing.

Virginia said, "It's not that funny!"

Norman was laughing too.

Mike went in the house, checking to see if it was still there, but then he came running out with the skunk right behind him. The look on his face was enough to make anyone laugh, and everyone did except for Mike.

Catherine thought they best leave before Mike got too mad at them. She yelled as they were moving in the jeep, "See you at dinner, and Mike, I hope you don't smell bad."

Catherine and Nicole bent over laughing, and Nicole said, "I sure did need that laugh!"

At dinner they saved a table for Virginia, Norman and Mike. As they all came in the door, Nicole and Catherine started laughing.

Mike was irritated, but started laughing too. "I guess it was pretty funny, wasn't it?"

Catherine chuckled and said, "It sure was. Mike, I wish you could have seen the look on your face. You looked scared to death, and I've never seen you run so fast."

"At least the skunk took off, so I guess I scared the daylights out of it. I wasn't looking forward to all that stuff I would have to bathe in to get rid of the smell, nor did I want to sleep outside and possibly attract another skunk to me. I'm just glad it's all over with, and I'm glad you all got the big laugh to make your day," Mike commented.

Virginia looked at Mike and lightly pinched his cheek adding, "We still love you even though we all laughed. I hope you can see the humor in all of this."

"I do." Mike responded. "I have to admit it must have looked pretty funny, but maybe not to me at that moment."

Virginia added, "I know it was my fault because I was trying to take the pot from the fireplace, as I had some cinnamon cider left in the bottom. When I took the pot off the hook some cider dropped on the hot ambers and smoke went everywhere. I opened the doors and the windows to help get rid of all the smoke. I am assuming the skunk saw a chance to get in, and it did. I'm sorry my mistake caused you to take the brunt of the humor."

After dinner, Catherine and Nicole returned to their cabin, and Nicole thanked her for letting her go to see Scott in the morning when she felt she should be helping at the resort.

Catherine stated, "Nicole, I know the weeks have turned into almost two months, and I want you to enjoy the rest of your stay here and be as happy as you can be. Your being here this summer has been a wonderful treat for me and everyone else. It has not been just a treat, but a real blessing. We have all enjoyed you so very much."

Catherine continued, "I know you have very loving feelings for Scott, and I have already talked to you a little bit about whirlwind summer romances, but I just want you to realize that those kinds of feelings very rarely pan out. That cliché of "*absence makes the heart grow fonder*" isn't always the truth. Right now you and Scott are in the "*sweet romance*" stage of your relationship. It's different from having a crush, and it feels good. Don't get me wrong, it is a wonderful time in your life, but a lot of things can happen to cause that feeling to turn into bitterness if you both move too quickly without truly knowing one another well. Like it was said in a children's film, you are both "*twitterpatted*," falling in love, but there's a life after romance, and it's different. You have to be intelligent about money, paying the bills, having enough money to treat yourselves once in a while, and when children become a part of your family, your love has to remain very strong for one another in order to share it with your children.

Children should never have to bear the brunt of wrong decisions. That's what is wrong with our society today. Too many young people get married without talking things through to make sure they are ready for the rough times in a marriage. And when they are not, the next thing you know, they are divorced with children having to split their home between two parents, and possibly having to share their lives with a step-parent, and step-brothers and sisters. We have made a mess of what God intended to be a perfectly good home with one set of parents. I know you know all about what I'm saying, as you must have seen it with friends in school. With you and Scott living in two different parts of the country, it will be very hard to keep things exciting and full of what you have right now. You will miss each other tremendously, and neither of you will be able to afford hopping on a plane on a regular basis just to see one another over a weekend, and still keep it fresh like it is now. You are an intelligent and beautiful girl, and I just want you to think about what I am trying to tell you. Be smart and let God guide you, and in time His answers are always going to be the best."

Nicole answered, "I will ponder on all the things you have told me. I know you know more about life and love than I do, and I appreciate you explaining the dos and don'ts of long distance romances. I know you are right, and I need to pay attention to not letting myself be led only by my heart, but by my head also. That was a very loving thing for you to say, but I know there will be a lot of give and take with my being away at college, and him working here in Colorado. I am hoping that love will conquer all the stepping stones of our relationship."

Catherine replied, "I do too, Nicole. I don't know about you, but I am tired and am ready for a good night's sleep. How about you? I know Bill will be here early in the morning to pick you up, so you might want to turn in too. If you want breakfast before you leave, have Charlie make something for you and Bill to take with you. Have a good night's sleep, and I'll probably see you in the morning before you leave."

"Catherine, I love you. I hope you have a wonderful restful sleep, and I too will see you in the morning," Nicole responded.

After a good night's sleep, Nicole was brushing her hair when she heard a jeep pull up outside the cabin. It was Bill, and he was a little early. She grabbed her sweater, purse and cell phone and ran out into the front room where Catherine was waiting.

Catherine said, "Nicole, you look refreshed this morning." Then she gave her a hug and handed her two paper bags with their breakfast.

Nicole thanked Catherine for getting their breakfasts, gave her a hug, then ran down the steps of the cabin and greeted Bill.

Catherine came down a few steps and said, "Have a wonderful day, and tell Scott we all said, hello. Bill, be careful, and Nicole give me a call when you arrive safely. Okay?"

Bill smiled and nodded as he held the door of his jeep open for her.

As they were leaving the resort, Mike and Norman were working on the resort sign, and they waved. Nicole was thrilled that she felt they were all her family, but now she was on her way to see her guy.

It was hard trying to talk over the wind in an open jeep, but every once in a while Bill would try to converse with her. He finally stopped at a gas station and asked if she was hungry.

Nicole said, "I brought, or actually Catherine got Charlie to make us some breakfast, so if you are hungry, we can eat it before we get back on the road. She opened the bag. Hey Bill, I hope you like scrambled eggs and biscuits plus a fruit cup. Thanks Charlie for the great breakfast!"

Bill answered, "I need some coffee to go along with what's in the bags. Would you like something to drink?"

Nicole answered, "I'll come with you if that's okay. I'm not really a coffee drinker."

Bill opened the door as they entered the restaurant portion of the station. He asked Nicole to select whatever she wanted to drink, and she picked a fruit smoothie while he got a cup of strong coffee. They took their drinks and breakfast to a little sitting area outside.

As they were eating, Nicole told Bill, "I can understand now why people love to live here. It is so beautiful and breathtaking with the mountains and all the lakes. You have all four seasons and can enjoy each one of them. I hope I can return here again and again."

Bill said, "I really like the mountains. Where I'm from we don't have mountains, only farmland and cities. My folks still farm the same property that belonged to my grandfather, and it was a great place to grow up and learn about nature, but I really like it out here much better."

Nicole asked, "Do you not want to farm with your father?"

Bill answered, "No, I really don't. I have always wanted to be a forest ranger. I love the land and the animals, but I've dreamed since childhood of being out in the wilderness with nature. "Well, if we are done eating, I think we better get on the road. I have that meeting at nine o'clock, and I don't want to be late."

Nicole replied, "Sure, I'm ready." Once Bill had filled up the jeep with gasoline, they started out again for Denver. The trip was pleasant and beautiful. Bill was an excellent driver, and Nicole felt very comfortable and safe with him.

Bill explained, "We're only about ten minutes out from the outskirts of Denver, and in just a few minutes you will be with your sweetheart."

Nicole was beginning to feel a little excited. She knew she would be seeing Scott very soon, and she could hardly wait.

She thanked Bill for the pleasant trip and for taking her to see Scott.

Bill stated, "I'll be back to pick you up when my meeting is over. Will you be all right there by yourself?"

Nicole smiled and said, "I won't be by myself, Bill. I will be with Scott."

Bill said, "Well, if you need anything, anything at all, leave a message on my cell phone, and I'll call you as soon as I can. Okay? Here is my card that has my number on it. I already have your cell number in my phone. I hope you enjoy your visit. Tell him we miss him and hope he is doing much better."

"Thanks again, Bill," Nicole answered.

As she walked down the corridor toward Scott's room, she felt anxious. When she reached his room, he was not there, but Emily was. Nicole looked startled and said, "Where's Scott and what are you doing here?"

Emily gave her a smug look before answering and then said, "Scott is in physical therapy, and he knows I am here waiting for him to come back. I've been here every day since he was brought here, and we have become very close. Now you can answer my question: 'What are you doing here'?"

Nicole could feel the hostility between the two of them, but she took a deep breath and replied, "I'm here because Scott asked me to come. Do you also have that same invitation?"

Emily remarked, "Look! He changed his mind about me not seeing him, so when I came back he was really glad to see me, and I'm not going anywhere, so don't expect me to leave when he comes back to the room."

Nicole replied, "I know he gets very lonely, so I am thankful that you keep him company. I just hope you don't feel that he has deep feelings for you. He wants a friendly relationship, and nothing more."

"What makes you think we are only having a friendly relationship? We are serious with one another, and I love him, and he loves me. Just ask him when he comes back from therapy," Emily stated.

Nicole responded, "I will do that."

Scott appeared in the doorway on crutches and hobbled into the room. He looked at Nicole with a big smile and hobbled over to her. He leaned over and gave her a hug. She stood up and hugged him back. He held on to her for a few minutes, and then he kissed her on the lips.

Nicole asked, "Are you sure you want to do this in front of Emily?"

Scott asked, "Why would you ask me that?"

Nicole answered, "Well, from what Emily has been telling me, you and she are very close and serious with one another."

"Emily, I think you need to leave," Scott said, "Why would you tell Nicole that? You and I are only friends, and I've told you from the beginning that we could never be anything more than friends."

Emily screamed, "Scott, don't do this again. You know we have a loving relationship, and I am not going to leave with you making her think that there is nothing going on between us."

"But there isn't anything going on between us, period!" Scott answered. "I appreciate you keeping me company and helping with the massages to help speed up the healing process, but that doesn't mean that I love you."

Emily cried, "You are so cruel to me when she's around. When she's not here you are very loving, and I'm not going to let you get away with this again. You have told me that you love me, and that means everything to me. I don't care what you tell her, but I know you do love me."

"Emily, I don't want to hurt you, but I have no romantic feelings for you," Scott said. "I appreciate you coming here every day to visit and help me, but that doesn't mean that I am in love with you. You do keep me company so I don't get bored, and we play cards, watch TV, and talk, but that doesn't equate to love. I thought we had a terrific friendship. I'm sorry that you have made it more than it is, but I'm in love with Nicole and have been for quite a while. I told you yesterday not to come today, but you came anyway. I want to spend the rest of today with Nicole and her alone, so I am asking you nicely to please leave. Do you understand what I am trying to tell you?"

Emily answered, "I don't need this kind abuse, so I'm leaving. Do not think that I'll come crawling back either! You are so mean to me when she's here, and I'm sick and tired of it. You know you love me, and you always will. You may have her buffaloed, but not me. I know after she leaves today you will be calling me in the morning to come be with you, but I won't be here. When you are ready to apologize to me and tell Nicole that it is over, then I'll come back."

When Emily left, Nicole was feeling sorry for her. Was Scott really leading her on, or was she really feeling that Scott loved her when he didn't?

Nicole said, "I don't really know what to think. I do know it is very difficult for you to handle your situation all alone, and I can understand that. I would not want to be alone either, but if you are using Emily, then I feel sorry for her. She truly feels that you love her, and she must have received some type of signals from you."

Scott responded, "I have told her that I truly care about her, and that I appreciate all that she does for me, but I never told her I love her. She knows how I feel about you."

Nicole stated, "Well, I'm not here to discuss your relationship with Emily. I came to spend time with you, so if you don't mind, let's put the subject of Emily to rest."

They discussed everything they could possibly think about, but mostly their upcoming decisions of her being away at college and him staying at the ranger's station in Colorado. She asked how he felt about them being apart for such a long period of time, and he became very quiet.

"I don't even want to think about that right now. I want us to remain close even if we are a thousand miles away." Scott said.

Sandy, the on-duty nurse came in to change the dressing on Scott's leg as he and Nicole were discussing their problem of distance. Nicole asked if she needed to leave the room, and Sandy said, "You can stay. His leg is healing, and the infection is gone, so there would be no problem if you would choose to stay."

Nicole noticed that there was a large indentation where part of the calf muscle was missing, and she asked Sandy, "Will the muscle ever grow back?"

Sandy shook her head, and said, "No. He will always have the indentation in his calf, but he can strengthen the muscle that he has left. It won't work as well as before, but if Scott continues the hard work that he is doing now, he will be fine. Because of his hard work, he might be leaving us sooner than we had anticipated, and now that the dressing has been changed, I will leave you two alone."

Scott smiled and responded. "Thank you for being such a great nurse Sandy, and thanks for the good news. That's possibly the best news I could ever expect to hear. I appreciate that very much."

Nicole cheerfully stated, "Scott, can you believe it? You might be able to go back to the station before I have to leave to go back to school. Isn't that the best news?"

"It sure is!" Scott replied.

It seemed Nicole had only been there a couple of hours when Bill came into the room. "Hey Scott, it's great to see you again. How are you doing, buddy?" he asked. "I see you and your lady have been in deep conversation. Am I interrupting anything?"

Both Scott and Nicole smiled, and almost in unison said, "No you are not interrupting anything."

"Scott, you missed a great meeting. We have some new equipment coming, and I get to train you and Todd on how to use it. It will certainly save us hours of time with our paperwork. If I get a chance this week, I'll come by and explain it to you," Bill stated.

Scott answered, "I would really enjoy your company, Bill."

Bill interjected, "Well I hate to break up this party, but I need to get back to the station. If you are you ready to go Miss Nicole, I'll go down and bring the jeep around, and I'll pick you up at the front door. Okay?

"Scott, it sure is good to see you again. Your coloring looks a whole lot better than when we saw you on the bluff. For a few minutes there I thought we were going to lose you. It's great to see you with that big smile on your face. Have they told you how much longer you might have to stay here in the hospital?" Bill asked.

Scott replied, "One of my nurses said that if I continue to work hard and continue healing, like I am now, I should be out of here soon, but I have no idea how long that will be."

Bill responded, "That is wonderful news. I know Todd will be really happy to hear your good news. We really miss you Buddy, and we will be happy to see you back at work. Take care of yourself, and we will try to come see you soon." Bill shook Scott's hand and said, "See you later."

"Goodbye Bill, and please tell Todd to give me a call when he has a few moments to talk," Scott answered.

Bill replied before leaving, "I sure will. You take care."

Scott looked at Nicole and said, "Well, I guess I only have a few more minutes to tell you how much I love you and miss you when we can't be together, but I am so happy that you were here to spend the day with me."

"I am happy I was here to be with you too, Scott. Hopefully I'll be able to come again with Bill or Todd. Call me before you go to bed, so I can tell you goodnight. I'm very proud of your accomplishments from therapy. Everyone at The Haven will be very happy to hear of your wonderful progress," Nicole replied. "I know Bill is waiting for me, and I need to go." She leaned over Scott's bed and gave him a very soft kiss, and he held her tightly.

As she pulled away from him he blew her a kiss. She walked out of the room and walked quickly to the elevator and rode down to the lobby. Bill was waiting in his jeep near the front door, so she hurried and got in. As they were driving away, she had a feeling that something was happening, but she had no idea what it was.

As they drove out of Denver the temperature dropped, and Bill noticed that Nicole was holding her arms tightly to her body. He pulled over on the side of the road, reached under his seat and pulled out a blanket. He told Nicole to wrap the blanket around her to stay warm, and then he turned on the heater.

Nicole said, "Thank you Bill. I didn't realize it would be this chilly on the ride home or I would have brought more than this thin sweater."

Bill asked, "Are you warmer now?"

"Yes, she replied, "Thank you very much."

It was so loud in the open jeep that it was hard for her to think about her day with Scott, but she tried until they drove into the driveway of The Haven.

"Hey Bill, have you had anything to eat today?" Nicole asked.

He responded, "I had breakfast with you, and half a sandwich that was provided at the meeting. I am a little hungry, but my brother, Jim, is flying in from Los Angeles, and we are having dinner together. He'll be flying out tomorrow heading back home to Ohio. I talked to him before I picked you up in Denver. I better get going. He has a ride to our station with a friend of his from college."

Nicole said, "Thanks for taking me to see Scott today. I hope you have a nice dinner with your brother. Goodbye Bill."

Nicole joined Virginia, Norman, Catherine and Mike at the dinner table. Everyone nodded when she sat down. Nicole said, "Thank you Father for the blessings of this beautiful day that you have given us, the time we have had to share with others, for friendships, for love that everyone can see on our faces, and for this food and its bounty. Thank you Father. Amen."

As they were eating, Virginia asked Nicole about Scott. "How is that dear boy doing?"

Nicole replied, "He is doing much better. The infection is gone, and his physical therapy is progressing nicely. The on-duty nurse said that if he continues to do well, he will be leaving them soon. His spirit is high, and he is working very hard to get back on his feet. Isn't that the best news? I am glad I got the chance to visit with him, and I want to thank all of you for letting me go."

Catherine looked up and said, "That is wonderful news!"

Virginia smiled and replied, "We want you to have the time of your life while you are here, so you don't need to thank us. We are just glad that you have given us an exciting summer, one that I know I will always remember."

Catherine and Norman nodded in agreement.

As they finished eating, Todd walked in the door and said, "Hello everyone! I passed Bill on the way here. Since I have a few minutes, I'd like to find out how Scott was today."

Nicole answered, "Come on over and sit down, and I'll tell you all about him."

Todd sat as close to Nicole as he could get, and Catherine noticed his body language with her. He had put his arm around her waist while she was talking with him.

"Scott is doing fine," Nicole responded. "His nurse said he is doing so well that he may get out of the hospital sooner than they expected, and then he will go to a rehab center until they release him to go back to work, and to a normal life. He looks good. His coloring has come back, and his spirit is high. I am so proud of him and his accomplishments."

"Was Emily there?" Todd questioned.

"Yes, but he asked her to leave, and after a few outbursts from her, she did leave, but I know she will be back," Nicole replied.

Todd asked, "How do you feel about that?"

Nicole answered, "I don't really like it, but there's not a whole lot I can do about it. She does keep him company, and I'm certain it is a one-way picture of love on her part, but not from Scott's. In her mind she believes he loves her, and she's not giving up on that belief."

Todd continued his questioning with Nicole. "How do you handle Emily being there with him every day, all day?"

Nicole said, "I have faith in him. I not only love him, but I trust him too. I saw how he handled her with me, and he let her know that there was nothing between them on his part. He appreciates her coming every day to keep him company, but friendship is all there is going to be. She cried, got upset, yelled, called me names, and then she left. I am hoping that she finally realizes that Scott and I are serious about one another, and that she will let go of him."

"Are you willing to take that chance? She's not about to give up on him, and the sooner you realize that, the better off you are going to be." Todd reminded her.

Catherine was really watching Todd and his body language. He was touching Nicole's back the whole time they were talking. She started to feel there was a little more to Todd's remarks than he let on. She decided that she wanted to watch him around Nicole.

Everyone was leaving the dining hall, and Nicole told Todd that she was going to take a shower and wait for Scott's call.

Todd said, "Please tell him that I will be calling him. I want to go see him in the next few days, and if you would want to go, I'll be glad to take you with me."

"That's very nice of you to offer. I will have to see how things are going here, because lately Catherine has been doing all the work while I've been gone, and I don't feel good about leaving everything for her to do alone," Nicole replied.

Todd responded, "Well, I will still call you to find out if you can get away."

They said their goodbyes as Nicole was walking backwards toward her cabin, and Todd left in his jeep.

Nicole was in the shower feeling the chill release from her body. She was tired and sleepy, but she knew Scott was going to call. If he didn't call her, she would call him.

After drying her hair and putting on her pajamas, she had her cell phone in her hand to call Scott, but it rang before she started to punch in his number.

"Hello my sweet princess. Are you ready for bed?" Scott asked.

"I have had dinner, a very hot shower, and I am on my bed talking to you with my pajamas on. Are you ready for bed too?" Nicole questioned.

Scott laughed. "Haven't you noticed that I'm always ready for bed, since that is where I always am? I've had my medication already, and I am about to nod off, but I needed to hear your voice before I do. Thank you again for coming to spend the day with me. It meant so much to me to have you here. I can hardly wait to see you again, and I hope it is soon."

Nicole replied, "Todd offered to bring me when he comes to see you in the next day or so, and I'll try very hard to make that happen. I've got to make up some time with Catherine. She's been doing all the work of two people, and I feel I need to get busy and help her. Goodnight my sweet prince! I will talk with you tomorrow."

After she laid down her cell phone she pulled up the covers and was thinking about her day, then she turned off the light. She was asleep within a few minutes.

In the morning Nicole heard Catherine in the front room. She got out of bed to see what Catherine was doing.

"Good morning, sunshine. Did you sleep well?" Catherine asked.

"I slept very well, thank you, but I'm really hungry. How did you sleep, and are you hungry too?" Nicole asked.

Catherine answered, "I slept well, and I am ready for breakfast."

"I will change my clothes quickly, and I'll be out in a flash." Nicole said.

Catherine smiled and nodded.

Catherine and Nicole were in line getting their breakfast when Norman and Virginia came walking in. Norman said to Nicole, "When you get your breakfast will you please come to our table?"

Nicole and Catherine both looked at one another wondering what Norman and Virginia wanted to talk to her about.

As they were ready to sit down at the table, Nicole asked, "Would it be all right for Catherine to sit with us?" They both nodded. Norman took Virginia's hand and then they both looked at Nicole. Nicole was wondering what was going on.

"Is everything all right?" Nicole asked.

Norman took Nicole's hand and said, "We just received a call from your mother, and we need to get you to the airport as soon as you can get ready."

Nicole was stunned and cried, "What's wrong?"

"Your father is in the University Hospital in Columbus, and is in intensive care. Your mother believes that he has had a stroke. We don't know the severity of it, but she has requested for you to come home."

Nicole was in a state of panic, and Catherine put her hand over Nicole's and said, "I will help you get packed and to the airport."

"I need to call Scott right away to let him know about my father, and will you please notify Todd and Bill for me?" Nicole asked.

Catherine replied, "Sure. I'll be glad to do that for you."

Mike looked at Nicole and suggested, "Don't panic. We will all help you get ready, and I will go along with you and Catherine to help you get your luggage into the terminal, and help you obtain your boarding pass. I am going to get on the phone right now and call the airport to try and get you the quickest flight out. Hopefully you won't have to wait very long. Just promise us that you will let us know when you have landed safely, and that you are all right."

Nicole answered with tears in her eyes, "Okay, and thank you, Mike."

She tried to call Scott's cell phone, but he must have been in physical therapy because he didn't answer. She left him a message saying, "Scott, I have to rush home because my father is in the Intensive Care Unit at the University Hospital in Columbus, Ohio. My mother called Norman and Virginia and requested me to come home immediately, as she thinks he has had a stroke. Mike and Catherine are helping me get everything ready. They'll be taking me to the airport to board the next flight to Columbus. I love you so much. I'll call you when I can. Goodbye Scott."

When Mike, Catherine and Nicole arrived at the airport, they walked quickly into the terminal. Mike took Nicole's luggage to the airline baggage check in clerk and told her that he had an emergency flight booked for Nicole Thomas to Columbus, Ohio. The clerk immediately found her ticket and boarding pass and asked Mike to put her luggage on the weight scale. She then handed Nicole her ticket and boarding pass.

The clerk said, "You'll need to hurry and go through security, then go quickly to Gate 26. I will call and tell them you are here and going through security so they won't close the gate. You must hurry though. Your luggage will already be placed on the plane by the time you get to the gate, so you won't need to worry about that."

Nicole said, "Thank you very much." Then she hugged Catherine and Mike and ran to the security gate. After she passed through security, an airline employee picked her up in a shuttle to get her to the gate quickly. Once there she handed the attendant at the gate her boarding pass, and was given permission to board. She found her seat two rows back from the wing section. She had a window seat, but there was a young man sitting in the seat by the aisle. He graciously got up and helped her with her overhead case. She thanked him, and then she sat down and put on her seat belt. She was out of breath and very nervous.

As they were taxing out to the runway, the young man said, "Hi, my name is Jim Martin. Are you all right? You don't get air sick do you?"

"I'm sorry. I am Nicole Thomas. I hope I didn't delay everyone with me being late getting to my seat. I have an emergency at home in Ohio, and my tickets were purchased a couple of hours ago, and

I have been rushing around ever since, and to answer your question, no I do not get air sick."

"That's good. Are you going to Columbus, Ohio?" The young man asked.

"Yes, I am," Nicole replied. "My father seems to have had a stroke, and he is at the University Hospital there.

Jim said, "What a coincidence. That's where I'm going too. I have just passed my medical exams, and I am interning at that same hospital. Has your father had a major stoke?"

Nicole answered, "I don't really know. I have been vacationing and working at our family friend's resort since the first of June, so I didn't get the chance to talk with my mother. She called our family friends, who happen to be the owners of the resort, and they let me know over breakfast. I've been rushing around ever since then, and I haven't had a moment to even think straight."

"Just take a few deep breaths and let them out slowly. That will help you calm down a little. We have a long ride to Ohio. Let's just talk, and that might help too." Jim advised.

"Okay. Are you from Ohio also?" Nicole asked.

Jim replied, "Yes, I am. I was raised on a small farm near a town called South Charleston. My father owns a farm that at one time belonged to my grandfather. My parents still live on that same farm where I grew up. I loved living there, and my brother and I used to help our father work it until he went to college to become a ranger, and I went to Ohio State to eventually become a doctor. We have a married sister, Bette, who lives in Fairborn. I've been in several different places assisting with victims of floods, hurricanes and a few other catastrophes, so I haven't been home in a while."

Nicole replied, "I'm from Springfield. You only live about twenty miles from me. You mentioned you have a brother who is a forest ranger. What is his name?"

Jim responded, "His name is Bill Martin, and he is stationed in Estes Park, Colorado. I don't remember what the station number is, but I talked with him the other day before I left Los Angeles on a connecting flight, and then I had dinner with him last night. He mentioned he went to a class in Denver and took a girlfriend of an injured ranger to a hospital to visit this guy. Bill said his fellow ranger got clawed by a grizzly bear. He also said the girl's name was Nicole. Is that Nicole you?"

"It's a small world isn't it? Yes, that Nicole is me."

"How's your friend doing?" he asked.

"He's doing pretty well for having lost over half of his left calf muscle. When he is released from the hospital, which should be soon, he will go to a rehab center for who knows how long," she said.

Nicole continued, "I would have had to come back home after Labor Day because I start back to Ohio State for my junior year. I just wasn't planning on coming back this soon."

Jim said, "Well, I'm doing my internship for up to two years in Columbus, so maybe we'll see one another from time to time. To change the subject, do you like take-offs or landings better? I, myself, like take-offs, but I like landings too because it means that I made it, and I'm still alive."

Nicole laughed. "I like take-offs the best. I don't really like the sound of the tires squealing on landings. We put our lives in the hands of the pilots, don't we?"

Jim answered, "Sure do! We really don't even think about it after we get off the plane. It's too bad we don't put that much thought regarding our beliefs and trust with God, like we do our pilots."

Nicole asked, "I'm glad to hear you say that. Are you a Christian, Jim? I am, and I pray to him for guidance and safety each and every day."

Jim said, "Yes, I am a Christian. I haven't been in a church building in a while, because where I've just been, they have church out in the open due to all the catastrophes they've endured."

"Say Nicole, are you engaged to this ranger?" Jim asked.

Nicole answered, "No, we are not engaged. I told him I needed to finish school before I even think about a future with anyone."

"How did he take that message?" Jim asked.

She replied, "He wasn't thrilled, but he understood."

Nicole continued, "Jim, how many people do you know who get on a plane, sit beside a complete stranger, and know some of the same people, come from the same cities almost, and then be heading to the same destination?"

"I guess you have a point there, Miss Nicole." He answered. "Do you know that you are a very pretty lady?"

Nicole responded, "Thank you, Jim. I think you are a pretty handsome guy yourself."

Jim said, "Well, when we get to Columbus, if you would like, we can ride to the hospital in the same taxi. I would like to keep in touch with you if you don't mind?"

Nicole smiled and answered, "That would be fine since I already know you, a little."

"I'm not planning on attacking you, you know? I wouldn't do that to someone I just met, but maybe after a few dates I might." Then he laughed.

Nicole blushed and put her hands over her face. "Are you serious? I didn't mean to make you think I was afraid that you would."

"Nicole, I am a nice person, and my parents taught me to be a gentleman and to be nice to girls, or I should say women."

"So you think I'm a young girl? Just how old do you think I am?" Nicole asked.

Jim answered, "I think you are a very nice and beautiful young woman that I would like to get to know better, and I think I better stop while I'm ahead."

"Are you hitting on me, Jim?" Nicole asked.

Jim answered, "Would you like me to be hitting on you?"

Nicole replied, "I think I would like for us to change the subject. Okay?"

Jim smiled and said, "Okay."

Nicole asked Jim where he went to school, and he replied, "I was schooled all twelve years in the Southeastern School District, and I graduated from Southeastern High School in South Charleston. Where did you go to school?"

Nicole answered, "I graduated from Springfield North High School. It was a very large school with lots of students. How big is Southeastern?"

Jim laughed and said, "It's a small school. There were only fifty-two in my graduating class. It was very small compared to Springfield North, but we got a fantastic education. There were only five students in my French class, so there was a lot of one on one attention if you needed it, and I sure did."

Nicole was amazed and said, "Wow! That sounds like a wonderful benefit for a small school. My classes were so large that it was hard to hear the teacher, but I did get a good education. I graduated with over 250 students. Were your classmates all friends?"

"Most of us were. Almost everyone participated in more than one activity. I was into sports, so I was busy all nine months with football, basketball, baseball and track. I wish now I had played golf, but I couldn't fit it in. It might have helped my game now. Do you like golf or sports in general?" Jim asked.

Nicole replied, "I love most sports. I'm not really into soccer, but I played volleyball, basketball, softball and ping pong, so I guess I was athletic too. I was really into music, and I played in the band, and I sang in chorus. Were you in the band or chorus?"

"Hold on a minute!" Jim emphatically said, "You played ping pong? I was the champion ping pong player at school, so that means we have to have a contest when we find a ping pong table somewhere. Are you up to the challenge? And I tried playing a trumpet in the band, but it interfered with my sports schedule, so I dropped out. I don't sing very well either, so now I'm a couch potato when sports are on television. What do you watch?"

"Before I answer your last question, I will challenge you to a ping pong match. That is if we can find a table somewhere. Now for what I like to watch on television; I watch anything and everything from ballet to football. I really like baseball, and my favorite team is the Atlanta Braves. They are a fantastic team, and have been for years. I like the Cincinnati Reds too, but I really am a number one Braves fan." Nicole said.

Jim answered, "Wow! I like to watch that team too. We'd be okay on the couch together except for the ballet stuff. I don't like to see men in leotards. It's just not right."

"You are such a manly man. Ballet is an art form of expression and skill," she said.

He replied, "I don't care. I still don't like to see men running around in tights."

Nicole laughed, "Jim, you are so funny, and I want to thank you for making me feel better. I was so nervous when I got on this plane, and now I am very relaxed and calm."

He took her hand in his and held it for a short time. "I have enjoyed talking and being with you also. You are a delightful person, and I meant it when I said I would like to get to know you better."

The flight attendants were coming around with the drink cart, and Jim asked Nicole if she would like something to drink.

"Yes, please. I would like a Sprite on ice."

Jim ordered her a cup of Sprite on ice, and a Coke for himself.

Suddenly the plane ran into some turbulence, and not even thinking, Nicole gripped both her hands around Jim's arm. He released her hands and put his arm around her and held her close to him. She had her head on his chest, and he kissed her on the top of her head. She didn't protest, he supposed out of fear of letting go, but to Jim it meant he wanted to become a lot closer with her. He was very much attracted to her, but he knew he would have to take it slow because she had stated that she had deep feelings for someone else. He thought his chances were better than the other fellow's, because he could be near her more often. But for right now, he just wanted to hold her in his arms.

As soon as the turbulence calmed down, she moved to sit upright in her seat. She looked at Jim and apologized for grabbing his arm, but she thought that it really felt good at the same time. She almost felt guilty for hugging someone other than Scott.

Nicole told Jim that she would like to rest for a little while, and Jim raised the arm rest so she could lean on him again. He took his jacket and placed it over her to keep her warm, and in no time at all she was asleep.

He was thinking to himself, "I know I would really like to see more of this girl. She is easy to talk to, and we have a lot in common. She has a guy in Colorado, but he's not here, and I am, so maybe she'll accept an invitation or two to dinner or a movie." For now, he would have to settle for this beautiful person just sleeping on his arm.

After an hour of sleep, Nicole woke up to find she was again laying on a man's arm, and it wasn't Scott. She looked at Jim and smiled. "I guess I owe you another thank you for letting me sleep on your arm."

"Hey," Jim said, "It was my pleasure except for the fact that my arm is asleep, and I need to move it to get some feeling back in it."

Nicole laughed. "I guess I shouldn't be laughing, but your arm was very comfortable, and I truly enjoyed my nap. Thank you for being my pillow."

"It is quite all right. Are you hungry? The flight attendant brought us some peanuts and pretzels while you were snoozing. Would you like some?"

She replied, "Yes, please. I am a little hungry. Do you know how long it is before we land?"

"I asked the attendant when she brought the snacks, and she said another hour, but that was about a half hour ago, so we're not that far. When we get into Columbus, do you want to get something to eat before we go to the hospital?" Jim questioned.

"I really need to get to the hospital to see my dad. I really don't know what his condition is, and I can't call Mom. I didn't recharge my phone before I left, so my cell phone is dead," Nicole responded.

Jim questioned, "Would it be all right for me to come with you to see your dad? I am almost a certified doctor, and I can read charts and ask questions regarding his prognosis that maybe you or your mother wouldn't know to ask."

Nicole sat up straight and said, "I would really like that a lot, but don't you have to report to the hospital to let them know you are there?"

"Yes, but I don't start work until I am put on a schedule," he said. "I won't be on duty until then. I have to find a hotel to stay in until I can find a group of guys to share a place and expenses. I won't make much money as an intern, so I've got to have time to look around for housing and roommates."

"If Dad is all right, I need to pay my fees and find a dorm near or on campus while I'm there in Columbus. I will probably do that tomorrow because I need to spend time with them today. I know I don't look forward to just sitting in a room while he is sleeping and watching to make sure he is breathing. I know that's what my mother will be doing," Nicole said.

"You and your mother do not need to stay in his room the whole time. It's not good for either of you to do that. That will wear you both out. If your dad is okay, I would like to go with you on campus if you don't mind," Jim asked.

Nicole answered, "That would be fun, and I would enjoy your company."

"Nicole, if it's okay, would you tell me a little bit about this guy of yours in Colorado?"

"Okay. He is a very handsome man, just like you. He works hard and loves his job, just like you, and he swept me off my feet when we first met. We were doing fine until a young woman named Emily came into the picture. She was a visitor at the resort, and she saw him with me and decided that he was going to be hers. After his accident, she moved from the resort to a hotel in Denver so she could be with him every day at the hospital, while I could not. She told him lies about me and his best friend, Todd, which weren't true at all. Now that I will not be there, I know she is making her move, and I can't do a thing about it. She is very beautiful, well-to-do, and very sure of herself. She's nothing like me, but maybe that's why he likes her. Even though he tells me he loves me, he likes her coming to see him every day. I realize he gets lonely, and she does keep him company. She gives him rub downs, and since I'm not there, why not?"

"I'm very sorry you are going through all this at one time. I know it must be hard on you not being with him, but for whatever it's worth, I would pick you over anyone else," Jim said.

She liked this person sitting next to her. She wanted and needed a friend like him since she was going to be so far away from the man she cares deeply about. It was even an extra bonus because she knew his brother, Bill. She really liked Bill. He was such a nice man, and she felt the same way about Jim. He was a perfect gentleman.

Jim was hoping that Nicole would find him more of what she needed and wanted in a man, but he knew he would have to give her time to come to that conclusion.

They seemed to have something to talk about almost the entire flight, but now they were preparing to land. The landing was smooth, and Jim looked at her and said, "The wheels squealed very little. Did you notice?"

Nicole smiled. "You are right, and I'm so glad we're on the ground again. Thank you Lord."

They walked to the baggage claim, and Jim got their suitcases. They rolled their luggage to a bus that read, "Ohio State University." Since the hospital was next to the campus, she told Jim that this bus might be the right one to get them there. Jim asked the driver, and he nodded his head, so they got on the bus.

Once they arrived at the campus entrance, the hospital was just across the street. When they went inside, Jim asked Nicole to wait one minute so he could notify someone in employment that he was there.

When he returned to Nicole, he said, "I don't have to report for two weeks, so I can keep you company if you would like. All I need to do while we are out is find a newspaper so I can look at the ads for apartments or rooms to share."

They got on an elevator and rode to the fourth floor. Her father was in room 421. When they found his room, they walked in. Nicole immediately saw her mother and walked over to her and gave her a hug. She looked at her father, and he was resting peacefully. Nicole turned back to her mother to introduce her to Jim. Her mother was elated that she brought him along with her. She thought that this was the young ranger that her daughter had told her about.

"Mom, this is Jim Martin, and Jim this is my mother, Connie.

"Mom, I met him on the plane coming here. I know his brother, Bill, from Colorado. Bill is a ranger where Scott and Todd are, so it was really unusual to sit beside someone on the plane that knew some of the people I do, plus he is from South Charleston. Can you believe that? He will be interning here in the hospital in a couple of weeks, and he asked if he could come and possibly explain some of what is happening with Dad."

"Do you mind if I take a look at his chart?" Jim asked.

Connie answered, "A nurse at the front station has his chart. I can ask one of them to bring it here, but I don't know if they will."

Jim asked, "Has his doctor been in to see him yet today?"

"Yes, he came in early this morning, but he didn't tell me anything other than Dean is doing fine."

"I can check his pulse and listen to his heart, but without permission from his doctor, I can't really tell you much." Jim put his ear to Nicole's father chest, listening for irregular heartbeats, and he checked his pulse. "He seems to have a pretty good heart beat. I don't hear any problems, and his pulse is good. What time does the doctor usually come in to see him?"

"He has been coming in around eight-thirty in the morning, but he told me he would be in tonight because he won't be here tomorrow. I'm hoping he will release him to go home," Connie replied.

Just then Nicole's father woke up, looked at Nicole and held out his arms. She hugged her father and asked how he was doing. He told her that he was feeling fine, but tired. While he was talking to her, she brought Jim to the side of the bed and introduced him to her father.

"Dad, this is Jim Martin. He will be interning at this hospital for the next few years. We met on the plane where we were seated beside one another. It was really weird, Dad, because he is originally from South Charleston, and I know his brother, Bill, who is a ranger at Estes Park, and I was dating one of the other rangers, Scott Thompson, and he met him too. That saying about "it's a small world," is really true. Anyway, Jim offered to come see you and possibly check out your chart, but the nurses have it at their station, and he doesn't believe he would be permitted to look at it.

"It's nice to meet you Jim. Maybe you can help keep her here in Ohio and not be so far away from us. I thought we were going to lose her to this Scott fellow, and I was hoping and praying she'd come home to finish her degree first. I didn't intend to get her home this way, but I'm certainly glad she's here.

Jim shook her father's hand and said, "I'm hoping to keep her here also. I want the chance to get to know her better. I learned enough in just the few hours we spent together on the plane. I know that I would like to spend more time with her.

"If I may, I would like to try a few things with you to see your range of motion.

Dean said, "Sure."

"Mr. Thomas, I would like for you to lift your left arm as high as you can lift it toward the head of your bed. Now your right arm please. Now keep your eyes open and I am going to shine a light in them one at a time. Don't blink unless you really have to. Thank you."

"Jim, what does all that mean?"

"Well, I'm not your doctor, Mr. Thomas, but to me it means you did not suffer a severe stroke. Without looking at your chart and seeing the tests you've had, I cannot actually tell you what is going on with you. Excessive stress and lack of rest can cause a body to act like it is going through a stroke, but your vital signs and your being able to raise you arms as high as you did suggests to me that you did not suffer even a slight stroke. Your eyes are clear, and your eyelids are working well, but I don't know what your doctor has seen, so we'll have to wait for his prognosis and treatment."

Nicole's mother took a deep breath. She was so happy to hear that he probably didn't have a stroke.

Just then the doctor walked in, and told Dean that he would be discharged in the morning. "The tests that were given have proved there was no stroke, so we're feeling that this was stress related. Spend the night here and get a good night's rest, and after you eat some breakfast in the morning you will be released to go home. I want you to contact your own physician in Springfield and let him know of our findings, and to keep up with you on a regular basis. We want to prevent you having a stroke." After he wrote on the chart, a nurse came back with some release papers for the doctor to sign. The nurse told Mr. Thomas that he could sign his release papers in the morning before he leaves.

Connie was elated with the wonderful news, and she hugged Jim, and said, "You will make a wonderful doctor." Nicole agreed and hugged him too.

"We are going to stay at the hotel tonight because I want to be close to your dad, and then we don't have to make two trips," Connie said.

"Jim, would you like to ride back to Springfield with us tomorrow and stay at our home until you can find a place in Columbus? I know Nicole is going to drive back here tomorrow to get everything squared away for her upcoming semester, and I'm sure she would enjoy your company. In the meantime we have an extra bedroom and bath, so you would have your own privacy. That is, if it's all right with the both of you?"

"What hotel are you staying at, and is it close to here? I will need to find one tonight myself, and if I can't find roommates in the near future, I will need to stay there if it's that close. I do appreciate your graciousness, and if I could get a ride to your home tomorrow morning, I could make sure your husband is all right, go over the doctor's instructions with you, then call someone in my family to come pick me up. I really need to stay at my parent's farm until I have to report to the hospital. I know my room is still vacant, and I want to spend some time with my family. I haven't been home in quite some time. I also have my car stored there in one of my father's garages. I will gladly pick you up, Nicole, and drive you to Columbus tomorrow or whenever you feel you need to leave. Just let me know."

Nicole answered, "I can't think of a better plan. We'll talk about it on the ride home and coordinate our time needed to get both mine and your things done. Mom, what hotel are we staying at tonight?"

Nicole's mother said, "The University Inn. Luckily classes have not started yet; during football season, they are packed. I have been walking to and from there and the hospital, and it is a nice short walk. I didn't see any sense in paying for parking to go two blocks that are well lit when it costs nothing for me to leave the car at the hotel."

"Mom, that is very dangerous for you to be walking at night alone. You could get mugged or something."

"Well, maybe so, but I haven't been so far, and I know with the two of you along tonight, I'll be safe."

Dean mentioned, "I'm getting sleepy, so why don't the three of you go get some dinner somewhere, and then go to the hotel to get some sleep. I'll be fine. I'm tired anyway."

"Okay, Dad. We'll be back to pick you up in the morning. If you need anything call Mom's cell phone. Mine needs to be charged, and I'll do that in the hotel. Love you!"

Connie leaned over Dean and gave him a goodnight kiss. "We'll see you bright and early tomorrow morning, so be ready to go home."

Jim, Nicole and her mother left to go to a restaurant to get something to eat. "I don't know about you Jim, but I'm starved. We only got peanuts and pretzels on the plane, and that was lunch."

Her mother said, "Well, I know the perfect place to have a meal, and it is right across from the hotel. We're going to The Family Restaurant. They have all kinds of dinners and sandwiches, and anything else you would possibly want to eat, and it's not expensive. I've been eating there every evening and a couple of lunches too. The food is great, so let's get walking."

After they finished dinner, they walked across the street to the University Inn. Jim got a room on the same floor as Nicole and her mother. They rode the elevator to the third floor and got off, noticing that their rooms were directly across from one another. Jim helped Nicole take her luggage inside her mother's room then started to walk out to go to his own room. Nicole tugged on his arm as he walked past her and said, "Thank you for a wonderful day. I truly enjoyed your company and look forward to spending tomorrow with you."

Jim kissed her on the top of her head and said, "I'll see you in the morning. Sweet dreams. Oh, and what time does your mother want to leave from here?"

Nicole asked, "Mom, when do you want to leave here in the morning?" Nicole asked Jim, "Could you be ready by seven? We'll get something to eat first then go to the hospital."

"Sure. I'll see you both in the morning. Goodnight."

Nicole immediately plugged in her cell phone so she could call Catherine and Scott. Her mother told her that would take too long so she let her use her cell phone.

"Hello Catherine! I just wanted to call and let you know that my dad is okay. He didn't have a stroke but suffered from a stress related problem that acted like a stroke. He is fine and we'll be taking him home tomorrow. You would never guess who I met on the plane coming home? His name is Jim Martin, and he is Bill's brother. You know, Bill, from the ranger's station? He is just as nice as Bill. His family lives in South Charleston, a town less than twenty miles from where we live in Springfield. It's a small world isn't it? How are Norman, Virginia and Mike?"

"We are all doing fine. We certainly miss you. You were the sunshine in our lives, but I am so happy to hear the good news about your dad. As soon as I get off the phone, I will let Norman, Virginia, and Mike know that you arrived safely, and all is well."

"Have you heard anything about Scott? My cell phone was dead before I got on the plane, and I'm recharging it, but my mother let me use hers to call you. I want to call Scott when we are finished."

"Nicole, Mike stopped in to see Scott after his class, and Emily was there hanging all over him. Mike asked him if he had heard from you yet, and he said he wasn't expecting to. Mike told him that you were called home because your father was in the hospital, and that he and I helped you get on a plane in Denver. His answer was, "Oh."

Catherine asked, "Did something happen that we don't know about between the two of you?"

"Nothing is wrong that I know about. I will call him as soon as we are finished talking, but I know Emily will take over now that I am gone, but if that is what Scott wants, then I'll have to live with it. I won't be coming back because it's too close to school starting, and my education has to take precedence now. I miss you, more than you'll ever know, and I'm sorry I had to leave you so quickly, but I appreciate all your help from the beginning of my being there until now. You are a very special person to me, and I want to keep in touch with you if that's all right."

"Nicole, you know that it's all right. You are like a daughter I never got to have, and I love you very much. I want you to have a wonderful life, with a wonderful guy, and with whatever good your future will bring. I want God's blessings to always be with you. You have a good night's rest, and give me a call when you get another chance. I know Norman and Virginia and Mike will also wish you the best of everything. Love you sweetheart, and goodnight."

Nicole was upset, but she didn't want her mother to see that she was, so she just punched in Scott's number and waited for him to answer.

"Hello."

"Scott!"

"Yes."

"This is Nicole. I tried to call you before I had to get on the plane, and I left a message on your cell phone. You must have been in physical therapy when I called. I didn't have my phone charged, so I couldn't call again until now. I'm in Columbus right now. My dad is coming home tomorrow, and he didn't have a stroke like the doctor thought he had. He was suffering from some stress related problem."

"I met someone you know. His seat on the plane was beside mine. I met Bill Martin's brother, Jim. He is a very nice person, and we talked about your situation and our long distance problem. I didn't know that Bill was from a neighboring town from us, but Jim told me about their father's farm. It was very interesting. Now, how are you doing?"

"I'm fine, but I'm a little upset that you left it up to Mike to let me know that you left. Are you coming back?"

"No, I can't come back now. My classes will start in a few weeks. I have to come back to Columbus tomorrow to get my fees paid and find housing, but I will keep in contact with you as much as I can. You can also call me."

"Are you trying to make me jealous, telling me about Bill's brother? I needed you, and you left without even a goodbye, and yet you discussed our situation with a stranger? If you really want to know the truth, I don't think this is really going to work out with you being so far away. I was really hurt that you didn't contact me, but maybe it's for the best. Emily is here with me right now, and I can always count on her, so I need to go. Just go and have a good life."

"I really want you to think about what you just said to me. I certainly don't feel that way, because I have very deep feelings for you, distance or not. I do hope you rethink this situation. I don't understand how you could give up on us so quickly, especially since we were just together almost all of yesterday. I guess I know that she will give you all the attention that I can't, and you seem to really need that. I'd better go. Goodbye Scott."

Nicole hung up before she started crying. She didn't want Scott to hear that. She was deeply hurt, and when she gave her mother's phone back her mother noticed that she was crying.

"May I ask what is wrong, and are you all right?"

"Mom, I don't really want to talk about it right now. Okay? I just want to take a warm shower and go to bed. I'm really tired."

"Okay honey, but please wake me up if you change your mind and want to talk. I'll leave the light on between our beds so you won't stub your toes. I love you sweetheart.

Nicole went into the bathroom and turned on the water in the shower. She was washing her hair when she started to cry. She couldn't understand how she could have lost Scott so quickly. The day before she was with him at the hospital, and they were talking about their future together. She still cared deeply for him. How could he not love her anymore and turn so quickly to Emily? What happened? The warm water helped her to relax a little, but she was so confused. She said a prayer to ask God to give her wisdom on how to handle her feelings.

Then she remembered the nightmare she had right after Scott was attacked by the bear and was in the hospital. Scott's leg was not healing right, and he couldn't walk properly. He lost his job as a ranger, and Emily had taken him away from her. It was a nightmare then but a reality now it seemed. "I can't think about this anymore tonight. I need some sleep and maybe things will look better in the morning," she said to herself.

After her shower, she sat on the edge of the bed and looked over at her mother who was sound asleep. She knew she needed some sleep to help her cope, so she turned off the light, crawled under the covers, cleared her thoughts, and laid her head on her pillow. "I can't think about this anymore right now," she thought to herself. "Tomorrow will bring about a new dawning, and I will deal with it then."

Morning was shining through the windows with a bright sun, blue skies, and lots of noisy activity coming from the hallway. Her mother was already up and dressed. She was finishing the packing of her suitcase, and was almost ready to go to the restaurant for breakfast, and then to the hospital to take her husband home.

"I was just going to get you up, so we can finish packing, go to the restaurant and then pick up your dad. Could you call Jim across the hall to see if he's almost ready?"

"Sure! I'm not ready yet but I'll hurry."

Nicole called Jim's room, and he answered quickly.

"Hi and good morning. Are you ready for this fabulous day ahead of us? I am ready, so I'll meet you in the lobby downstairs."

"That will be great. I've got to finish getting ready. I just woke up a few minutes ago, so I haven't even brushed my teeth yet, but I'll hurry. We'll see you in the lobby in a few minutes."

Nicole got ready very quickly. She cleaned her face, brushed her teeth and then brushed her hair. She dressed, packed her suitcase, and was ready to go.

Her mother looked around the room to make sure they didn't leave anything behind, then walked out the door, got on the elevator and rode down to the lobby. Her mother turned in her key, and paid their bill. Nicole had already gone over to the couch where Jim was sitting and said, "Hello."

He looked at her and smiled. "Your eyes look a little puffy. Have you been crying?"

Nicole looked away a little, and said, "I had a rough night, but I don't really want to talk about it. Okay?"

"Sure. Are you hungry? I already have a menu in my mind, and I want pancakes, eggs over medium, a slice of ham and a big glass of milk. Doesn't that sound good to you? Am I drooling yet?"

"You make me laugh, and I really need that today."

"Are you ever going to tell me what happened?"

"Maybe, but not right now," she said.

"Okay, I'll settle for that for now."

Nicole's mother walked over to them and said, "Are you two ready to go have breakfast?"

Jim was up and grabbed everyone's luggage and was off to put everything in the car. Nicole's mother looked at her and said, "I really like that young man."

Nicole looked at her and said, "I do too. He is very sweet."

Her mother said joyfully, "Well, let's get going, okay?"

Once they were in the restaurant, they were seated in a booth, and Jim and Nicole were looking over the same menu together. "What looks good to you Nicole?"

"I think I want the French toast, some juice and fruit."

Jim's face was all scrunched up, and he said, "Ooh! That is a healthy breakfast. What's wrong with you? I'm having ham and eggs, toast and pancakes with lots of syrup, and a glass of milk. Now that's a breakfast to remember."

"I thought you were going to be a doctor? Is that any way for a future doctor to be eating? Look at all those calories and sugar you are putting into your body. Jim Martin, I am so surprised at you."

He laughed and responded, "Why, because I'm a healthy man already, and I want to splurge this one time, when you want to watch your girlish figure?"

"No, because I want the same breakfast as you, so we can enjoy the calories together."

"Now you're talking. I like a woman who likes to eat hearty once in a while."

"Well, if you two are through throwing egg in each other's face, I want to order and get going. I want to get your dad home with me as soon as we can."

"Sorry Mom, but we do have to wait on the waiter to take our orders, and then we'll have to eat, so we can't hurry up the system.

Dad will still be there when we get there. If you're worried about him, call him on your cell phone. He has his cell phone with him, doesn't he?"

"No, I have it in my purse. He was afraid someone would take it."

Jim said, "Just call the hospital and ask for his room number. There is a phone in every room. Do you have the hospital's number? I have it if you don't."

He gave Nicole's mother the number for the hospital. She dialed it and asked the person answering for room 421, and the call went right through.

"Hi honey! How are you feeling this morning, and are you ready to go home? We're going to eat our breakfast and then we'll be right there to pick you up. You have been released right? That's wonderful. Are you dressed and ready to go? Have you already had your breakfast? I'm glad they fed you well and that you are dressed and ready to go home. I have missed you so much. Yes, Nicole and Jim are with me, and we will be taking Jim back with us. He'll call one of his relatives to come pick him up so he can get his own car to drive back to Columbus. Hopefully he'll stay a few days with his folks and with us. Yes, I like him too. Our breakfast is coming, so I will see you in a little bit. Love you too."

After they ate, Jim picked up the ticket and paid for their breakfasts. Nicole's mother was very appreciative of Jim's gesture and gave him a hug.

"Hey, that's the least I can do. You are taking me back closer to home, plus I really enjoy being with all of you. Once I start being an intern, I probably won't have a lot of time to go home very often, so I want to do that now while I have the chance."

Nicole said with some excitement, "Well let's get going, pick up Dad and head for Springfield. I haven't been home in a while either, and I'm looking forward to familiar surroundings for a change."

After they left the hospital, with Nicole's dad, Jim offered to drive so her mother could spend time with her husband, and he could relax in the back seat. Connie was grateful for the offer. Nicole sat in the front with Jim.

When they arrived in Springfield, Nicole gave Jim directions to their house. Jim noticed that they had a lovely home that looked neat and tidy on the outside as it probably looked on the inside. This was a very loving and good family, and he really felt drawn to them. Once he helped unload the car and brought everything inside, he looked around the living room. It was such a peaceful looking place with a huge fireplace. The furniture looked very comfortable, and it made him feel at home. He mentioned to Nicole's mother how much her taste in furniture and décor reminded him of his home on the farm. Nicole invited him into the kitchen where she fixed them all some hot tea. Jim wasn't really a tea drinker, but because Nicole was making it, he wanted to try some. He sipped it and said, "This is really good, and I don't normally like tea."

Nicole smiled and asked him to sit down while she poured some for her mom and dad. She took a tray to them and left them alone to spend time with one another. When she came back to the kitchen, she went over to Jim and gave his a kiss on the top of his head. He looked at her and said, "We need to talk. I know something happened with you and your guy in Colorado, so before I let my feelings get any deeper than they already are, I need to know where I stand with you. I realize we've only known one another for a couple of days now, but I really want to know if we start a relationship, is there going to be a future for us."

She looked at him and said, "We need to take it slow. I am not going to jump from him to you too quickly. That's not fair to you or to me. I truly enjoy your company more than I ever imagined I could, but we need to take it step by step and not rush our feelings for one another. I want to get to know you a lot better, as I am sure you do with me. A good relationship takes time, and I have really learned my lesson on that subject. I'm still not up to talking about the Scott issue yet. My feelings are still very raw, and I want to get him out of my system so that I don't pull you into this tangled web. Right now I want to run to you, but that's not fair to you because I have not had enough time to get over what I thought was a real commitment between Scott and myself. Do you understand what I'm trying to say?"

"Yes, but I want to help you with it. You need to have someone you can turn to, and I want to be that person for you. I don't mind you talking about him to me, and I know it will cause tears and regrets, but I already have feelings for you, and have since we got to know one another on the plane. I will help you through this, Nicole, so if we are going to be seeing one another, I need for you to let me help you."

"I really appreciate you saying that because I know I will need help with this, but I don't want to hurt you. I already care about you, and maybe too much too soon."

He answered, "That's not a bad thing as far as I can see. If it were me in your situation, wouldn't you want to help me through it?"

"I guess you're right. I just hope I won't be sorry for doing this. Well here goes. I was with Scott the entire day before I left Denver. When I got back to the resort, Norman and Virginia told me that my father was in the hospital, so Mike and Catherine got me all set up to fly home. I know you don't know these people, but they were my family while I was in Colorado. Norman and Virginia own the resort. Mike helps Norman run the resort for the summer. He is working on his master's degree in hotel management. Catherine was my mother away from home. I worked with her, shared a cabin with her, and would do almost anything for her. Anyway, I tried to call Scott before I left, but he must have been in physical therapy, so I left a message on his cell phone. Emily, the girl who was trying to take him away from me, probably erased my message, as she is always there at his side except when he's in therapy. Anyway, he didn't get my message, and my cell phone went dead, so I couldn't keep trying to call him. The next day he heard that I flew home from Mike, who stopped in to see him after his class in Denver. I assume that it made him angry with me, that he had to hear that I had left from someone else. He was very short with me when I called him last night. I could tell he was upset, but then he told me that he didn't think our relationship was going to work because of the distance between us. He said he could always depend on Emily, and she was there, and he needed to get back to her. I told him I didn't understand how he could so quickly abandon our relationship, especially since we were so close together the day before. He was so abrupt with me, and I could tell he wanted off the phone, so I said my goodbyes and wished him a happy life. That's the reason why my eyes were so puffy."

Jim got up from his chair and came over to Nicole. He pulled her from her chair and gave her a very gentle hug. She could feel the strength in him holding her, and she liked it.

Jim said, "Look, you cannot expect him to give up on both of you, and since you were no longer there, at least he would still have Emily. I don't believe he loved you as much as he let on. No man can handle two women at the same time, and it's impossible to give back to both of them when they are both there together. I met him once when I visited my brother, but I didn't get a chance to know him that well. He seemed like a really nice guy, but he must not have known how to handle you both, especially when the two of you knew one another and were together some of the time with him. He let her down to encourage you, but he let you down to encourage her. He probably knew that Emily would always want him no matter what he would say or do, and it felt safe. If he has chosen Emily, then I would suggest you let him go. If he has done this once, who's to say he won't do it again, and I don't want to see you get hurt any more than you already are. She's there, and you're here. You have me, and I would never do that to you. You need to let him go. He has chosen Emily over you, and I thank God that you weren't married to him. I will help you get through this. I want to help you, so please let me do this with you. My schedule will never be the same every day at the hospital, but because you will be close by, I can see you more often than he would ever be able to. I know my own heart, and Nicole you have touched me in a way that no one else ever has. I will always be here for you."

Nicole had tears in her eyes. She knew everything he said was right, and she laid her head on his chest and hugged him tightly.

Her mother and father came into the kitchen and saw them hugging, and her mom looked at her father and smiled. They both approved of this man for their daughter, even though they hadn't known him very long. They were hoping something very special would happen for them.

Jim called home and asked his mother if she would come pick him up at Nicole's address. His mother told him she would be there within an hour, so it still gave Jim a little time to spend with Nicole and her parents.

Jim looked at her parents and said, "Mr. and Mrs. Thomas, I care very deeply for your daughter, and I want to help her get through her problem with this man from Colorado. I promise I will be there for her, and not hurt her in any way. I was raised to be a gentleman, and to treat women with respect and dignity, just as I would want to be treated. I realize she needs time and distance from her existing problem before she can become involved in another relationship. As I will be in Columbus close by, I will be meeting with her as much as my schedule will allow. She needs time to heal from this hurtful relationship, and I promise to be there for her if she will accept my help.

They all sat in the living room talking about Jim's family and the farm where he was raised. Nicole's dad liked that he had been raised with a good work ethic, and that he was now truly working toward becoming a doctor where he could help other people. They talked about Nicole's goals in becoming a teacher where she would be helping young people. They liked this young man very much, but time would tell if he would become their son-in-law.

Jim's mother rang the doorbell, and Mrs. Thomas greeted her and asked her to come in. Jim got up and hugged his mother, and made the introductions. "Mom, this is Nicole, and her parents, Dean and Connie Thomas. This is my mother Nancy Martin. They talked for a few minutes and then Jim went over to Nicole and hugged her. "What time would you like to leave in the morning to go to Columbus?" he asked.

"I will be ready to go by nine o'clock. The administrator's offices don't open until nine, and I don't necessarily want to be standing in line when they first open. Would you like to have breakfast with us?"

"Thank you for the breakfast offer, but I'd like to have breakfast with my folks. We eat early there, so I'll have time to gas up my car and make sure it runs well before I come to pick you up. I'll be here by nine though."

He grabbed his suitcase, shook Mr. Thomas' hand, hugged Mrs. Thomas and said his goodbyes to everyone. On the way home Nancy asked if Nicole was his girl, and if so, are you serious about her? It seemed that her parents really like you."

"I'm hoping to have Nicole in my life, but first she has to get over a guy that was trying to have two women at the same time. I've only known her for a short time, but she is everything I have been looking for in a woman. She goes to Ohio State, and I'll be working at the University Hospital right beside the entrance. I met her on the plane coming back to Columbus. We were seated beside one another, and if we were comparing her in baseball, she was a homerun."

"So you're smitten with her?" Nancy asked.

"Yes, I guess I am. We can talk about anything. We have the same values, and she is not only very attractive, but she's smart too. She's not stuffy, but fun to be around, and I have had a very enjoyable time with her, and her parents are really good people."

"Sounds good to me, and I know your father will be pleased. Your brother, Bill, called to tell us about one of the rangers that got attacked by a grizzly bear and is in a rehab hospital. He said his workload has really increased since that accident."

"The ranger he was telling you about was Nicole's guy. He seems to have had two women on the string, and when she had to come home because her dad had a scare of a possible stroke, the guy decided he no longer needed her. He told her over the phone that distance was the reason for their breakup, and that the other girl in the picture would always be there for him."

"How did she take it?"

"It really hurt her, but I told her in time she would let it go, and then she and I could have a chance with our relationship. I think he was her first love, and it's going to take some time before she'll really let go. But I'm hoping it won't take too long."

When Jim arrived at the farm, his father was walking from the barn to the house. When he saw his son, he embraced him. "I've missed you son, and I'm glad you're home. I've hired a young man, Art, who lives in South Charleston. He comes out every day to help me, but I give him Sunday's off so he can go to church with his family. I'm not milking anymore, so he helps me with feeding the livestock, mowing and all the other stuff you and Bill used to do. I'll introduce him to you if you're going to be here for a little while."

"Dad I'll be here off and on for two weeks. I don't start my internship until then, so I'll be here to help you some. I met a girl on the plane coming home, and she is from Springfield."

"Is she pretty?"

"She sure is, and I think she's just as pretty on the inside too. Her name is Nicole Thomas. Maybe I can bring her out to the farm tomorrow after we get back from Columbus. She's a student there, and I have to look for housing, something cheap to be shared with several other guys while she's there to pays her fees, get her schedule and find out about housing."

"Are you specializing in one area of medicine?"

"I don't really know yet. After I have been in the program for two years, then I'll pick what area I want to specialize in, or what they pick that fits my skills. Right now I'll be in emergency care and some different types of surgeries. I'll be learning more than doing much for a while, but I've already passed my testing, so the next two years will determine what I want to do, and where I'll do it, then on to more experience as a resident doctor. After that, I choose the area of medicine I want and where I would like to be located. Then the interviews begin."

"Well, your mom and I hope you will be closer than your brother. I know you don't want to be in farming, and that's okay. We raised you all to have a mind of your own, and all three of our kids do. Bette comes to see us at least two or three times a month, but she has her hands full teaching. Maybe while you're here she'll come over to see her brother."

"I'll call her to let her know you're home for two weeks, but you'll have to let me know when you're going to be here."

"Okay, Mom. Is it all right if I bring Nicole over tomorrow after we get back from Columbus? She would like to see the farm and meet Dad."

"Could I count on you to be here for dinner? I need to know how many to cook for."

"Sure."

"Well, after I get settled in, I need to get my car gassed up and ready for the drive tomorrow."

"Son, I've loaned your car to Art, but I'll call him to bring it back. He's taken good care of it. I think he polishes it every day. He's not changed anything on it."

"Dad, he'll have to find some other transportation, because I will need my car from now on."

"Okay. I'm sure he'll be all right with that. Maybe I'll loan him my old truck. He's a good driver, and a good young man. I trust him. Well, look here, I don't have to call him because he's driving up the driveway."

"Art, I'd like you to meet my son, Jim. He's the owner of the car you're driving. I'm sorry but he's going to need it back from now on. I'm going to loan you my old truck. Sorry about that, but I didn't know he was coming home until today. It's his car, and I really didn't have his permission to let you use it, but I needed your help, and you needed transportation, so I thought until he returned, you could drive it.

"That's okay Mr. Martin. I've taken really good care of it, and it runs smooth as silk. I can fix up that old truck to look like new, and make it run just like I did the car."

Jim looked at Art and his car and said, "Thank you Art for taking such good care of my vehicle. It looks great. Thanks again."

Dan and Art walked back toward the barn where the old truck was parked in an open garage. Art got in and tried to start it. It wouldn't start, so he asked if there were some jumper cables, but he remembered he saw a set in the other garage, so he ran to get them. When he came back with the cables, he jumped it with another truck in the barn, and it started right up. He told Mr. Martin that he needed to let it run for a while, so he unattached the cables, returned them to the other garage, and let it run for about ten minutes.

Dan told Art to go ahead and drive it home and do whatever he needed to do to keep it running. He told him if it needs a new battery to go ahead and get one. He handed him some money to pay for it, and then Art left in the old truck.

Jim was amazed at how clean his car looked on both the inside and the outside. Art had done a terrific job in keeping it clean. He wasn't expecting it to look like a new used car. He thought to himself, "She's going to really like this car of mine."

He went into the house and saw his mother slicing up tomatoes for dinner, and asked, "Would you like some help?"

His mother said, "You can help me set the table for three, thank you. It's so good to have you home. We have missed you so much. Even though you don't want to farm with your dad, we appreciate and are so proud that you are going to be a doctor who helps other people. I know that God must be very pleased with you also. I called your sister, and she will be coming over to see you tomorrow evening. I told her you were going to Columbus and taking Nicole, and she wants to see you and meet Nicole. Is that all right with you?"

"Sure Mom. Then Nicole will have met everyone in our family. I know she will be happy about that. She's a very sweet person with a terrific personality, and she's a Christian. She prays at meals, goes to church, and devotes time to reading the Bible. I hit the jackpot, Mom."

"Son, just don't get your heart broken. You did say she isn't over that ranger who got hurt. Is that correct? Give her the time she needs."

"I will. I don't want to mess this up."

After dinner, Jim helped his mother clean up the kitchen, and then they went into the living room where his father was asleep sitting in his recliner.

"This brings back a lot of memories for me to eat dinner and see Dad asleep in his chair, and I see you're still making quilts by hand."

"Yes dear, I am. I guess it's just a calming therapy for me. I've made so many of them I finally started a notebook with a color picture of each one I've made, the date I made them, and the type and name of the material, so if I want to make a duplicate for someone, I would know exactly what material to buy, the dimensions, and so on. The pictures in the album also told what they were about. I really liked making quilts with log cabins and scenery on them. They always looked nice on the beds at the cabin. Maybe one of these days all of us could go back to the cabin for some rest and relaxation. Maybe Nicole would like to go. You know that I already like her. Do you know if she has any hobbies like mine? That would give me even more to like about her."

"I don't really know. I haven't had a whole lot of time with her alone except on the plane, and she slept a good bit. I will ask her tomorrow on our drive to Columbus. I think her mother does because I saw a lot of pillows with cross stitching and some with quilting. I know Dad didn't like it much when you taught Bette and me how to cross stitch. I haven't done any of that since, so I know I wouldn't remember how to do it. Dad didn't mind you teaching Bette, but he sure didn't want me doing any "girly stuff."

Nancy answered, "It doesn't hurt for a boy or a man to learn some of the sewing skills. It should come in handy with you being a doctor. You'll be sewing kids and older folks up if you become a surgeon. So don't pay any attention to your dad in that respect."

"Dad wanted one of his sons to be a farmer, but I have always had an interest in wanting to save people's lives rather than tilling the land. I use to pretend that I was a doctor with the livestock. I had a pocket watch that I attached to some twine and checked the cow's heart beat. Maybe I should have been a veterinarian. I'm glad I was brought up on this farm though, but I knew from an early age that I really wanted to be a doctor.

"I know Bill always wanted to be a forest ranger. He likes the out of doors and being among wildlife. He always liked to climb trees and pretend to watch wildlife from the tops of them. He even called them by some name like the dog was a bear. He scared me once, yelling at me to look out for the mountain lion that was Cuddles, our cat.

"Bette always wanted to be a teacher, and that is what she's doing. She wanted me to play school with her all the time on the steps. If I passed her questions then I got to go down one step. I never did make it to the twelfth grade on the steps. I know she is happy teaching, and I bet she is a very good teacher. I will certainly be glad to see her and introduce her to Nicole. She wants to be a teacher also.

"So, see, your three kids turned out to be what they always played they would be, and that shows that you and Dad gave us a solid foundation, and freewill to do our heart's desire. I thank both of you for that. You have been there for each of us with love and solid advice, and for that you are to be commended." Jim continued.

Dan had left his recliner and snuck out the door while they were talking. He came to the back door and called for Jim. "Can you come help me for a few minutes?"

"Sure Dad. I'll be right there."

Dan needed Jim to help him lift a plow tongue off the hitch of the tractor. "How did this get so jammed on the hitch?"

"I was in a hurry and I backed up too fast. It is stuck pretty hard, and I think I bent it a little, but I know you can help me get it off."

"Dad, I will push it back while you steer the tractor forward, but don't go fast, or I'll be pulled under the plow or the tractor."

"Okay son. Are you ready for me to start?"

"Yes, but remember, go slowly."

Dan's foot slipped on the clutch and the tractor jerked forward. The hitch came loose, and Jim's arm got hit hard with the plow tongue. He was in a lot of pain. "Oh! That really hurts."

"What happened, Son?"

"I think my right arm is broken. I need you to take me to the hospital to see if it is."

"I'm going to go get your mother, and we'll all go together. I'll be right back. Just try to get it in a comfortable position."

Jim's mother and father were running back to check out Jim's arm. Nancy noticed that his right forearm was bent, so she knew it was broken. She ran back to the house to get a cold pack from the refrigerator to put around his arm along with a towel to help him keep it in one place. Dan brought the car to them and Jim got in the backseat along with his mother. He wedged himself next to the door so he could keep it still. When they arrived at the hospital emergency room, he was immediately taken for an x-ray. An emergency doctor came into his room and said it was broken, and he would need to reset it, put it in a cast and a sling.

"You will need to rest tonight. I have given your mother your prescription to be filled at your drug store, and you should take one when you get home. You'll sleep well tonight, so no strenuous activities for the next few days. You will have to wear the cast for six weeks, so don't do any lifting until the cast comes off. Are you living near this hospital?"

"No, I am just visiting with my family for two weeks, but I have to be back at University Hospital to begin my internship, so I can get it taken off there at the hospital. This certainly won't look good for my first few weeks there."

"I'm sorry that you will be inhibited on some of the things you won't be able to do, but observing isn't always a bad thing. Sometimes you learn just as much watching as you do by working in the Emergency Room or doing rounds. You can have someone at hospital take your cast off, but you need to wear it for six weeks. Okay?"

"Yes, I understand, and thank you for the blue cast. I was afraid you were going to hassle me with a hot pink or a red cast. Thanks again doctor."

Dan and Nancy walked Jim to their car, and Jim sat in the front seat with his dad. Dan drove to the nearest pharmacy to get Jim's prescription filled and then they headed home.

Nancy said, "Are you still thinking about going to Columbus tomorrow? I could call Nicole and tell her you can't go for a couple of days."

"No Mom, I'll let her drive my car tomorrow, and I'll be the passenger. She has to get her registration stuff done, and I need to find an apartment or house to share with some other interns. I really need to go too."

"But the doctor said you should rest for a couple of days, and you being on these sedatives won't allow you to drive. I can call Nicole for you."

"No, Mom. I need you to drive me to her house by nine o'clock tomorrow morning, and then she and I will bring you back here. I trust her with my car and with me. That way, when we get back, she can meet all of you here except for Bill, but she already met him in Colorado. I know you want to mother me, and I thank you for wanting to, but I don't really need it right now. I will keep it elevated. I will also have Nicole bring us here to the farm in time for dinner. I want her to meet Bette and us as a family. I know Bette and Nicole will get along well. The pill has taken affect, because I am very tired, so when we get to the house, I really want to go to bed. I know you fixed dinner for three, but I can't eat right now. I'm very sorry about the dinner. If you save it, I'll eat it later. Okay?"

"Sure honey."

Dan pulled into the driveway and said, "Son, we are home."

Jim got out of the car and went upstairs to his room. He got his clothes off and went into his bathroom to clean up, brush his teeth, and put on his shorts and tee shirt. He found it wasn't too difficult because he is left-handed, and he had broken his right arm. He pulled the covers down on his bed and got in under them. He set his alarm clock for seven thirty, and then went to sleep.

"Dan, I really think he should stay in bed for a few days to give his arm a chance to heal, but he doesn't want my advice. Maybe you can say something to him."

"Nancy, he's a grown man, and he's going to be a doctor himself, so I don't think we need to put any demands on him right now. He'll be fine. We are done raising our children, and now we need to give them some space and trust their own judgment. I'm quite sure he knows how to handle his broken arm, after all he's almost a doctor."

"I now you're right, but a mother will never get over seeing her child hurt, no matter how old they are, and I know he hurts. He's just trying to hide the pain from us."

Dan answered, "You think you feel badly, I'm the one who broke his arm. How do you think that makes me feel?"

"It was a freak accident, Dan, and accidents do happen. I'm just happy that the plow tongue didn't hit him in the head."

Dan said, "Me too!"

The alarm went off at seven-thirty and the sedative had not completely worn off, but Jim knew he would be all right once he got cleaned up, ate breakfast, and then let his mom drive him to Nicole's.

Nancy was already up, dressed and fixing breakfast for the three of them. "Okay guys, breakfast is ready. Come and get it."

Dan was the first one to the table, and then Jim came down the stairs and into the kitchen. He looked over the scrambled eggs, bacon, buttered toast, coffee and juice, and the smell was almost good enough to eat by itself. Jim sat across from his mother and said, "Mom, this looks and smells delicious, and thank you for fixing us breakfast."

"You're quite welcome, Son."

Dan said, "I think you need to come back and live with us so I can have breakfast like this all the time. Usually your mother makes me eat fruit and one egg for breakfast. I like this spread better."

"You act like I never feed you, but you don't look thin to me, and your usual habit is to go sit in your recliner after breakfast and relax before you go out to water and feed the stock.

"Nancy, I like my routine just fine."

"Okay you two. If my being here is causing you to pick on each other, then I'll just stay in Columbus so you'll be civil to one another again. Play nice. That's what you always told us kids."

"I'm sorry son. Your mother has gone to all this trouble fixing this wonderful breakfast, and I think we are both very concerned about you breaking your arm. It was my fault, but it still hurts us both to know you are suffering from my mistake."

"I'm okay with it, and it wasn't really anyone's fault. I just happened to be at the wrong spot at the wrong time. Please let it go. I have."

"Mom, I will help you clean up the kitchen, and then can we go get Nicole? I told her we would be there at nine o'clock, and I don't want to be late."

"Sure Jim. We will leave as soon as we get the kitchen cleaned up. I am already to go after that."

"Great! Mom, you look very nice in that outfit you have on. Is it new?"

"Heaven's no! I don't buy anything new anymore since I've retired. I no longer have a need for really nice clothes, because I don't go much of anywhere except to church on Sundays, and I have plenty of dresses, skirts and blouses, and even slacks. I just wore this to impress your Nicole and her family."

"Are you putting on a fashion show to impress them?"

"No, I just want to look nice for a change. I get tired of wearing jeans and an old shirt, so this is a nice chance for me to look a little better. Your sister and Nicole will be here for dinner, so I'd like to look nice again, just as I did when I was working."

"Mom, don't you know you always look good to me no matter what you're wearing? It's what is good on the inside that counts, and you're always beautiful to us, plus you are an attractive lady, and you should always feel good about yourself. I saw Dad looking at you this morning with that sparkle in his eyes. He still thinks you're a knockout."

"Thank you son. I appreciate all the compliments, but now we need to go if we are going to get there on time."

Nancy drove Jim's car to Nicole's with no problems. "This car sure does run good. Maybe I'll have Art take a look at mine. Hopefully it won't cost me an arm and a leg to get it fixed."

"Why, is something wrong with your car?"

"I don't know, but I know it doesn't run as well as your car."

"Well, just ask Art to look at it, and maybe he can tell if there is something wrong with it."

"I will have to do that this week when he's helping your dad."

They were driving on the street of Nicole's home, and Nancy asked, "Is this the right house?"

"It is and your memory is very good."

As they were walking up the sidewalk and the steps to the front porch, Nicole was already there with the door open. She looked at Jim and said, "What happened to your arm?"

Jim replied, "The plow tongue broke it. I'll tell you all the details on the way to Columbus, but for right now we need to get on the road. But first I want to say my hellos to your folks. Dean and Connie were staring at Jim's cast, so he told everyone the story of how he broke his arm. "I'm doing fine. It doesn't hurt, but I'm on low-dose pain pills, so I am asking Nicole to drive us to Columbus in my car. We need to take my mother home first because she had to drive me here."

After saying their goodbyes to Connie and Dean, Nancy drove Jim's car to the farm where she got out of the car and said, "Have fun you two. Don't forget that dinner is at six o'clock, and your sister will be here to meet Nicole. So don't be late. Okay?"

Nicole answered, "We'll be there on time Mrs. Martin."

"Nicole, please call me Nancy. Mrs. Martin seems so stuffy and proper, and I don't feel that you need to address me that way. I am Jim's Mom."

"Yes Mrs., I mean Nancy."

Jim and Nicole were on their way to Columbus. Nicole commented on how nice the car drove and that it was so clean.

Jim said, "A young guy, Art, works for my dad, and he was using my car while I was away, and he cleaned it up and worked on it too. He did a great job, and I'm very pleased with what he did."

"I really like the way it handles."

"Nicole, how are you dealing with the Scott issue?" he asked.

"I know he was using me, and I'm finally realizing that. You have been so wonderful to me, and I told myself to let go and go forward, and that's what I am trying to do. With your help I will soon be able to completely let go of that involvement. He gave me this engagement locket to wear around my neck. It had a picture of both of us in it, but I took our photo out and took the locket off the necklace. Now I just wear the necklace, and if you're good about resting when you should, maybe I'll put our picture in the locket."

"Yes dear! I will be on my best behavior and do as I am told. I'd love to give you a locket myself, but I'm afraid it would only remind you of him."

Nicole replied, "We can talk about that later. Right now I need to know where we are going first."

"Would you mind if we went to the hospital first to find out if my broken arm will affect my work schedule, as I am supposed to report for work in a little more than a week. I can also look on the intern's bulletin board to check if there are some guys looking for a roommate. I also need to find a newspaper. Is that all right with you or do we need to do your itinerary first?"

"That will be fine with me. We need to get your running around done first so you won't be dragging. With my scheduling, you can sit on a bench and rest. The only thing I may have you do with me is to check out my housing. That way you will know where I will be living and how far it will be from the hospital."

"You are so smart. I was hoping you would let me see where you will be living. You know that I want to see you as much as possible. Thank you, Nicole."

"It's my pleasure, Jim. I will also want to see you every day if it is possible." As she was pulling into the hospital's parking lot she asked, "Jim, where do I need to park here at the hospital?"

"If you don't mind dropping me off at the Emergency door, then you can park along the walkway over there. I'll be out in just a few minutes."

"Okay, I'll be right over there," she said.

Jim wasn't gone but about ten minutes. When he got into the car, he told Nicole that he would still be able to work after he brought a work release from the doctor who set his arm. "I don't remember the doctor's name and I don't remember him wearing a name badge either."

Nicole said, "When we get back to your house we can call the hospital and ask for his name, but your family physician can fill out the form you will need. The reason I know that is because my cousin had to have a release form before she could take physical education, and her doctor filled out her form, even though he wasn't the doctor who saw her."

"We will have to do some walking because the parking lots are small near the Administration Building, but there are other lots we can use. If you would rather sit where it is beautiful, you can sit on a bench close to the center of the campus. Will it bother you to walk some distance?"

"No, I'll be fine. If I get tired I'll sit on a bench until my stamina will allow me to catch up with you. I'll be fine."

They walked together, and Jim did not seem to get tired. As they walked into the Administration Building, Jim was standing right with her in line. When she received her forms, they went to a table for her to fill them out. When she was finished, she took them to another window and paid her fees for the first semester of her junior year. Then she went to another area of the same building to find out about housing. They both sat down with the lady in charge of housing, and it was going to be cheaper if she lived in a dormitory. Nicole chose Bradley Hall because it was very close to the hospital where Jim was going to be. She would be on the fourth floor in a double room with one other girl. She was offered a sextet room with five other girls at a cheaper rate, but she thought she could study better with having just one roommate.

She applied for her parking permit, but she found out that she would have to park in a parking garage closer to the hospital because there was nothing available close to her dorm, and then she would have to pay a parking fee to have it stored there.

Jim looked at her and said, "Why don't you just leave your car at home as I have free parking at the hospital. Anytime you need to use the car, you are more than welcome to do so, and it won't cost you anything. That's a lot of money to pay to store it in a parking garage, when you won't be using it much."

"Jim, I don't want to be an imposition to you in any way. If I need to go home I would keep you from being able to go anywhere, and what if you needed your car while I was using it?"

"There are a lot of what ifs, but when I'm off, I can take you wherever you need to go, and possibly I would want to go with you. My schedule will vary from night to day or day to night or week to week and possibly day to day, so it won't inconvenience me in any way. Your folks have a double garage and only one car, so I know they stored your car in their garage while you were in Colorado, didn't they? And besides that, your mother would be able to use your car if your dad was using theirs. Does that sound reasonable to you?"

"Yes, but I don't want to inconvenience you in any way."

"The only inconvenience I would have is if I didn't get to see you."

Nicole sighed and replied, "Okay, but I want to help with the expenses with your car."

"Nicole, the expenses will be minimal, and if anything happens I can take care of it, or have it taken home and let Art work on it. Then we would possibly have to use your car. Does that seem okay to you?"

"Yes. You are always so sensible about everything. I know I haven't known you very long, but you make me feel so comfortable around you, and I really appreciate you being so sweet to me."

"I have feelings for you Nicole. I never thought I could feel this way about someone in such a short time, but I am smitten with you. I realize you need some time to totally let go of Scott, but I am here for you, and I hope your feelings for him are diminishing."

"They are, Jim. I saw the writing on the wall long before now. I saw how he let Emily be so close to him, but I didn't want to believe what I was seeing. It hurts less and less the more I am around you. Catherine even tried to tell me to beware, but I didn't listen. He paid so much attention to me until Emily came on the scene, and he even turned her away in front of me and around others, but I don't know what happened. I do know now that he loved us both in different ways. Now it's time to move on, and you have been so gracious to allow me the healing time I need."

Just then Nicole's phone was ringing in her purse. She found it and answered it. It was Scott. He told her that he missed her, and that he didn't mean what he said about them being over. He told her he still loved her. He was upset that she had to leave without even saying goodbye. He wanted to pick up where they had left off.

"Scott, where is Emily?"

"She left a little bit ago. Why are you asking about her? You know you are the one I love, not her."

"Scott, I realize you were a summer romance for me, but I don't like to be treated as a twosome for anyone. You have feelings for Emily, and I know it. Why else would she hang on to you the way she does? No girl wants to be second fiddle to anyone, and that includes me. When I'm not there, you have Emily. When I was there along with her, you treated her so badly, but she kept coming back. You had to be enticing her in some way, and as I said, I will in no way be a twosome for anyone. You've made your choice, and you must live with it. I am no longer yours, and I don't need to hear from you again. Have a wonderful life with Emily, but do yourself a favor and love her with all your heart. Don't share yourself with anyone else. She deserves better than that. Goodbye Scott."

As Nicole put her cell phone back in her purse, Jim took her hand and pulled her to his chest. She was crying.

"I am so proud of you. That took a lot of courage for you to tell him what you did. Now I truly know that you and I are free to possibly be together. Thank you so much for that reassurance."

"Jim, I am sorry you had to hear that, but it hurts to know that he was still trying to use Emily and myself. What's wrong with him? Can't he find happiness with just one person?"

She continued to keep her head on his chest, and her arms were hugging him.

"It's okay to cry, Nicole. I am here for you. You don't have to worry about me. I have a very clean past. I have dated, but nothing was ever serious, and there are no loose ends dangling out there."

Nicole interrupted, "I need to think about something else. I don't want to dwell on a lost cause, and we need to get on the road to be on time for your mother's dinner. I am looking forward to meeting your sister, Bette."

Jim put his arm back in the sling, put her hand in his and squeezed it gently. "I know you are going to like my sister. She's a very sweet person. I have never brought anyone home to meet my entire family before. Even in high school I wasn't dating that much. I had my mind on my career while a lot of my friends were doing things like getting drunk or smoking, and treating girls like they were objects for them to toy with. I don't know how they could stand themselves. I wasn't a part of that crowd, and I'm glad that I wasn't."

Nicole stopped Jim on the sidewalk, reached up and held his face in her hands and kissed him. "Thank you for being so kind and good to me. I know it must have been hard for you to listen to my conversation with Scott. You are not the type of person who might have taken my phone and told him to never call me again, but you just listened and let me have my moment. That's why I hugged and kissed you."

When they were at the car, Jim unlocked the driver's door and started to open it, but he turned Nicole toward him and kissed her tenderly. He felt they were now a couple. He closed her door and walked around to the other side. He sat down on the seat and looked at her. She had tears in her eyes again, but she looked at him and said, "Thank you."

Nicole was driving toward the farm, and Jim was just looking at her most of the time. She finally said, "Please quit looking at me. You're making me nervous."

Jim said, "I want to memorize your beautiful face and lock your image in my brain. I will never forget what you did for us today. You made me feel so good, and now I know I can tell you that I really want us to have more than a friendship. I seem to be one of those people who, right from the beginning, know that there is something there."

"I want us to go slow with our relationship, and not because I still have deep feelings for Scott. I don't. I am hurt more than anything else, but that's my own fault, and I would never want to do anything that would hurt you. I hope that you will understand what I'm trying to say. I will not rush from one interest to another. I have to be true to myself, and that way, when it is happening again, I will know that it is right. You and I are in the beginning stages of a very good friendship, and I want it to grow, as it should with no other attachments. I cannot totally get over Scott and what he did to me in a day, a week or however long it takes, because I trusted him with my heart, and my feelings. It hurts to know that I was so gullible. I believe that you are a different person from him, and that you wouldn't do that to me, but I have to have time to get over that situation. I trusted him with me. We never went beyond my boundaries, which I am really happy about now. I felt that I was competing with another woman, and I was. I went through jealousy, anger, not trusting myself, abandonment and loss within a few weeks. I didn't like any of those feelings, and I don't really want to go through that again. I'm not saying that you would, but for your sake, I want to go slow and let it build into something we will both want and need. I want our lives to be built on a solid foundation."

Jim responded, "I can give you all the time you need, but I still want to be with you as a trusted friend, a confidante and eventually a person you can love. I will remain someone you can come to with anything, and I will be there for you."

They were almost at Jim's parent's house. They were talking, listening to music when her cell phone was ringing again. She could see that it was Scott, but she didn't want to answer it. Jim looked at her and smiled, and she smiled back.

Jim said, "I can see that you're beginning to let go of him, and that's a good sign for me. You are too nice of a girl to let someone mistreat you, and that is all I'm going to say for right now."

As they drove up the driveway Nicole saw a blonde haired woman talking with Jim's mother. She asked, "Is that your sister, Bette?"

Jim answered, "Yes, that's her."

After Nicole stopped the car, Jim got out and gave his sister a big hug. He introduced Nicole to Bette, and they instantly starting talking as though they had known one another for some time. He knew that Nicole fit in very well with his family, and he was going to give her the time she needed, but he would also be working on becoming someone she could trust and love.

Bette and Nicole helped Nancy set the table. When everything was ready, Nancy called Jim and Dan to come to the table. When everyone was seated Nancy, asked Nicole if she would say a prayer. Nicole began to thank God for His many blessings, and for this family that she was beginning to know and love. Jim looked up at her and smiled, but her eyes were still closed. After her prayer and an Amen, she looked at Jim and grinned. All of them talked continuously about any subject that came up, and Nicole felt as though she truly fit in with this sweet family.

After dinner, Bette and Nicole helped Nancy clear the table and clean the kitchen. When the three women were done, they went to the living room where Dan and Jim were talking and watching a baseball game. Nicole sat down between Jim and Bette. The girls started talking about teaching and Nancy listened and added some things to the conversation. All of a sudden, Jim put his hand on Nicole's. She looked over at him and smiled and squeezed his hand.

It was getting late, and Nicole said she needed to call her mother to come pick her up, but Bette said, "It's right on the way home for me, so I will be happy to take you there. I enjoy talking with you, so we can get to know one another even more in the car. Is that all right with you, Mr. Broken Arm?"

"It sure is, Sis. Mom needs my car tomorrow anyway. She's having Art look at hers."

Dan asked, "What's wrong with your car? This is the first I've heard about you having a problem with it."

Nancy replied, "I like the way Jim's car drives, and I want Art to fine tune mine. It's making a funny little noise, and has for a while, but I'll feel better if he checks it out."

Dan said, "Okay. I have some work for him to do, but it can wait. Your life in that car is more important to me than what I was going to have him do. Besides, he'll be working here for a long time."

"Dad, Is there anything I can help you with?"

"No son. You need to let your arm heal. I'd hate to dirty up that pretty cast of yours, and besides you just got it fixed. By the way, what did the hospital say about you reporting for duty?"

"I'm still on for light duty starting in a week or so. I can observe surgeries and help with whatever else they find for me to do. It will put me a little behind, but I know I can catch up. I've already done a lot of what's on the list when I was helping with the Red Cross in Haiti and Louisiana. Hopefully, I'll be a little ahead on some things."

Bette said, "Well Nicole, are you ready to get on the road with me?"

Nicole answered, "I sure am. I just want to thank you Nancy and Dan for the wonderful meal and company. I have totally enjoyed myself. I know I will be seeing you again soon. Goodnight."

Jim walked both Bette and Nicole to Bette's car. He told his sister to be careful with her precious cargo, and she laughed. He turned to Nicole before she got in the car and gave her a hug and a kiss. She looked into his eyes, and said, "Goodnight my sweet prince," and she kissed him back.

Jim told her that he would call her in the morning. He watched as they backed out of the driveway. She was waving at him, and he waved back.

When Jim came back in the house, Dan and Nancy said "We approve and really like your girl. She's a keeper all right."

Jim replied, "I am already falling for her, but I need to give her some time to get over someone she met in Colorado and thought they were going to have a future together. He didn't treat her right, and she needs some time to forgive and forget. I totally understand and will give her all the time she needs, but in the meantime I will be helping her through it, which will give me an advantage to further our relationship. I just have to honor her wishes and give her the time she needs."

Nancy said, "Don't push her if she's not ready. Just remember you only met her less than a week ago. Very few people find that perfect person for them in that short of time."

"I won't Mom. But for now, I am going to bed. I took a pain pill with dinner, and I'm really getting sleepy, so I'll see you both in the morning. Remember Dad, if you need some help with something I can do, don't hesitate to ask me. Okay?"

"Okay son."

Nancy gave Jim a hug and said, "Sweet dreams."

Bette and Nicole talked all the way to Nicole's parent's house, and Bette said, "I hope I can remember how to get here again. I was talking with you the whole time I was driving, and I wasn't paying close attention to where you were directing me. Please write down your address and number, and I will call you tomorrow sometime to get directions again. I have a new GPS system, but I don't have it programmed right, so it's really useless until I can figure it out. It was wonderful meeting you, and I am so happy for my brother. He is such a nice guy, and I know I'm prejudice, but I want him to have the best, and I really think you fit that bill. No pressure, right? And maybe the next time you can meet my husband, Russ, and our son and daughter. Our son was not feeling well, and I didn't want to take our daughter without him. He would have had a fit if she got to go to Grandma and Grandpa's without him."

"Bette, I enjoy your family so very much, and I already have feelings for your brother, but I want to take it slower than I think he wants to, but he says he understands. I know he's a great guy, and he is very compassionate towards me for having met me on a plane several days ago. We could talk about anything and everything. We'll see what happens with some time on our side. I really have enjoyed talking with you about teaching. You must have heard that I want to become a teacher, and you have enlightened me even more to help me know that is what I really want to do. Thanks again for accepting me as all of you have, and also for the lift home. I do appreciate it. Drive home safely, and I hope to see you soon. Goodnight."

When she walked into the house her mother was cross stitching a piece to be put on the quilt she was finishing, and she asked Nicole if she had a good day.

"I did, Mom. I'm all set with my classes for this upcoming semester, and I paid my fees. Jim went with me, and then we looked at the room in Bradley Hall where I will be staying. It's a great room with a lot of light, and I had a choice between a room with six girls or a room for two, and I picked the room for two. I thought I would have a better chance of being able to study. I don't know who my roommate will be, but I will find that out when I get there. I will not be driving my car there because there is no parking near the dorm, so Jim said I could use his car when I might need it. He will be at the hospital right across the street and up one block. I would have had to pay to store my car two blocks away, and it would be very costly. So, I took Jim up on his offer. The only time I would need a car is to come home, but if he's not scheduled to work then, we'll come together."

"That's sounds really good. How was your meeting with his family?"

"Mom, it was wonderful. You already met his mother, but his dad and sister are so nice. They made me feel like I was one of the family, and I felt so comfortable with them. His sister, Bette, brought me home. She lives in Fairborn, so it was a little out of her way, but we had such a fun time talking and getting to know one another. I couldn't have asked for a better day. Jim was so kind, even though I knew he was hurting. He kept his arm in a sling, but I know he needed to take a pain pill, but he waited until we got to his parent's house. We did go to his hospital first to find out if his schedule would be changed due to his broken arm, but he is to start in less than two weeks. He'll have light duty of watching surgeries, and fetching things for other doctors. He's okay with that. I'm just happy that we will be close to one another."

"Are you having serious feelings for Jim?"

"I told him I needed some time to get over Scott, and I don't want to jump right into another relationship with anyone else until I have some time to let go of what I thought we had together. While we were on campus Scott called me and said he didn't mean what he had said about us being over because of the distance. He told me that he missed me, that he still loved me, and that he wanted to pick up where we left off.

"I asked him where Emily was, and he said she just left. He wanted to know why I was asking about her, and I told him that he has feelings for Emily, and she should not be treated like a second fiddle. No girl wants to share her guy with another girl. He said he loved only me, but he probably has told her that too. I told him to have a wonderful life with Emily, but love her with all his heart, and don't share your love with anyone else. She deserves better than that. Then I said, 'Goodbye Scott."

"Nicole, he called here about six o'clock, and I told him you weren't back yet, so he said he would call later. I just wanted to give you a heads up. I know you did love him, but sometimes we learn lessons for life through pain, and I know he caused you a great deal of pain. Your father and I would prefer you not get involved with him again."

"Those are true words spoken, Mom. I will not be going back to Scott. I need to call Catherine to see if she knows what's going on with him."

"That sounds like a good idea."

"I think I'll call her after I get ready for bed. She is three hours behind us, so she should be in her cabin by then. I haven't talked to her since the other night, and I want to keep her posted on what's going on here. She was my confidante while I was there, and I couldn't have asked for a better sister."

"Where's Dad?"

"He went to bed early. He tires so easily, but the doctor told us that he would regain his strength once his body gets used to the medication."

"I sure hope he will be all right."

"I'm sure he will be, but he needs to rest and not worry about things that need to be done. Those things can wait."

"I'd be glad to mow the lawn and trim the bushes tomorrow."

"I may take you up on that, Nicole."

"Okay Mom. I'm going to get ready for bed and then call Catherine. I love you." She leaned over and kissed her mother on the top of her head.

"I love you too, sweetheart. Goodnight."

After Nicole readied herself for bed, she thought about all the questions she wanted to ask Catherine, so she picked up a pad of paper and wrote them down. She was dialing Catherine's number when her phone rang. She answered it before she looked to see who was calling, and it was Scott.

"Hello Nicole. I know I talked to you today, but I didn't feel that it went very well, so I thought I would try a different approach this time. Emily and I are only friends, and she has accepted that. She does still come to see me every day to help me with my therapy. I very much appreciate her help because if I didn't have someone to help me, I wouldn't be as far along as I am now, so I really have depended on her, but I don't love her. I love you, and she knows that. So can we talk to each other and start where we left off before you left?"

"Scott, words were spoken by you in the presence of Emily, when you told me that our relationship would not work out due to distance. Those were your words, not mine. I don't know what your motive was to say what you did, but I will not compete with another woman, and you do have feelings for Emily, and you know it. I am not interested in picking up where we left off. I think you were right about the distance, because there is no way we can continue on when we can't even be civil toward one another, and because we don't have the ability to see or be near one another on a regular basis. My life is back here, and I will be attending college here. I'm sorry that you don't want to understand my side of things, but I, in no way, want to go back to the misery I was put in. I have never been a jealous person, but you brought that out in me, and I don't want to become that jealous person ever again. I also think it thrilled you to know you had two women to love. Now you have one, and that is Emily. Have a good life, Scott. I'm through. Please don't call me anymore. Goodbye."

Nicole immediately called Catherine's number before Scott would be able to call her back. Catherine answered the phone on the first ring.

"Hey my little sis, how are you?"

"Hi Catherine, I'm fine, and you?"

"Well, to tell you the truth, I miss you terribly. It is so quiet in this cabin, even though you didn't make much noise when you were here. I truly miss you. Norman fell yesterday and broke his left big toe and little finger. He and Mike were cleaning the outside wall of the diner, and he stumbled on a rock, and down he went. He is fine, but a little sore. Mike is okay and still trying to work his man act on some new girls who are visiting here, but he tells me at least twice a day that he misses you. Virginia continually asks me about you and your dad. I told her what you told me a few days ago, but how is your dad?"

"He is really tired most of the time, but his medication makes him tired and sleepy, so he sleeps a lot in his recliner or in their bed. He is doing as well as can be expected. Hopefully after his medication is gone, he'll feel like doing a little something."

"So he didn't have a full-blown stroke?" Catherine asked.

"No, he did not, but if he would have continued down the path he was going, he would have had one eventually. It scared him into doing what the doctor told him to do, and now he eats what is on the suggested menu, and Mom is feeling better also."

"To change the subject, I was trying to call you a few minutes ago and Scott called me again. He called me this afternoon while I was on campus, and I had a friend with me. He told me he wanted to start up where we left off. I told him no. He told me he didn't mean to tell me we were over, because he was still a little angry with me for not telling him I was leaving. I told him that he is trying to play two women at the same time, and I'm not interested in playing that game. I asked him if Emily was there, and at least he was honest enough to tell me that she had left a little while ago. I asked him why he was calling me, because I know he has feelings for Emily or else she wouldn't be hanging around. He tried to tell me that he didn't love her, but she was there to help him with his therapy, and he really appreciated her loyalty. I told him not to call me anymore because I don't want to be a part of his life ever again. I made up my mind to let him go."

"Nicole, are you seeing someone else?"

"Yes Catherine I am. It is nothing serious, but I am seeing Jim Martin, Bill's brother. We are close friends right now, and I like it that way. There is no pressure to make our relationship more than it is right now, and that's what we both want. I have told him I need time to get over my relationship with Scott. I truly loved him, but loving Scott was difficult, and I was beginning to become someone I didn't like. His actions made me jealous with Emily always being there, and I had a hard time sharing him with her, but he wouldn't change anything. He had us where he wanted us. I guess it thrilled him to know he had two women wanting him for themselves. I don't believe it was worth the fight anymore, because nothing was going to change."

Catherine asked, "Nicole what time was it when he called you this afternoon and this evening."

"It must have been around two or three o'clock this afternoon, and then ten o'clock tonight. We are three hours ahead of you, so it would have been twelve o'clock noon and then seven tonight, your time. Why did you ask me that?"

Catherine told Nicole, "Todd called me earlier and said that Scott got Emily an engagement ring today. Todd picked him up to take him to the jewelry shop. He said it was a beautiful ring, and he thought it might be for you, but when he took Scott back to the rehab center, Emily was there, and he gave it to her. I don't understand how such a terrific guy turned into someone I don't even recognize. I thought so much of him when he was with you, but you never know, do you?"

"No, you don't, and neither do I. I don't feel that hurt now because I gave him his walking papers, but I don't understand why he called me twice especially when he knew he had put a ring on Emily's finger. Well, I hope they are both happy. This gives me the freedom to have a decent relationship with Jim, if we both choose to do so."

"Go slow, sweetheart. I wouldn't want this to happen to you again."

"Catherine, I won't let this happen to me again. I'm not as vulnerable as I was with Scott. He was my first love, but first loves rarely work out from what I've heard. Remember who told me that? Has Todd found someone yet?"

"No, I think he is still trying to get over you. He said he asked Scott since he was now engaged to Emily, if he would have any objection with him pursuing you, and Scott said 'yes', and Todd told him that he couldn't marry both you and Emily. Scott told him that he was going to try and get you back, but if he couldn't, he would marry Emily."

"Catherine, I don't want to hear any more about Scott. I'm sorry now that I ever had a relationship with him. I truly wasted my time not helping you when I was visiting with him. I'm sorry Catherine."

"You don't need to be sorry about anything that happened. We had a great time, and we worked well together. We had fun and that's all that matters. You can't blame yourself for what happened with Scott. He is the only one who has to answer to a higher power for what he's up to. If you want a suggestion as to what I think is happening I'll be glad to tell you."

"Sure Catherine. I want to know what you think."

"I might be wrong, but I think Emily was getting a little tired of being his nursemaid without a commitment. I actually think Scott bought the ring for you, but when he thought he couldn't have you anymore, he offered her the ring to keep her coming back. Todd told me that Scott may not be able to be a ranger anymore because he is considered disabled, and he won't be able to really help them on hunts or other things that require a healthy able-bodied man to do. Maybe since he knows that Emily's family is wealthy, he could get a sit down position in her father's company. I am just surmising at that possibility. I don't know if that is true or not, but it would make sense.

"Catherine, did you see this coming while I was there with you?"

"Yes, dear, I did. Don't you remember me telling you to not go so fast with your relationship with Scott? I was mostly worried that he would try to do something with you, but I know you told me that was not going to happen, and I believe you told me the truth."

"I did tell you the truth. Nothing happened between us even though he tried a few times. I told him I wanted to wait until I was married, and he told me I was being very old fashioned. I was beginning to see the writing on the wall early into our relationship, but I was blindsided with Emily in the picture. I thought as you did that he was trying to get even with me because he could have Emily anytime he wanted her. I don't know if they have done anything, but

I just want her to be happy with him. She certainly spent a lot of time pursuing and helping him, and I hope for her sake that it paid off.

"Catherine, when is it a good time for me to call you again? I do want to keep in touch with you. I feel badly about not be able to ride back to Ohio with you. I don't like the fact that you will be driving all that distance by yourself."

"Oh, I forgot to tell you that I won't be driving alone. I will be driving Norman and Virginia's car, and we'll be towing mine behind theirs. They live in Dayton, and after we get to their house, I'll stay over for a couple of days, and then I'll drive up to my place in Cuyahoga Falls, where I'll spend the winter. Norman isn't healing as quickly as we thought he would, and Virginia is worried about him. She thinks this may be their last time at the resort, but she said if anything happened to Norman or her, they would leave it to me and Mike. Let's just pray that Norman will heal completely, and that they will have many years left to be at their resort. To answer your first question, you may call me if you are awake at eleven o'clock your time, it would be eight o'clock here, and I should be back in my cabin by then.

"You take care of yourself, and please go slower with this fellow. You know I love and care very deeply for you, so take care and know that all of us here love you immensely. Bye now, sweet girl."

She had just hung up with Catherine when her mother came in her room. "Do you have enough blankets on your bed? We don't want you to catch a cold, you know. We don't heat the upstairs too much at night, so it may be too cold for you. If it is, come and wake me up and I'll fix it for you.

"Thank you, Mom."

While Nicole was sleeping, her cell phone was ringing. It awakened her from a sound sleep. When she did answer it, she was still a little groggy. "Hello, yes this is Nicole. Who is calling?"

With a little hesitation he said, "It's me, Scott."

"Why are you calling me? I told you that you and I are through, and I understand that you gave Emily an engagement ring today, so again, why are you calling me? You have made a promise to Emily by asking her to marry you."

"I want to marry you. The ring I gave her was for you, Nicole, but Emily was threatening to leave me if I didn't make a commitment to her. I acted foolishly, but I don't want to marry her. I want to marry you."

"Scott, are you drunk?"

"I've had a few drinks, why?"

"Scott, you and I are over. I want you and Emily to have a good life together. She loves you so much, and she's given you so much love and attention, that she deserves a commitment from you. I talked with Catherine before I went to sleep, and she told me that you might not have a job as a ranger anymore because of your disability. If that is so, then Emily's father can probably give you a job in his company. Is that true?"

"Yes, but I don't love her like I do you, and I don't want to lose you."

"You have already lost me, and I'm not going back to that kind of a relationship. It did not make me a better person. I finally came to the conclusion that you were playing Emily and me against one another for your affections, and I don't like a guy who wants two women at the same time. Do not call me anymore. I am over you, and you need to go on with your life with Emily. And for Pete's sake, try to truly love her, and her alone. I do not want you back. Goodbye Scott."

She was unable to go back to sleep, so she got out of bed and walked around the room for a while to get rid of her frustration.

Her mother came upstairs to her room and asked, "Are you all right? We could hear you pacing above us. What's wrong?"

"Scott just called me for the third time today. He wants me back even though he just gave Emily an engagement ring. Today! He said the ring was really for me, but I told him not to call me anymore. If he does, I will have my cell phone number changed. I don't want to hear from him ever again. He just doesn't want to let go of me, and I want to let go of him. I don't want a man who loves two women at the same time. That's a disaster ready to explode. Emily was ready to leave him if he didn't show some type of commitment, so he gave her the ring he actually bought for me, so he said. I told him that

I am through with him, and do not bother me again. Then I said, 'Goodbye Scott,' and then I hung up. I was in a sound sleep, and now I'm upset. What's wrong with him, anyway?"

"Honey, you did the right thing, and he probably won't call you again. Was he drinking?"

"He said he had a few drinks, but I don't know how many is a few to him."

"Well, he will have to face the fact that you are no longer in his life. He can't have both of you, so if you said goodbye, then he'll have to accept that. Is that how you really feel?"

"Yes, it is. I don't want to hurt anymore over him. Besides, I really want to have a relationship with Jim. I want it to go slowly, and have it turn into something solid for both of us. I don't exactly know how he feels, but I'm hoping he will want a relationship with me also."

"Well, we'll just have to pray that Jim sees it the same way you do. Just don't rush into things. Slow is always better when it comes to relationships. You learn more about one another in a way that becomes everlasting."

"Thank you Mom. I'm going to try to go back to sleep if I can. Scott really messes with my mind. He seemed to be so sincere with me, and I believed him, but not anymore. Now he has to live with his own consequences, but I feel so sorry for Emily."

"It seems to me that he was messing with your heart, and you fell for him. Good looks and first impressions don't always make for a good relationship. Do you know if he had any other girlfriends besides you and Emily?" her mother asked.

"No, I don't know. If Catherine had known I'm quite sure she would have told me. She kept telling me to slow things down, and give it some time, but I let him have my heart before I knew what was happening. It almost makes me afraid to trust anyone else, but from what I know about Jim and his family, they don't seem like the type of people who would rush right in regarding anything. I don't know them that well, but they are nice people to everyone they meet. Scott's background was not that good. His father was disabled and couldn't do things that most fathers and sons do, and his mother had to work several jobs all the time to put food on their table and pay the bills. I knew he had a hard life growing up with very little attention, and I think it angers him somewhat. Maybe he thought if he had two women desiring his affections, then he would feel he had control. I don't really know. I'm just assuming my thoughts may be correct."

"Why don't you turn your cell phone off, so you won't get disturbed any more tonight?"

"That's a very good idea. Thanks again Mom for the advice."

Nicole slept later than usual. Her own bed felt so familiar and comfortable. From the large window in her room that faced the front of the house, she saw the sun and a blue sky out the window. She turned and looked at her clock on her night stand and saw that it was ten o'clock. She jumped out of bed and went to the bathroom to get ready for the day.

She came downstairs still brushing her hair, and asked, "Mom, did you get any sleep last night after I kept you up?"

"Yes dear, I did get enough sleep, and I'm feeling fine. How are you feeling this morning?"

"I know I am well rested. My bed felt so comfortable to me. The bed I slept in at the resort was also very comfortable, but there is something very comforting about your own things in your own room. It really feels good to be home."

"You know that Dad and I are very happy to have you back here with us, even though we know you will be gone again in a week or so. But the nice thing about it is that you won't be that far away from us. We can still visit once in a while, and you can call us whenever you want without a time change to think about."

"The phone is ringing, can you get that for me. I am up to my hands in dough."

"Sure Mom."

"Hello. Oh, hi Jim. How are you this wonderful morning? It's nice to hear your voice too. I don't know what's going on today. I just got out of bed a little bit ago. You say that Art already fixed your mother's car? What was wrong with it? So it wasn't a costly repair? That's good. You want to go to the Clark County Fair today? Let me ask Mom if she has anything she would like for me to do here at home. What time do you want to go? I will help her do a little cleaning, and then I'll get ready. Okay. How about three o'clock? That's great. I'll see you then. Bye."

"Mom, don't you have some ladies come on Fridays to play Bridge?"

"Yes, and I'm happy you told Jim to come a little later so you can help me a little. You remember Frances who lives on High Street, and Jean who lives on Fountain, and Sharon is just two doors down from us. We've been playing bridge for many years now."

"After I eat some breakfast, I'll dust and run the vacuum, and clean the bathroom. I'll do the kitchen too if you don't have time."

"I can do the kitchen as I'm finishing up the pies I am making for dessert. Thank you for all your help. I really appreciate it, honey."

As Nicole was finishing up the guest bathroom, she thought to herself, "What am I going to wear to a fair?"

Her mother must have read her mind, and said, "Nicole, you will need to wear something that is cool in the mid afternoon, and something to pull over you for the evening. As soon as the sun goes down, it gets chilly, so I just thought I would give you a suggestion."

"Thank you Mom, because I had no idea what to wear."

She decided to wear a pair of jeans and a roll-up sleeve blouse. She tied a cardigan sweater around her neck. "This looks pretty good." She decided to wear her white tennis shoes and some white socks.

When Jim came to the door, the four ladies were playing Bridge. Nicole ran to the door and invited Jim to come in. The ladies stopped playing long enough to be introduced to Nicole's guest. Nicole was ready to leave so she walked over to her mother, and Nicole gave her a kiss on the cheek. Her mother put her right hand on Nicole's face and told her to have a good time at the fair.

Jim asked what the ladies were playing, and Nicole said they were playing Bridge. She told Jim that those four ladies have been playing Bridge together forever it seemed.

"The apple and peach pies sure did smell good."

"Mom is saving a piece of each for us when we get back this evening."

Jim said, "All right and yum! Did you help your Mom bake the pies"

"No, but she taught me a long time ago on how to make pies, and also how to keep a house clean and neat. My high school friend was always embarrassed to have anyone come in her house, because it was so cluttered and messy, so I had the opportunity to know the difference, and I like a clean and uncluttered home. One day, she and I cleaned her house and boxed up the clutter, and when her mother got home from work she was really pleased, but the house only stayed that way for a couple of days. That's when I learned a valuable lesson. If you want your home to look nice, you have to take care of it every day. It sure doesn't clean itself."

"Did your friend try to keep it clean?

"I don't think so. She wouldn't let any of us back in her house. I think she saw the difference by seeing her friend's homes, and I knew she liked coming to my house all the time after school. Mom always had a snack for us, and we'd go to my room to study. Sometimes she used to stay for supper."

"Didn't her mother object to her not coming home?"

"I don't know. She never called to find out where she was. Linda called home once in a while, but her mother was never there. I know Linda said they ate a lot of boxed meals. My mom taught Linda how to cook some things, and Linda really enjoyed that, so Mom tried to teach her how to cook an entire meal and then how to clean a house. Linda liked my mom a lot. I think she liked her more than she liked me. She hugged my mother when she graduated from high school, and she got married right away and left town. I never heard from her again."

"Wow, your mother really helped her. Did you know the guy she married?"

"No, I didn't, and she never mentioned that she was seeing anyone. I heard he was an older boy, maybe in his twenties, but that's all I know."

"Nicole, she wasn't raised on a solid foundation like we were. Kids like your friend, Linda, were raised on shaky ground, or shifting sand, and I have seen a lot of that in my helping in Haiti and Louisiana, especially Haiti. It's sad when no one takes the time to teach you, and because they don't know any better, it gets passed down to another generation, and the poverty level grows even more. That's why we need to teach kids from an early age what is an acceptable way to live and give them hope. We know, but do we teach others like your mother did? I tried to teach cleanliness with your body. We took a lot of soap, wash rags, towels, toothpaste, toothbrushes, hair brushes, shampoo, and a lot of other items and showed them how to use them. Some learned; some didn't want to learn. It's sad when you go help with a catastrophe, and very few people know how to care for themselves."

"Did you enjoy helping those who were left with nothing?"

Jim said, "Yes and no. I found you can only help those who want your help. When a lot of families lost their homes and were thrown into tents until things were stable again, they lost hope. I talked to them about God. We tried to have them understand that He cares for them, and that He understands their problems and He will help them rebuild their lives. Some listened, some didn't. Some were angry with a God who would destroy everything they had with an earthquake or a flood. It was really sad. We tried to teach them that God didn't bring on these catastrophes, and He is always there to help you when you pray to Him and ask for His help."

"Did some of them pray and see a different light on what had happened to them?"

"Yes, but not enough. We only had a two-week period to help them, and when most of them pray to an idol rather than Jesus, it is difficult in a short time to have them accept Jesus. They were inquisitive about Him, but very few turned their lives over to Him. I understood it was not numbers that we were trying to convert, but that the souls of those who accepted Jesus would be changed forever."

"Jim, I am so proud of you for all you have done. You are a remarkable person who allowed God to use you as an instrument of His peace and love."

"Well, thank you, but I didn't do much. I wanted to help those in need, and there were so many that we didn't have time to even talk to. To lose your family and especially your child was too much for me to take. I know this may not sound very manly, but I cried every night when we prayed and then went to sleep, but I knew Jesus was with me the whole time we were there.

"Well, enough on the sadness we endured there, let's go have some fun at the County Fair. Okay?"

"Sure, but may I say one thing about what you just told me?"

"Sure, go ahead."

"I have never known a person like you, and I am so proud of all you have done to help those in need, and I know that you will definitely be a wonderful doctor, one with compassion and care."

"Thank you, Nicole. I really appreciate you saying that to me."

"I bet your parents are really proud of you too."

"They don't really know that I was at either place. I haven't been home very much, mainly because Dad wanted me to give up on being a doctor and be a farmer instead. I have told him that my passion is in medicine, not farming. I know he was hurt because he wanted to pass down his father's legacy to me. Bill chose to move so far away that he knew he couldn't persuade him to be a farmer. I tried to explain to Dad that he grew up where father's passed on their legacy to their oldest son, just like in the Bible, but Bill didn't want that, and neither do I. I will help him all I can, but I want to help people, not grow crops or feed livestock. I am in the people business, not in corn or cattle, pigs or sheep. Bill and I actually ran away from home, but we are accepted now and our folks finally got the picture, so now they welcome us with open arms."

Nicole said, "I would never have thought there was any tension in your home. They seem so loving and kind and accepting. I truly care for your family."

"I'm so glad to hear you say that because one day I would like you to be a part of my family and for me to be a part of yours."

"In time I hope that is the direction we will take together." She said.

"Enough of this heavy stuff Nicole, let's go on the Ferris Wheel so you can see for miles around."

Nicole said holding her breath, "Wow, I didn't realize you could see so much from up here."

Jim asked, "Have you ever ridden on this ride before?"

"No, I never have, and all the years this fair has been here, I have never ridden it."

"You've got to be kidding me! Well, I guess this means you need for us to have a little rocking since we're stopped on the top."

"Don't you dare rock this cart! I will scream and maybe even get sick on you. Would you like me to do that?"

"No, not especially! I won't rock it if you don't want me to."

"Jim, I am really afraid of heights, so please don't do that. Okay?"

"Okay, I promise. I'm sorry if I frightened you. Why didn't you tell me you were afraid of heights before we got on this ride? I would never have wanted you to be afraid."

"I wanted to try something new because I trusted that you would help me get over my fear of heights, and maybe I might like it and want to ride it again. See how much I trust you?"

"I'm glad you trust me, but let me know about some of the things that frighten you, so I won't do any crazy antics with you anymore."

After they rode the Ferris Wheel, they decided to walk around and see the different displays, and then go to the animal barns. The displays of pictures that children drew from each of the county schools, the canned vegetables, pies and cakes, and the 4-H displays were fun to look at. There was so much to see in the two buildings that they decided to stop at a church owned restaurant to eat dinner before they toured the animal barns.

Their dinners were delicious. They had ordered a homemade meal and warm peach pie with melting ice cream for dessert.

"I don't know about you, Jim, but I am really full. I do need to walk some of this off."

"Okay. Are you ready to go see the animals?"

"I sure am."

First, they went through the sheep barn. There were so many different types of sheep that were all trimmed and looked so neat. "Look at those sweet faces. They are really cute."

"Well, now we're on to the hog barn." Jim stated.

"I've never seen such large hogs. They must be well-fed, and they're so clean."

Jim said, "The kids wash them every day and feed them a mixture of grains to help them grow that large. Their skin is pink because of the daily washings. They don't get the chance to roll around in the mud here. The black ones with the white ring around their necks are called Hampshire pigs."

"Did you raise them on the farm and, are they mean or friendly?"

"They're friendly to their owners, just like a pet would be, until they have a litter, and then they'll do anything to protect them. We did raise different breeds on the farm. I wouldn't suggest you try petting them though. See the sign over there? It says, 'Please do not touch the animals.'

"Okay! I guess I should read the signs, huh?"

Next they went to the rabbit and chicken barn. Nicole said, "Look at those beautiful bunnies. They are so cute. Doesn't it make you just want to cuddle them under your neck?"

"No, not me. That cuddly stuff is for girls."

"Oh, Jim, don't you like pets?"

"Sure, dogs and cats, but I'm not into animals that reproduce that frequently. And the chickens smell. They are only good for eggs and fried chicken."

Nicole said, "I was only talking about the bunnies."

"I know, but let's go to a non-smelly barn. All right, no more bunnies and chickens. The next five barns are for cattle."

Nicole questioned, "You don't think they smell?"

"Not as bad as those chickens. Look over there. The first four barns are for dairy cows, and the last barn is for some bulls. I would think they wouldn't want to put all the bulls in one barn. They are very territorial and don't like any competition. When I was about twelve years old, I took an almost two-year-old Holstein calf to show at the fair. That breed is the black and white ones like those over there."

"Did you win?"

"No, because she came in heat, and the bulls were very interested in her, so I had to take her home. With that many bulls there, it wasn't safe for her or for me, so we loaded her up and took her home."

"Was she all right?"

"Yeah, she was, but I wasn't, because I had worked with her every day, teaching her to accept wearing a halter, to walk with me, trimming and bleaching the white tip of her tail, buffing and shaping her hooves, bathing and brushing her, and more. Luckily she didn't have any horns. My dad put some salve on where she would have had horns, and that eliminated that problem. You can really get hurt if a cow has horns. I called her Black Beauty. She was so pretty. She had a white star on her forehead, and white lower legs, like high knee socks. She was a sweet girl."

"What happened to her?"

"She wouldn't breed, which meant she wouldn't become a milk cow, and that's all I'm going to say on that subject."

"What are the pretty faced tan cows?"

"They are called Jerseys. Their milk has a lot of butterfat, which is good for cream."

"Don't Holsteins have butterfat?"

"Not as much. We use to always have a Jersey or a Guernsey cow with the milking Holstein herd to have more butterfat in the milk sold.

"Why does whoever you sold the milk to want cream on the top?"

"Because that's what they use to make butter."

Nicole stated, "Boy! I have a lot to learn about farm animals, don't I?"

Jim stated, "I hope that when I have children, they will love the farm. I really loved the farm itself, and the animals, but I have always wanted to be a doctor."

"Did you ever think about becoming a veterinarian?"

"At one time I did, but I like working with people better. They can tell you what's wrong, and an animal can't. You can really get hurt by animals when they're sick. They don't realize you're trying to help them. Their first responses are fright and flight, or let me out of there. I didn't like getting kicked either. The cows can kick hard. A neighbor got kicked in the leg and lost the use of it. He had to give up milking and sell his herd. That put a real damper in his income.

"Nicole, now that you've seen most of the cows how about us seeing the horses in the horse barns?"

"They have horses here too?"

"Sure, they're also animals."

"I know that, but I didn't think of them as being farm animals."

"We just have to walk a little further. They are in horse barns over by the track."

"Wow! Some of them are really huge, and some are smaller."

"Haven't you ever seen the big horses that pull the beer wagons or stage coaches from the Old West? Those on the right side are called Clydesdales. They are massive in weight and strength, and the rest are work horses. The next barn is generally riding horses, but I call them pets. Most farmers don't use horses anymore to till the land because they use tractors to hook plows and different implements onto the back of them. The tractors can pull more than the horses, and the only feed they get is gas and oil."

"Jim, you know so much about farming, and it is so interesting to hear about it. I'm really surprised that you don't want to farm. I love most animals, but dogs and cats especially. My family had a pet dog, a black cocker spaniel, named Buttons, and I had a pet gray cat, named Whiskers. When they died, it was like losing a member of your family. It has been so much fun learning about the animals, and I have really enjoyed this entire day with you at the fair. Thank you for bringing me."

"Well you'll find a lot of cats and a dog or two on a farm, but they don't really bring in any money, as the larger animals do. I guess you could breed dogs to sell, but cats are good for keeping mice out of your feed. I always had a pet dog and cat, but my horse was my favorite pet. She ate grass, some hay and feed. The vet bills are pretty costly for the larger animals. I hope we'll have many more days like this together. I'm also glad we came to the fair. Thank you for accepting my invitation."

"How's your arm holding up?"

"It's beginning to throb a little. I didn't bring my medication because I'd get sleepy, and I'd rather be with you than sleep."

"Well, I'm ready to go whenever you are. I don't want your arm to throb, so let's go to your house to get your pills. Okay?"

"Nicole, if I take a pill I'll be asleep in about fifteen minutes, and I want to spend more time with you."

"If we go to the farm, I can have my dad pick me up when I'm ready to come home. I'd like to spend some time with your folks and see their farm."

Jim replied, "Your folks may not want to leave to come after you."

"I want them to meet your mom and dad together. They already have met your mom, but I also want my folks to see what a nice farm your parents own. They will get a better idea of who you are, and why I like you so much."

"Oh! So you like me?"

"Yes, I do very much like you."

"Well, I like you very much too, and I'd like that to become something more in time. You are everything I have been waiting for, and here you are."

Nicole said, "What happened to the slow idea?"

"This is slow, isn't it?" Jim replied.

Nicole couldn't help but laugh. "You are so funny, and I love the way you make me laugh."

"I am at your beckoned call, my dear, but may I escort you to the car?"

"If you so desire, my lord."

"Hey, I'm not your lord. I'm your prince in shining armor, and I'm here to sweep you off your feet directly into my arms, or should I say into my one good arm?"

"Jim, you make me laugh, and I feel so good. I haven't worried at all, and you make me feel so at ease. I don't remember how long it's been since I've been able to just let loose and have some fun. I enjoy being with you. When we get to the farm, let's get your arm elevated and talk about what each of us needs from one another. I have always thought I'm not the needy type of person, but I do have some thoughts of what I want and need from a significant other."

"Okay. Let me call Mom, and see if she will invite your parents to dinner. We'll help her get things ready so she won't have it all to do."

"Good idea!"

"I'll need your house phone number because I only have your cell number. You know what that means, don't you Nicole?"

"No, what does that mean?"

"It means to me that I have connection to you and your parents, so you better behave."

"Ooh! I'm scared. Now you can tell on me plus keep tabs on my whereabouts."

"Yep, you're right!"

"I'm calling Mom right now, so you better behave. "Hi, Mom. Nicole and I are coming home shortly, and I was wondering if you would invite her parents to come to dinner. I know this is short notice, but I will stop and get anything you need on our way there. Nicole will need a ride home, and if her parents come, Dad will get to meet them, and they can take her home afterwards. I've told them about us living on a farm, and Nicole thinks they would really enjoy seeing a little of it. Would that be okay?"

"Yes, Jim, that would be fine. Do you have their phone number? Thank you. You can pick up some rolls at the store, and that's all I will need. I have a chicken all thawed out, so it won't take me very long to fix it. Where are you right now?"

"We're on our way out of the fair, so we'll be home shortly to help you."

"That sounds fine, Son. Have you taken your medicine yet today?"

"No, but I will when we come home. Thanks again, Mom, and I love you. See you in a little bit. Bye."

"Was she after you about taking your medication?" Nicole asked.

"Yes. You women worry too much about taking medication at a certain time every day."

"That's because it works better if you take it the same time every day."

"Who's the doctor around here?"

"I don't know. It seems you would take the advice of your doctor since you're going to be one."

"Okay. You win that one."

"Jim, I'll run in the store and get the rolls so you can rest."

"Okay. I am hurting a little. I think it is swelling because it feels tight in the cast."

"When we get to the farm, you are going to lie down and put your arm on a pillow and take your pill. I will help your mother get everything ready. Do you understand what I am telling you?"

"Yes dear, I understand."

"Hey Nicole, I appreciate you looking after me. I really like you more and more every day. Would it bother you if I said I love you?"

"Jim, I don't want to rush this because I want it to last. I won't mention the last person's name, but it happened in a whirlwind, and look what happened. I thought I knew him, but I didn't. I want to make sure that you and I are reaching for the same goals; an education, a relationship, and a future. I don't want this to only be an infatuation. I want it to last."

Jim replied, "I will give you all the time you need. Just realize that my schedule when I start working at the hospital will be long and never on the same days or time. Do you think you can deal with that?"

"Yes, I will be studying in my room in the dorm. Your upcoming schedule will be unknown for some time, so the surprise of us seeing one another should be very pleasant, and we'll make the most of it."

Jim responded, "We'll do all right, you'll see."

Nicole asked. "Do you know where things are in this store? I don't want to run all over the store trying to find rolls."

"Sure, just go inside and take a right, and they will be on the far wall. You won't be able to miss them."

"You weren't gone very long," he said.

"The rolls were right where you told me they would be. Thank you."

When they arrived at the farm and went inside, Nicole handed Nancy the rolls. "What may I do to help you?"

Nancy told Jim to go lie down and elevate his arm. "Nicole, can you make him take his medication for me?"

"Sure, and then I will come help you with dinner."

"You can set the table for six. Your parents were very gracious and accepted my invitation."

"Thank you for inviting them. I know this is an imposition for you, but I know they will enjoy meeting with you again and meeting Dan, plus seeing the farm."

As Nicole was setting the table, she got a call from her mother. "Hi Mom, what's up?"

"Nicole, you have a visitor here at the house."

"Who is it Mom?"

With a delay, she said, "It is Scott."

"What is he doing there?"

"He flew in from Denver this afternoon and rented a car to come talk with you in person."

"Mom, put him on the phone, please."

"Hello Nicole. I came to see you, but your mother told me you were out for the day."

"Yes, I am out, and I'm not coming home until later this evening. What is it that you want from me?"

"I want to talk with you face to face."

"Scott, I don't want to talk with you anymore. You are engaged to Emily, and you should be thinking only of her and not me. I have nothing more to say to you, so I'm sorry you made the trip, but you should get right back on a plane and go back to her."

"I guess you haven't talked with Catherine lately, have you?

"No, I talked with her right after I came home. Why?"

"Emily dumped me."

"Well, you haven't treated her very well. Now have you?"

"No, and I feel very badly for the way I treated her, but she broke off our engagement and was in an accident on her way home, and was killed instantly. Her sister, Sandy, called to tell me. I assume they didn't know she broke off our engagement. I didn't tell Sandy that because I didn't want to be blamed for her accident. She missed a curve and went through a guard rail. The car tumbled and rolled down into a ravine. I'm sad about the accident, but that doesn't change the fact that I have always been in love with you, and that's why I'm here to tell you that I love you more than ever. I want us to get back together. I'll move here if it means I'll have you."

"Scott, I am so sorry to hear about Emily's death. I know you truly had feelings for her. Even though you no longer have Emily that doesn't mean that you have me. I let go of you when I was told that you were engaged to her. I don't want to go through that hurt ever again. So I'm sorry Scott, but you need to go back to Estes Park. I don't want you here. I will not see you. I am moving on with my own life."

"Nicole, you can't mean that. What we had was real, and I believe we can have it again."

"Scott, we cannot go backwards. Go back to the airport and catch a flight home. I will not be seeing you."

"I can wait."

"Well, you'll be waiting a long time, and not at my parents home. Do yourself a favor and go back to Estes Park."

"I am no longer a ranger. They let me go because I'm considered disabled. I have no job except for monthly compensation from the government. I need you to help me through this."

"Scott, find you a good therapist, but I'm not available anymore."

"Nicole, please. I need to talk with you. I'm lost without you."

"Scott, I have someone else now. I don't want you back. I went through so much misery and hurt feelings, that I won't accept that anymore. You need to go on with your life and find someone else.

You're a healthy, good looking man who should have no problem finding someone other than me. I wish you the best of everything, but I'm not taking you back. This is the last time I want to speak to you, and please leave my parents out of this. I don't want you in my life anymore. Do you understand me?"

"I hear you, but I don't believe you."

"Well, I don't know what more I can say. I've told you how I feel, and I have no more room in my heart for you. You cannot repair the damage you did. I'm sorry for your loss, but I won't be your soft pillow anymore. Goodbye Scott."

When she hung up Jim noticed that she was disturbed.

"Are you all right?"

"I'm shaken up a little, but I know where I need to be, and it's with you."

"Do you want me to contact this Scott fellow?"

"No Jim, but thank you. I want to call my Mom and see if he's still there."

"Hi Mom, is he still there?"

"Your dad is talking with him on the porch. I don't know what they are saying to one another, but your father knows you no longer want him in your life. Scott's head is down, and he's looking at his shoes. He has a crutch and a brace on his left leg. We heard his end of the conversation, so we knew you didn't want him back, so I think your dad is telling him in a nice way to go back where he belongs, and that would not be here. I'll tell you more when we come out there for dinner."

"Just make sure he's not following you. I don't need Jim's family caught up in that mess. I feel sorry for him, but not enough to give up Jim. I really have good feelings about my relationship with Jim. He is not only good to me, but he is fun, intelligent, and he respects me. I can't say that for Scott. I hope and pray he goes back to Colorado. I'm quite sure they can give him a desk job because I don't think they would just let him go because he got hurt on duty, and from of all things, a grizzly bear.

"Make sure you get a good look at his rental car, so you will be able to tell if he's following you. If he is, have Dad take you to the grocery store, call me, and then both of you go in and act like you're are shopping. If he's still there, give me a heads up, and I'll think of something. I will let Nancy know you will be a little late so she can keep things warm."

Jim got off the couch and went directly to Nicole. He hugged her and kissed her on the top of her head. She looked up at him, and he tenderly kissed her lips. He said, "If you need me to go back to your house and confront this guy, I will."

"I don't think that will be necessary, but thank you for wanting to be my knight in shining armor."

Just then her cell phone rang, and when she answered it was her father. "I think we lost him. We went around several blocks and luckily we had a green light that turned red as soon as we made a left hand turn. He couldn't turn because there was a police officer sitting in his patrol car at the same intersection. We are on our way to the farm. Your mother is still checking the mirrors to make sure he isn't behind us. If by any chance he is, we will call you again."

"Thank you Dad!"

Nancy asked Nicole if there is some trouble.

Nicole told her, "I was going with a park ranger who worked with Bill. He and I were seeing one another, but he was also seeing a beautiful girl who was a guest at our resort. He got hurt and had to go to three different hospitals, and I just couldn't be there all the time and she was. He led us both on, but she was persistent and he finally gave her an engagement ring. I was on my way home to be with my parents when we thought that my dad had a stroke. That plane ride home was where I met Jim. I found out once I got home that Scott gave the other girl a diamond ring, but he still led me on at the same time."

Nicole's phone was ringing, and she answered it right away. "Nicole, this is Catherine. I need to tell you something."

"What's wrong Catherine?"

"Todd called me and said that Scott had Todd take him to the airport, and he caught a flight to Ohio. He also said that Emily gave him back the ring. She was in an accident. It wasn't her fault but she is all right."

"Catherine, Scott is here. He was at my parent's house. My mother gave him the phone, and he said he wanted to talk with me.

He said Emily gave him back the ring, but her sister, Sandy, called him and told him that Emily was in a deadly car accident, and she was killed instantly. Now you are telling that she was in an accident but she is all right. I can't believe he would lie to me about that."

"Honey, he is desperate. He has no one, so he's counting on you to take care of him. He had an opportunity to answer calls for the rangers, but he wouldn't take it. Todd said he has compensation, but it's not enough for him to live on for a long period of time. Maybe Sandy did call and tell him that so he wouldn't bother Emily anymore."

"I'm at Jim's house now, and my parents are coming here to eat dinner. Dad said that Scott was following them in a rental car, but they lost him, but I bet you anything that he will be at our house when we get home."

"Nicole, be very careful. Scott is very upset with Emily and with you. He has no one now, and he doesn't like it."

"Catherine, why did Emily break up with him, do you know?"

"Todd told me that Scott talked about you to her all the time and she got fed up with him, so she threw the ring back and walked out."

"I don't care what he talked to her about. He's not getting me back. I am happy right now and in a very good place with a wonderful guy and his family. May I call you later? My parents just got here for dinner. I love you for the heads up. I will call you when I get home. Thanks again for the head's up. Bye for now."

Nicole's parents were there and she introduced them to Dan.

Dan said, "It is very nice to meet you. We are very happy that our son picked such a nice girl. We truly love her already."

Dean said, "Thank you for saying that. We really love her too, and we are pleasantly pleased with your son."

Nancy called everyone to come to the table. "Everything is ready, and I want to thank you Nicole for being such a great helper. I really appreciate all you have done."

"It wasn't much. I was on the phone most of the time. I'm sorry for the intrusion."

Jim asked Nicole's dad, "Mr. Thomas, do you think this Scott is a threat to all of you?"

Dean said, "No, I don't feel that way. He just wants to talk with Nicole, but she doesn't want to talk to him. I'll be with her if she does decide to talk with him.

"Since he doesn't know where she is, would you want her to stay with us until he's gone?" Jim asked.

Nicole replied before her father could answer, "No, but thank you for the offer. This problem does not need to be your problem, and I don't want to leave my parents alone to settle this. If he is still there, I will handle it. He will not win this one. I will call you and let you know we are all alright. Okay?"

"You know I will worry about the three of you." Jim replied.

"We'll be fine. I promise."

"Mr. Martin, If there is still some daylight, could you please show my parents a little of your farm? I love it here with the wonderful smells of fresh mown hay, and the many sounds of the animals, and the landscape is so beautiful too."

Dan asked, "Would you like to be a farmer? I can't seem to get either of our sons to be one. I have accepted their paths, but I wanted to pass it down to one of them."

Jim answered, "Dad, I like farming, but I want to be a doctor more than I want to be a farmer. You love the land and the animals, and I love dealing with people. They don't kick as hard."

"Well, you do have a point there. I really don't hold any animosity against you and Bill deciding not to farm. I just wanted to be like my dad and hand it down to one of you."

"I know Dad, and I appreciate you wanting Bill or me to follow in your footsteps, but maybe Bill will change his mind. After I become a doctor, I may just come back to South Charleston and open a clinic. I have thought a little bit about that. All the doctors here have retired, and I see a need for one who could cover the town and the surrounding towns, and there is an empty building already set up for a doctor's office."

Nancy was delighted with the thought of Jim opening a clinic here. She said, "Jim that is a fantastic idea. As it is now, we have to either go to Columbus or Springfield to see a doctor or a hospital."

"Mom, it is just a thought in the back of my mind right now. I have no clue what my specialty might be. If I would choose to open a clinic then I would be an internist. I would have to go back to school every year to learn new methods and treatments. Learning about all the old and new drugs and the tests run on them is mind boggling. You must learn to almost be a pharmacist too. Medicine in so complicated now because of all the different drugs and all the diseases, but I still want to be a doctor. Maybe you could even work for me. You know how to run a business, and I would be able to take care of the patients and not the books."

Nancy asked Nicole what she wanted to do once she graduates from college.

"I want to be a teacher like your daughter, Bette. I want the opportunity to open up a child's mind to learning. There is so much to learn about in this world, and helping children from the ages of five to twelve years old is my goal."

"So teaching high school is not a desire for you?"

"I don't believe so. Older kids are going through so many changes in their lives, and from what I've seen, a teacher has to deal with hormones, attitudes, laziness, and disrespect from the kids and the adults. I don't think I'm up to dealing with that yet."

Connie said that Nicole was a very good student all through her twelve years of school and two years of college. "We are very proud of her accomplishments and her desire in wanting to help young people open their minds to the world around them."

"Thank you Mom for saying that. I had a wonderful upbringing with loving parents plus terrific schooling. That should be what children have today. Opening their minds is one thing, but teaching them respect must also come from the home. Too many parents feel that is the teacher's job, but if there is no respect taught at home, then there is not going to be respect anywhere else."

Dan commented, "You sure do have that comment right. I know I've hired a few teenagers during the summers to help me bale hay, but it's like pulling teeth to get them motivated and stay motivated. Some of them always had a negative comment to throw back at me, and that's when I told them to go home. I paid them for the work they did, but I thought sending them home would cause a change in their attitudes. Whether it did or not I don't know. I wouldn't hire them back again to find out."

Nancy said, "Dan, let's show them some of the farm. We still have some daylight to see where we're going, but we'll have to take a short tour because it will be dark soon." She looked at Nicole's parents and said, "That will give you an excuse to come back again."

After a very short tour of the barn and some of the grazing pastures with some of the cows munching on the grass, it was time to say goodbye. Dean and Connie said they needed to head for home.

"Dan and Nancy, we have thoroughly enjoyed the delicious dinner, the hospitality and the tour. You have been very gracious to us, and we thank you."

Jim and Nicole were in another room, so Connie called out to Nicole to tell her they were leaving.

Jim told Nicole, "If you have any trouble with this Scott fellow, please call us. We will come help you if we're needed."

"Thank you, but I don't think it will get that far. He will leave if I tell him I have someone else in my life now."

"Nicole, you mean a lot to me, and I don't want you or your parents to get hurt, so please call after he leaves to let me know everything is all right."

"I will."

Jim leaned over and gave Nicole a kiss, and she kissed him back. He looked at her, put his left arm around her and said, "I love you."

Nicole looked into his eyes and said, "I love you too. I will call you after he leaves if it's not too late."

"I don't care what time it is. I won't be able to sleep not knowing if you are all right, so call my cell phone, and it won't disturb anyone else. Promise me you will call."

"All right, I will call you no matter what time it is."

They kissed one another again, and Nicole ran to her parent's car where they were waiting.

Jim helped Nancy put away the dishes and Nancy asked him, "Are you in love with her?"

"Yes, I am. Mom, I knew when we were on the plane coming back here that she is the one. I feel so good around her, and I think she feels the same way. She wants us to take one day at a time, and not rush into anything. She says it takes time to learn about one another, and we need to give ourselves that time. I will do that, but in the meantime I am going to continue to tell her that I love her because I do."

"Well, she is a beautiful and smart girl. How much younger is she than you?"

"I am almost three years older than her, but she is so down to earth, intelligent, and full of common sense. What more could I need?" he asked.

"Just give both of you the time needed. It takes more than a few weeks to really know someone, and sometimes it takes years. I have loved your father since we were in the seventh grade, and that was fifty-five years ago. We are still together, and we know each other very well. With God's help we will have many more years together."

"Mom, I have been searching for someone like Nicole, and I am praying that we will have a marriage, if it is to be, just like yours. I truly think we can have that too. She is so different from any of the girls I have dated. I think God placed her in my arms at the perfect time. I hope this ordeal she is about to have will end smoothly. She no longer has feelings for that summer romance with that guy. He was in love with two women at the same time, and she was the one who got hurt. She is happy that they only had about two and a half months together, and there wasn't anything sexual about their relationship. Maybe he did with the other woman, but Nicole told him no. I totally believe her. She had a lot of people looking out for her, and Scott was told he better not mistreat her. She said he did mistreat her mentally but not physically."

"Well, just be kind to her, and I know you will treat her with respect and dignity. Your father and I think very highly of her and her family."

"Thanks Mom, I appreciate that."

Dean, Connie and Nicole pulled into their driveway and noticed that Scott was sitting on the front porch. His car was parked across the street.

Dean said, "I will remain out here with you for your protection, and Connie you need to go inside and stay near the phone in case we need help from the police. Is everyone ready?"

They all vacated the car at the same time and climbed the steps onto the front porch. Connie put the key in the door and walked in. Dean and Nicole stayed on the porch with Scott.

"Mr. Thomas, I will not harm her in any way. I just want to talk with her," Scott said.

"Scott, I feel I need to stay here with her, and I won't be leaving, so anything you have to say, you must say it in front of me."

"Nicole, do you think I would ever hurt you? I love you more than you'll ever know. I need to explain some of my actions, and ask for your forgiveness. Please let me at least talk to you."

"Scott, I don't want to be alone with you. I talked with Catherine, and Emily is not dead. She was injured but survived with only scrapes and bruises, and her car did not go through any railing, nor was her car in a ravine. Did you just tell me that for my sympathy or are you still fabricating your way to get me to come back to you?"

"Nicole, I swear that Sandy called and told me that Emily was dead. Now that I know the truth, I assume she just didn't want me to contact her anymore."

"Do you blame her?"

"No not really. I wasn't very good to her. I didn't want to marry her, but when you left me without a word, I turned to her, and she wanted some reassurance of our relationship. I did buy the ring for you, but you left, so I gave it to her. Everything was fine until I missed you so much, I guess I talked about you to the point that she knew I wasn't over you. She said she got tired of sharing me with the ghost of Nicole."

"Scott, do you realize what you have done?"

"Yes, I've lost both of you."

"That is correct, and I will not be taking you back. You need to return to Colorado and accept that desk job with the rangers. At least you'll be among your friends and doing some of the job you loved, and hopefully someday you will find someone who will love you unconditionally without your past clouding the relationship. You'll be all right, but I'm not coming back to what I thought we had only to find we didn't have anything. The relationship we had was tainted. No one can love two people at the same time and not get caught. You got caught. You will find someone else, and I wish you the very best in life. Now I need to ask you to leave. There are some motels close to the Dayton airport, and you will be able to catch a plane tomorrow back to Denver. Goodnight Scott. I wish you the very best of everything."

"Could I at least hug you one last time?"

"No, that will cause a problem for you and for me."

"All right, I will leave. Goodnight Mr. Thomas and goodbye Nicole."

"Goodbye Scott."

Dean and Nicole went into the house and her father watched to make sure Scott got in the rental car and drove away before he turned to Connie and Nicole.

"Nicole, I thought you handled that very well, and he didn't look as though he was going to be aggressive. Now maybe we can relax and enjoy the rest of the evening. Thank you for having Nancy and Dan invite us to their lovely home. The dinner was delicious and we enjoyed the tour and their company."

"The invitation was Jim's idea, not mine, but his mother agreed. I am really tired. Jim and I made a day of it at the fair, and we did a lot of walking, so if you don't mind I am going to get ready for bed. If you see Scott's car out there again, call the police. I won't stand for him stalking me."

"Do you think he might do that?" Connie asked.

"I don't really know. I thought I knew him, but I was wrong. I guess some guys want more than one girl on their arm at a time. That's not for me. I don't want to have to deal with a girl-crazy person. I really didn't think Scott was like that. It's just that the circumstances of him being in a hospital that was far away, he evidently became very lonely. When I couldn't give him the attention he needed, he accepted Emily's affections, and I know she definitely wanted him for herself. I assume she got tired of me always being in the picture, whether I was there or not."

"Do you think he will accept your demands?" Dean asked.

"Dad, I don't really know. I am just going to live my life the best way I can without him in it. I am so tired, so I am going to bed. I have to take a shower, so I hope you have a wonderful evening. I love you both. Goodnight."

After she took her shower she called Jim.

"Hello Jim."

"Are you all right?" he asked.

"Yes, we are all fine. He is gone, and we didn't have any trouble. Dad stayed on the porch with me while I told him there was no longer a relationship between us of any kind. I asked him to catch a plane back to Colorado and accept the job he was offered as a ranger dispatcher. He apologized to me and to my family, but I didn't back down. Everything is okay. He left and hopefully he'll take a flight back to Denver tomorrow morning."

"Were you afraid he was going to do something?"

"No, not really, especially with my dad standing right there listening to every word. Dad told Scott in the very beginning that he was going to stay with me on the porch, and Scott would have to accept that or leave. Scott wasn't angry; he was hurt that he no longer had anyone now. Emily, if she's smart, will stay away from him, but I don't know about her. She wanted him in the worst way. I am so relieved. I appreciate that you have been concerned, but I am all right. I just took a nice warm shower, and I'm already in bed. The fair really wore me out. I guess it was from all that walking."

"Nicole, I am so glad you called me to tell me you are all right. I know that we have just begun our relationship, and I know it will be a long relationship, but I also know that I have very deep feelings for you, and I hope that it stays this way for the rest of my life."

"Jim, I feel the same way. I am going to get some sleep, and so should you."

Jim replied, "I took a pain pill a few minutes ago, and I'm already feeling its effects, so I will call you tomorrow. I love you. Goodnight."

Jim got up out of bed and looked at the clock. It was eight o'clock in the morning. He decided to get dressed and go downstairs to see what his mother was cooking.

Nancy said, "Breakfast will be ready in a few minutes."

"Thanks Mom. Do I have time to call Nicole for a few minutes?"

"Sure Honey."

"Good morning Sunshine! Are you up and about this morning? My mother is fixing breakfast, and she told me I have a few minutes, so I wanted to call and see if you are all right."

"I'm fine, but I am so glad you called me."

"Why, what's up?"

"Nothing is up. I just wanted to hear your voice."

"Is he still parked outside your door?"

"I don't think so, but I'll look." After a few seconds, she said, "No, he is gone. Whew, I got scared for a minute thinking that he might have spent the night in his rental car, but it's gone. Wait a minute, there's a parked rental car down the street, but I don't see him in the car. Maybe he's asleep in the backseat. I'll have my dad check it out. I can't believe he wouldn't leave when we told him to."

"Are you sure it's the same rental car?"

"No not from this distance. I'll have my dad walk down on this side of the walk to see if it is him. He saw the car too, and he would remember the logo markings."

"What are you going to do if he's still there?"

"I want to call the police, but he's not actually bothering us, and he's not trespassing, so we don't really have any grounds to make a charge against him."

"Hold on a second while I ask Dad. He said he would go now and check it out."

"Nicole, Mom has breakfast ready, so I will hang on the phone to keep you company while you worry yourself silly."

"I'm not afraid of him. I just want him to go back to Colorado."

"Dad's back. He said it was not Scott, and he even looked in the car. It looks like the same rental, but there was no one in the vehicle."

"Well, keep an eye out just in case, okay?"

"I will. Why don't you call me back after you eat your breakfast?"

"I will do that," he said.

Nicole wanted to call Catherine to give her a heads up as to what's going on, but it is way too early to call her now. I'll have to wait another two hours.

Just then Nicole's cell phone rang, and she quickly answered it.

"Hi, it's me, Jim. I was just thinking. I can call my brother, Bill, to see if he's heard anything from Scott. If he might have accepted the job he could have called Bill or Todd, and I'm quite sure they would tell one another if he is going to accept the offer."

Nicole said, "I was going to call Catherine in a couple of hours, because there is a two hour difference from our time zone, and she's probably not up yet. Don't you think you should give them a few more hours of sleep before you call them?"

"Yes, you're right again. That would be very rude of me to call them at that hour. I do think they would know before Catherine would."

"You are right, but I want to talk with her anyway, and keep her abreast of what's going on here."

"Have you had your breakfast yet?"

"No, but I am going to fix pancakes and scrambled eggs. Mom and Dad are reading the paper, so I will surprise them."

"I wish I was there for you to surprise me!"

"What do you mean by that Mr. Martin?"

"I'd like to surprise you every morning with a cup of coffee and a breakfast fit for a queen."

"Well, thank you, but I'm not a queen. I am just an ordinary girl from the Midwest, who is going back to school the end of next week. By the way, have you been able to locate any roommates?"

"No, I thought I would ask you if you would like to go to Columbus with me tomorrow to look at some places, and also check the bulletin board at the hospital to see if any of the new interns need a roommate."

"I'd love to go with you. Maybe I'll be able to find out who my roommate is going to be."

"Good, I'll pick you up at nine o'clock in the morning, and we'll make a day of it. Okay?"

"What are you going to be doing today?" she asked.

"I'm going to help Dad on the farm then Mom is going with me to the doctor's office this afternoon to see how my arm is healing. Maybe we'll stop by after my appointment if that's all right with you?"

"That will be wonderful. I can't wait to see you both. Be careful."

"I will, and Nicole, I love you."

"Jim, I love you too. Bye."

Jim helped his dad with some fence mending and throwing hay in the outside feeders. It was a little difficult with the cast in his way, but he managed all right. One of the horses ran over to him and shook its head and scraped the ground with its hoof. Jim went over to her and rubbed her head and ears, and she nuzzled him. He laughed at her antics and gave her a hand full of hay. She ate it from his hand. She was a beautiful horse with a loving disposition. It had been a long time since he had seen her, but she still recognized him.

"You remember me, don't you girl?" She continued to nuzzle him, so he fed her another hand full of hay.

"Jim's mother came to the fence and yelled, "It is about time for us to leave and, you have to get cleaned up yet."

"I'm coming!" He gave his pet another hand full of hay and said, "Girl, I've got to go, but I'll see you later on today."

When he was heading for the house, he turned around and saw that she was following him. He climbed the fence, rubbed her head, and said, "I've got to go girl. I'll see you later."

She snorted and went back to the feeder.

He got cleaned up and put on a clean shirt and jeans. Nancy was waiting on him in the car. He ran down the steps and jumped into the car.

He said, "Mom, the horse still remembers me. She came right up and nuzzled me. I'll have to pay a little more attention to her when we get back. I thought that after my appointment we could stop at Nicole's unless you have to get back early."

"That would be fine with me. I have to ask Connie about fixing an old quilt that was my grandmothers. Connie does quilting, cross stitch, and rug weaving, and we decided we would have a day to do some stitching together."

"I'm glad you two get along so well. It seems you have a lot in common."

"We do, but since I have worked all those years, I never had the time to really learn how to do some of those crafty things very well, and Connie was kind enough to offer to teach me properly. I really like Nicole's family. They are good people and very friendly."

"That's a good thing Mom, because one of these days they will be my in-laws and your family friends."

"Remember what Nicole told you about going slow and not push. Give her the time she needs to be really comfortable and ready for a permanent commitment."

"I will Mom, but I know she is the one for me, and I don't want to mess things up."

"Good idea!" Nancy said.

When they arrived at the doctor's office, Jim went in to see the doctor by himself. Nancy wanted to go in with him, but he laughed and said, "Mom, I'm old enough to go in by myself now." She looked at him and smiled. "I will tell you everything he said."

After Jim was finished with the doctor, he walked over to his mother who was reading a magazine, and he said, "Mom, are you ready to go?"

"Not until you tell me what the doctor said."

"I can tell you in the car just as well as tell you here where everyone can hear it to."

"Okay, I'll wait until we get to the car." Jim was smiling all the way to the car about keeping his appointment to himself.

"Okay, we're in the car and now you can tell me."

"The doctor said I am healing just fine, and I am permitted to drive again. The bone is mending all by itself. I will need to wear the cast for another two to three weeks, so I have another appointment with him two weeks from today. Okay?"

"Well, your father will be very happy to hear that it is healing. He has felt so guilty about the accident, and he'll be relieved to know that it is healing well."

"The doctor told me to finish the prescription, and if I need more to call his office, and they will call our pharmacy. That's the news from the doctor's office."

Nancy said, "With that being said, let's head over to Nicole's."

"Now that's the best thing I've heard all day." Jim replied.

As they pulled up to the curb at Nicole's, Jim saw a man sitting on the porch, and he recognized him to be Scott Thompson. He remembered him from the ranger's station where Bill worked.

"Hello Scott. What are you doing here?"

"I could ask you the same thing?"

Nicole opened the door when she heard people talking on the porch.

She first saw Jim and Nancy, and then she was startled to see Scott sitting on the swing. "What are you doing here? I thought we made it clear to you to not come back here but to catch a plane back to Colorado."

Scott asked, "What is he doing here?"

"Scott, this is none of your business. If you must know, Jim and I are going together, and I don't have room for you in my life anymore. I thought I made that clear to you last night when Dad and I told you to leave."

Nicole said with a frantic voice, "Nancy, I'm so sorry, please let me open the door for you. Mom is waiting on you. Jim, I would like you to stay here with me."

"I can't get a plane out of here until Saturday, so I still wanted to talk to you alone, but I guess that is out of the question?"

"Yes, I said all I needed to say last night, and I don't want you here, so please leave."

"I don't have enough money to stay in a hotel until Saturday."

"What did you expect me to do? Give you enough money to get you back to Colorado?"

"Well, I was hoping I could borrow it, and pay you back when I get home."

Jim asked Scott, "How much do you need?"

"I figure with food and hotel, around five hundred dollars. I already paid for the plane fare, but without paychecks I don't have enough to cover it on my credit card."

Jim said, "I will give you the money if you promise to leave Nicole alone from now on. She and I are together, and I don't like it when another man tries to steal my girl."

"I appreciate your kindness. I really did love Nicole, but I was weak when I should have been strong, and I lost out."

"Scott, how did you get here? I don't see a rental car." Jim asked.

"I walked part of the way and hitched a ride the rest. A guy who lives near here gave me a lift. I didn't have enough money for the rental car or a bus, so this was the only place I thought I could come to get help."

Jim replied, "I'm going to call my brother and tell him about your predicament to see if he might have a solution. I know Bill and Todd will want to help you."

Jim pulled out his cell phone from his pocket and called Bill.

"Hello."

"Is this Todd?"

"This is Todd, and to whom am I speaking?"

"This is Jim Martin, Bill's brother."

"Oh! Hello Jim."

"We have a problem here at Nicole's. It seems your fellow ranger, Scott, needs a ride home to Colorado. He has plane fare taken care of, but his flight doesn't leave until Saturday morning, and he has no more money for a hotel or food. I told him I would loan it to him, but he needs five hundred dollars. I first wanted to see if you might have someone near Dayton, Ohio, who could assist him?"

"Jim, you don't need to give him any money, as we will take care of that. It just so happens that we have a rangers' convention in that area near the airport. I will call my buddy there and see if he can assist him. I'll call him right now, and call you back within ten minutes. Okay?"

"Thanks Todd."

As they were waiting on Todd's call, Scott had his head down. Nicole went into the house to get them some lemonade. When she returned she noticed that Scott and Jim were talking to one another. She served them the lemonade, and sat on the bench beside Jim.

"Nicole, I am so sorry to involve you in this, but I didn't know anyone else. My cell phone is dead, and I didn't bring a charger, so I couldn't call anyone. I know you told me to leave you alone, but I need your help."

Jim's phone was ringing, and he answered it. "Yes, this is Jim. Thanks Todd for helping us. Yes, I can get him to the airport but at what time? Okay, Nicole and I will leave right away. What did you say the man's name is who will help Scott? His name is Steve Granger? Steve Granger will be at the front desk and will help him get his refund on the Saturday ticket, and give him his new ticket and boarding pass. Yes, we will take him to the front desk to meet Steve then he is to go to Gate 5. It's a direct flight to Denver. Okay, and thank you so much. I will call you to tell you that he got on the plane. And someone will pick him up at the airport. His cell phone is dead, so he won't be able to call you. You will be there to pick him up at the baggage area. Okay I will relay the message to him. Thanks again Todd."

"Well Scott, it looks like you're going home tonight. We better get going."

Nicole said, "I'll go tell Mom and your mother where we are going. I'll hurry."

Jim drove with plenty of time to get there, so Jim and Nicole helped Scott manage all the instructions they were told by Todd. Steve Granger was very helpful and gave Scott a total refund for the Saturday ticket. Steve told Scott he needed to hurry to Gate 5.

Scott looked at Jim and Nicole and said, "Thank you for helping me. I wish you both the best of everything. I know I couldn't give her all of me, and I lost her. I will straighten myself up so you can be proud of me again. Thank you again for all you've done to help me."

Jim turned to Steve and asked him if he could let him know if Scott got on the plane.

Steve said, "Sure. His boarding pass will show up on my computer to tell me he is on the plane. It will take a few minutes. Well, he must have hurried, because he is on board. The plane will take off in five minutes. If you look out that window over there, you will be able to see it take off."

Jim looked at Nicole and said, "I want to make sure he is up in the air and on his way back to where he belongs."

"Thank you for doing all this for him, and for me. I surely didn't want him staying at our house or for you to give him five hundred dollars to last him until Saturday." Nicole said.

"That's why I called the ranger's station. I was pretty sure they would help their own. Hopefully he will accept his new job, and learn from his mistakes with women. I hope he finds happiness with someone, just not with you."

"Why, Jim Martin! I am already taken."

Jim laughed and hugged Nicole. "You bet you are, my girl!"

They both laughed. Steve Granger called out, "There goes his plane to Denver."

Nicole and Jim hugged one another, and Jim leaned over and kissed her.

When they returned to Nicole's house, their mothers wanted to know what happened. Jim explained the situation, and Connie said, "I didn't even know he was on the porch."

Nicole responded, "Neither did I, but I heard Jim talking to someone, and I opened the door to find Scott sitting on the swing. What a shock that was after Dad and I told him he was not longer welcome here. Jim handled it so well, and I am so proud of him. He didn't even punch him!"

Jim laughed. "Did you think I would stoop so low as to deck someone on your porch?"

"Well, you knew the situation I had with Scott, so I didn't know what you would do to him, but you were a real man about it all, and I am so proud of you."

Jim hugged Nicole and kissed her on the cheek. Nancy looked at them and smiled. She looked over at Connie, and she was smiling too.

Nancy said, "Connie, I think we're going to be seeing a lot of one another, don't you?"

"I certainly hope so. Maybe we'll have a chance to do a wedding quilt together."

Nancy replied, "I love those quilts, and I can hardly wait to get started. I don't know how much time we'll have before that might happen, but it's nice to think ahead and be prepared. Don't you think so?"

Connie nodded and said, "I do think so."

Jim looked at his mother and asked, "Do you mind waiting on us to return or do you want to drive yourself back to the farm? Nicole and I are going to go to the mall to do some school shopping. She says notebooks and paper and other things are a lot cheaper at the stores here than buying them on campus. I'm just going along because I want to be with her. You know how Dad and I hate to go shopping."

"Jim, then why are going? Do you just want to make her miserable like you and your father do with me?"

"This is different. This is my girl. We're not going shopping for girly stuff. We're going shopping for school supplies."

"Do you need school supplies?" Nancy asked.

"No, but I want to be with her."

Nancy sighed and said, "I will never be able to understand men. Once he gets married, he'll become just like his father. You just wait and see."

Nicole heard all of that conversation, and told Nancy, "I'm taking advantage of him right now, because my dad is the same way. I think it's a man thing. After we've been together for a while, he'll not want to go shopping with me."

He said, "Hey, I heard that."

Jim and Nicole had been shopping for a couple of hours, and Nicole's cell phone was ringing. She took it from her purse and answered, "Hello. Oh! Hi Catherine. What's going on? I know I didn't call you back, and I was going to call you this morning, but it was too early with the difference in time zones. Yes, Scott was here last night, and he came back this morning, but Jim and I took him to the airport to catch a flight back to Denver. I think Jim talked him into accepting the dispatcher's job at the ranger's station. Yes, he told me about Emily's accident, but he said that Emily's sister, Sandy, told him that Emily was killed. He acted very sad about it, but was elated to hear that she wasn't dead. He realized that Emily probably didn't want any more to do with him, and that was probably the reason Sandy told him that story. He seemed very depressed. Todd took care of Scott's ticket. He had everything set up for him, so I hope Scott realizes what a true friend he has in Todd. Scott even said he was happy for me and Jim, and he asked Jim to take good care of me. That was a very nice gesture on his part.

"Are you all getting ready to close the resort?"

"Yes," Catherine said, "We are securing all the cabins that are empty now, and we only have a few more bookings left. Since I am in the dining area, everyone in the kitchen and laundry area said to say hello to you, and to tell you they miss you."

"Ah, that's so sweet of them. How are Mike, Virginia and Norman?"

"Norman is still having trouble with his foot, but Virginia is catering to him like a nurse, and Mike is doing really well. I've grown to appreciate him. He's learning how to treat people, women especially, and he does miss you. He asks me every day if I've heard from you, and for me to tell you he said hello."

"Be sure and give my best wishes to everyone. Tell them all that I miss them too. I still feel badly about leaving you when I did. I know it couldn't be helped, and I wanted to stay. But if I had stayed, I doubt that I would have run into Jim like I did, and that would have been a bad thing for me. We are taking it slow, which is my rule, and he is abiding with it. I know that I would have been miserable with the Scott and the Emily situation. Jim doesn't know that I am watching him, but I see he has walked over to a jewelry store here in the mall, and I hope he is not looking at what I think he is looking at. I am going to finish college first, and he has two years of internship, and then residency, so it will be a while for both of us before we can even think about marriage. We've only been together almost a month, so it's too early in our relationship to be thinking of marriage."

Catherine asked, "Has he popped the marriage question to you yet?"

"Not in so many words, but he hints a lot about our future together. I'm in no hurry, and neither should he. I am too young to be going to school and take care of a family too. I think that can cause a lot of animosity between a husband and wife."

Catherine said, "I am so glad to hear you say that, because you are right. Most young married couples, or at least one of them, who are attending school end up quitting classes to take care of the family and the home."

"Please give everyone my love, and give me a call before you leave Colorado. I want to say goodbye to Mike and the staff. I'm looking forward to be able to talk with you, Norman and Virginia face to face when you stop by my parent's house. They are looking forward to seeing the three of you again, and I can hardly wait to see you also. I love you my sweet Catherine. Call me if you find out how Scott is doing. I just want to make sure he is okay and back at the ranger's station."

"I love you too Nicole, and I will call when I hear anything about Scott. Bye for now. Maybe I'll go visit them before we leave."

Nicole walked over to where Jim was looking at some jewelry. She startled him when she touched his back.

He said, "Hey! I didn't know you were right behind me. I wanted to give you some time to talk with Catherine. How are things at the resort?"

"Catherine told me they are securing the cabins that are empty, and they only have a few more guests booked, so they are winding down. She said it wouldn't take them long to finish closing. She's going to call me from the dining hall while everyone is there so we can all say goodbye to one another. Once they leave, Mike will secure the gate so no one can come in. They have an alarm system. If someone should try to enter the area the rangers would answer the call, and if they are needed, the police would be contacted. Sometimes an animal like a bear, cougar or deer could set it off. The rangers have a set of keys to the alarm and the buildings."

"Have they ever had break-ins at the resort?" Jim asked.

Nicole replied, "I don't know. I never asked Catherine that question, but they will be here probably two or three days after the resort is closed, so we can ask them about that. I'm interested in that question too. I do know that I want you to meet them. I think they should be here before we both have to go back to Columbus."

"Yes, and I would like to meet them. Even though I don't know them personally, I feel like I already know them from you telling me about all of them. Are they going to stay here over night?" Jim asked.

"I always hope they will. We've invited them several times on their return trips, but Norman and Virginia live in Dayton, and it's not that far from here, but Catherine might. She is towing her jeep behind their SUV, so she would probably help them get home and then come back here. She lives further north of us. It all depends on how much time they all have to whether they stay for a while to visit. I really miss them. I had such a wonderful time with the staff there at the resort. Maybe someday you and I will be able to go there for a vacation. It is such a beautiful place, and the scenery is amazing. That reminds me that I need to get my film developed. I have an old Canon AE-1 that takes fabulous pictures, but I still have to get them developed. If I would have thought about it, I would have brought them to the developing center here in the mall."

"By the way, what are you looking at?" she asked.

Jim smiled and said, "I'm just looking around."

"I've been watching you while talking with Catherine, and you haven't moved from this area of jewelry."

"Ok, I'm busted! I am looking for something special for someone very dear to me."

"May I ask who that special person is?"

"You don't know her yet."

"Oh, okay." Nicole was puzzled at his answer, but she let it go. Maybe he has a grandmother he would like to buy jewelry for. "Do you need some help?"

Jim answered, "Yes, I do. Can you tell me what you would like if the gift were for you?"

"Are you talking about rings since we are in the ring section or would you want a bracelet or a necklace?

"I think maybe a ring."

Nicole asked, "Is this for an older person?"

"It could be, but not necessarily," he said.

"Well, I don't know the taste of the person you are thinking about giving a ring to, or the age of this person."

Jim replied, "Well, just pick out something you would like in the ring section, and I'll tell you if she might like it."

"Okay. I like the simple ring that has the gold band and the diamond set in white gold. That's the one right there."

"I like that one too, but I don't know what size to get. What size do you wear?" he asked.

"I wear six and a half in a ring. Is this person tall and thin, average sized or heavier?" she asked.

Jim answered, "She's about your size. Do you think I can bring it back if it doesn't fit?"

"I would think so. You probably need to ask a clerk what their policy is on returns." she said.

"Will you try it on to see what it looks like on a finger?"

"Okay."

The clerk came over to the ring department and Jim asked to see the ring that Nicole had picked out. "What size ring do you want?" The clerk asked.

Jim said, "Is that one a six and a half in size:"

The clerk said, "Yes it is."

Jim replied, "Then that is the one I would like her to try on."

Nicole tried on the ring and it was a beautiful fit. It looked so nice on her finger. Nicole was beaming at the sight of such a magnificent ring.

Jim asked, "Do you like that one."

Nicole answered, "Yes, Jim, it is beautiful. I think whoever you are getting this for will be very pleased with your selection."

Jim looked at the clerk and said, "I will take this one."

The clerk took the ring, polished it and put it in a case for Jim to take with him.

Jim paid the clerk and thanked him.

Nicole was puzzled, but she didn't say anymore about it. She thought to herself that maybe it was for his mother because she never noticed any rings on her fingers. But why would he buy her an engagement ring? "I'm just not going to think about this anymore," she told herself.

As they were leaving the mall, Jim asked, "Would you like an ice cream cone? I know a place not far from here where they have the best ice cream."

"Sure, I'm all for ice cream." She said.

Nicole let Jim drive her car to the ice cream place. He ordered a double chocolate caramel swirl. Nicole thought that looked too sweet for her, so she ordered a vanilla raspberry swirl. They both licked and talked little. When they were done, Nicole said, "You were right. That is the best ice cream I have ever had."

Jim nodded and said, "I come here whenever I'm home. I didn't know if it was still open, but it is, and I'm glad you liked it. We'll have to do this again."

Nicole told him about a place her mom and dad use to take her. It was called Riverdale Dairy, but it closed a long time ago. "I would always get Red Drop ice cream. It had crushed red hot candies mixed with cream and vanilla ice cream and was red in color. You could even smell the red hot candies. I've never been able to find it again. It was so good that I can still taste it. My uncle used to buy a huge ten gallon tub of it, and he kept it in his freezer. He shared it a couple of times with me, but it tasted better at the store."

"You mean to tell me you can still taste red hot ice cream even though that place has been closed for over ten years?"

Nicole asked, "How would you know how long it has been closed if you've never been there?"

"Did I say that I've never been there?"

"Well, no, I guess. When did you go there?"

"I use to go there with my parents on Sundays after church to get butter and ice cream. We would try to eat out, but the three of us kids always had something going on, so we didn't make it every week. I loved their ice cream, but since they've been closed, we would go to the Ice Cream Parlor, and it has been open since Riverdale closed. My parents knew the owner, but his sons didn't want to continue the business, so he just closed it. Sounds kind of like my dad and his two sons who don't want to farm."

"It's really nice that we can talk about things that we both knew and loved, and of all things, it's about ice cream."

"Well, I guess we'd better head for home. Don't you think?"

Jim replied, "I guess you're right, but I'd rather spend the rest of the day with you."

Nicole said, "You can stay and have dinner with us, and then I'll take you home."

"Now that wouldn't be right. I can't have you take me home and drive back in the dark by yourself. I don't like that idea at all. I don't want anything to happen to you. Anyway I am taking us to Columbus tomorrow. Remember? I need to find a roommate, and you wanted to find out about your roommate. Remember?"

"Yes, I remember, and I'm looking forward to tomorrow so that I can be with you the entire day. We'll be all alone for the whole day almost."

"That sounds very interesting. You think we could stand to be together that long?" Jim asked.

Nicole said, "Yes, I do. Don't you?"

"I'm looking forward to it. I know when we get back to your house this afternoon my mother will want to go home if she's still there, so we'd better get going. She has to fix dinner for three, but maybe I'll surprise her and get some fried chicken. Then all we'll have to fix is the veggies and a salad. Doesn't that sound good to you?"

"That sounds wonderful, and I know she will appreciate not having to cook tonight. Do you want to stop now and get the chicken? There's a great chicken take-out place right up the street from here," Nicole replied.

"You are such an asset to me, because you know where everything is," he said.

"Springfield isn't that big, and I've lived here all my life. Wait until we go to Columbus where neither of us will know where anything is."

Jim answered, "I'm quite sure we will have some opportunities to get familiar with what will be around us. You already know the campus, so we'll make it a habit when we have free time to explore. Does that sound good to you?"

"Any time I can spend with you Jim, will be amazing for me"

"Well, I look forward to any time we can spend together," he responded.

When they arrived at Nicole's house, Connie and Nancy were discussing projects they wanted to start. They had already started planning out a quilt that they seemed to want to keep secret, but Nicole had overheard them before they left. They were going to work together on a wedding quilt for when Jim and Nicole were to get married. Nicole was elated with that thought. Now if she could only find out the mysterious person who would be receiving that beautiful ring. She would watch to see if Nancy would be wearing it. Maybe she would ask Nancy about her mother. Maybe she would be the one he purchased the ring for. She was tired of thinking about it, and was sure she would find out soon enough.

When Nancy and Jim were ready to leave, Jim told her that dinner was in the car. She looked at him and said, "What did you get?"

"I got some fried chicken and biscuits. All we need to fix are some vegetables and a salad, and dinner is done."

Nancy came over to Jim and gave him a hug, and he said, "It is nothing big, Mom. I just didn't want for you to have to cook. I know Dad will want to eat as soon as we get home, so now you don't have to worry about what to fix."

"I really appreciate you doing this for me. You always surprise me with your thoughtfulness," Nancy said.

"Well we better get going before it gets too cold. Warmed up chicken just isn't the same when it's reheated."

As they said their goodbyes, Nicole followed Jim to the car. He pulled her to him and kissed her. "I'll be picking you up around nine o'clock, unless that's too early.'

Nicole answered, "That will be fine. I'll be up and ready to go." She stood on her toes and kissed him back, and they hugged. Jim got behind the wheel, and he waved as they drove off.

Connie asked Nicole if they had a good time at the mall, and did she buy everything she needed for school.

Nicole answered, "I think I did. It's so much cheaper here than on campus."

Connie asked her, "Do you love him?"

Nicole replied, "Yes, I do, but we want to take it slow. I just left one man, and now I am jumping into another man's arms, but I know for sure that this one has my interests at heart, and not someone else."

As Connie and Nicole were preparing dinner, Nicole's cell phone was ringing. She said, "They can't be home already. Oh! It's not Jim, it is Catherine. Hello Catherine. How are you?"

Catherine answered, "We are all fine, but I thought I would give you an update on Scott. I talked with Todd today, and he said that Scott is working with them as a dispatcher, plus he takes inventory and other odd jobs they find for him. He seems to be much happier and not showing signs of depression. He also called Emily and apologized to her for the way he treated her. Todd didn't know if they would be getting back together, but he knows that she really loved him, and he wants her to give him another chance. I guess she told him that she would have to think about it. Other than that, I don't know anything else about Scott. If I do, I'll either call you or tell you when we drive back to Ohio."

"How are things going at the resort? Did Norman ever go to the doctor to find out if he broke a bone in his foot?"

"Things are going great. Our last customer is this weekend. We are all ready to close. All but that one cabin, plus mine, and of course Virginia and Norman's are left to clean. They are almost ready to be closed. I've been helping Virginia ready their cabin so they won't have that much to do. Charlie will be taking all the excess food with him, so there will not be anything to attract bears, mountain lions, or any other critters. Our plans are still to leave the day after Labor Day. The people coming in this weekend are only staying for one night. They are on their way to Oregon, and they didn't want to stay in a hotel. They must have a pet with them, and you know what that means. I will have to shampoo the carpet and let it dry before I can close it up. Mike said we could use a blower to dry it out quicker, but I'm not too sure about that. We'll see. I told all the staff that you wanted to say goodbye to them, and they are all going to meet in the dining area on Labor Day to say goodbye to you. Just make sure your cell phone is well charged. I have no idea how long that call will take, but they really liked you, and they all miss you, including me. My cabin has been so empty. It's almost creepy."

"Catherine, you know how much I care about you, and everyone there. We were like sisters, and I've never had a sister, so it is nice to finally feel as though I have one."

"It felt good to have a little sister. My sister was older than me, and she has passed on, so it felt good to have that feeling too. Well, I better let you go. I know I've probably reached you at dinner time. The next time we talk I want to hear more about this fellow you seem to be in love with. Love you much and give my best to your folks. Bye for now."

"Bye, Catherine,"

"Sorry Mom; I haven't helped you very much. It was good to talk with Catherine. I feel so close to her. She's a very special person in my life, and I hope they do stop in to see us before she takes Norman and Virginia home."

Connie said, "I hope they stop here too. I know your father wants to see them. If they don't get to stop, we'll all have to go to Dayton to visit with them."

"Norman and Virginia were so good to me. They paid for my plane fare to come home. I will repay them for the ticket when we see them."

"You won't need to do that because we already paid them."

"Mom, you didn't need to do that. I want to pay you back. I have the money in the bank."

"Nicole, we prepaid for your going out there and your return home. So, you don't need to worry about it. That was our gift to you for being such a wonderful daughter who just happens to get excellent grades."

"Well, thank you. I really appreciate all you do for me."

"Sweetheart, you are quite welcome. We couldn't have more children, so we raised you not to be spoiled, but you could stand a little spoiling, so we were happy to give you a vacation. The college education money was put away every week we got paid so you, nor us, would need to worry or take out a loan against the house. I am so glad we did what we did because we don't have to scramble around trying to find a way to pay for your education like some of our friends at church are doing. Times are tough right now, and so many people are getting laid off from their jobs. Some of our friends have had to tell their children that they can't afford to send them to school, so that makes me feel good to know that we sacrificed way back when, and we aren't in that same situation."

"Well Mom, I do appreciate all you and Dad have done for me. Someday it will be my turn to help you, and I'll make sure I will be prepared for that time to return the favor. I have the best parents, and I've known that for many years. Thank you, Mom, and Dad too."

Connie said, "Dinner's ready, will you please get your father. He's probably out in the garage or down in the basement."

"Sure."

Dean was in the garage, and Nicole told him it was time for dinner.

He asked, "What are we having?"

Nicole answered, "It's a surprise. You'll just have to come in and see."

"Okay. I like surprises," he said.

"Wow! Connie, you fixed my favorite meal of ham and sweet potatoes and cranberries. Hey! Is it Thanksgiving already, and I've missed the months in between?"

Connie said, "No dear. I just wanted to surprise you with your favorites."

"Dean said, "You are something else Connie, my dear."

After they ate dinner and cleaned the kitchen, they all went into the living room to relax. Connie was working on a quilt and Dean was reading the paper. Nicole decided to go on to bed so she would be ready for her day with Jim. "Goodnight Dad and Mom. I'm going to bed. I'm a little tired tonight."

Dean said, "We'll see you in the morning. Sleep tight, and don't let the bed bugs bite."

"Okay. Dad you used to tell me that all the time when I was a little, girl, and I never did feel any bugs biting me. Now there are epidemic outbreaks of them everywhere, and they do live in beds and coverings, so we're back to that age when that saying is absolutely true. I hope I never find any though. It will be your fault, Dad, if I do, she said with a smile. "I love you both and goodnight."

The morning sun was bright, and Nicole knew it was going to be a sunny day. She woke up with a smile, and she knew her day with Jim was going to be a day filled with fun.

When she went downstairs, she could smell the coffee, and she saw her parents sitting at the table drinking a cup of the fresh brew.

Her father said, "Well there's the reason for the sunshine. You look beautiful today. Are you seeing Jim by any chance?"

"Yes, Dad, we are going to Columbus for Jim to see if he can find a few roommates to share expenses, and I'm going to see if I can find out who my roommate will be at the dorm. While I'm there, I'll pick up my schedule for the classes I signed up for, go to the bookstore to purchase my books, and then we're just going to do some sightseeing around Columbus. Neither of us are familiar with the sites of the city, and we'd rather locate some of them now while we aren't saddled down with studies and work. We also want to do something fun today, but I don't know what that is.

"On a different subject, I talked with Catherine yesterday. They are preparing to close the resort. They only had one booking for a day of this weekend, and then they are going to close for the season. Catherine said they would probably be leaving in a day or two, but she'll call to let me know. She said that Norman's foot is not healing the way it should, and he wants to go see his doctor in Dayton. They are going to call me before everyone leaves so that I can say goodbye to them. I got pretty close with all of the staff, and they were all so kind and fun. Well, I better eat something before Jim gets here."

Dean said, "I'd like to talk with that boy. He's a nice fellow, and he comes from a good family. I really enjoyed our visit and dinner with them at their farm. That's a pretty place. I hope we get to see more of it one of these days."

"Dad, are you taking your medication on a regular basis as prescribed?"

"I do when I remember to take it," he said.

"Dad, that explains why you're looking a little gray in the face."

"I'm fine."

"Where is your medication?" Nicole asked.

"It's in the bathroom cabinet," he said.

"Well, you're going to take it right now. Do you feel tired?

"I always feel tired. I'm old, and old people feel tired."

"You don't have to feel tired, Dad."

Just as he was taking his medication, Jim knocked on the door.

Nicole asked him to come on in. "I'm trying to get my dad to take his medication on a daily basis. He doesn't remember the last time he took it, and he's looks a little gray to me."

"Let me look at him," Jim said.

"Hello Jim. Don't pay any attention to her. I told her I'm old, and old people look gray."

"Let me check your blood pressure and your temperature. Do you feel clammy and tired?"

"I'm always tired, but I feel fine."

Jim told Dean, "You need to take your medication as prescribed. How long has it been since you took your last dose?"

Dean answered, "I think I took it a couple of days ago. I don't really need it. It doesn't make me feel any better."

Jim said, "We need to get you to the hospital right now. Your blood pressure is very high, and you are sweating."

"Ah, I don't need to go to the hospital. You kids go ahead and go on to Columbus as you had planned."

"No sir, we are taking you to the hospital. Tell me who your doctor is, and I will call ahead and see if he will meet us there."

Connie said, "I will get the information for you."

"Thanks Mrs. Thomas. We need to take all of his prescriptions with us."

Connie said, "I'll get everything ready. Here is his doctor's name and number."

Jim called his doctor and told the receptionist that he needed to talk with the doctor, as it is an emergency. After he got off the phone, he told Nicole and Connie to get in his car and he would drive them all to the hospital.

Dean said, "I don't want to ruin your day together, so go ahead and just drop me off."

"You are more important to us than that, Dad. We can go tomorrow if we can't go today. We want to make sure you are all right."

When they got to the hospital, Dean's doctor met them at the Emergency Room entrance.

"Hello sir. My name is Jim Martin, and I found Dean to have a very high blood pressure. He is clammy to the touch, and his coloring is gray. He also told us that he has not been taking his medication on a regular basis, and that he probably took a pill about two days ago. He did take one about a half an hour ago. Mrs. Thomas has all his prescriptions with her."

"I am Dr. Roberts and I thank you for bringing him here so quickly. Are you a doctor?"

"No sir, I am not one yet. I will be interning at University Hospital in Columbus starting next week. I didn't have my stethoscope in my car, so I don't know exactly what his heart rate was. I tried to get it from his pulse, but it was so fast I couldn't get an accurate count."

"Young man, you may have saved his life. We are stabilizing him right now. He could have died if you hadn't noticed and brought him here."

"Thank you sir, but I want to make sure he is totally okay before he goes home," Jim said.

Dr. Roberts said, "Dean needs to spend a couple of days in the hospital. He is going to have a stroke if he doesn't take care of himself and take his medication daily. You may visit with him until he is taken for testing, then he will be returned to this room, but he will be getting a sedative to relax him, so he'll remain groggy for some time. I suggest you all go home and come back in the morning. I will be doing my rounds starting at seven o'clock tomorrow morning, so you can come back then, and I will tell you the results of his testing."

Connie was worried and asked Dr. Roberts "Is he going to be all right?"

Dr. Roberts said, "Connie, I will tell you tomorrow what our test results reveal. Don't worry because that won't help him or you. You need to get some rest yourself, so have an early evening, and in the morning you'll feel better and we'll be able to understand what we need to do to help him. Okay?"

"Yes, I will do what you've told me to do. Thank you very much."

"Mom, Jim and I will stay at home with you."

"No, you must go to Columbus to do what you need to get done. You can't help me or your dad by just sitting around and waiting. I need you to have your day together to enjoy one another's company. I will be okay at home by myself until you get back. Just make sure your cell phone is charged just in case I need to call you."

"Mom, I hate leaving you alone at home. I know you will worry yourself silly. We can go tomorrow."

"No, Nicole. You are going today, and I don't want to hear anymore about it. Now please take me home, and then be on your way."

Once they returned Connie to her home, Jim said, "Mrs. Thomas we will go, but if you need anything at all, please call Nicole's cell phone, and if we can't be here right away, please call my mother. You have her number don't you?"

"Yes, I do, and thank you Jim for all your help with Dean."

"You are quite welcome."

Jim opened the car door for Nicole, and she sat in her seat looking straight ahead with tears running down her cheeks. He took her hand, kissed it and said, "Your dad will be all right. He's in good hands right now, and your mom doesn't want us to worry, so we need to get done with what we were going to do with the exception of looking around the city. We can do that later when we won't have this cloud over us."

After driving for awhile Nicole looked over at Jim and thought, "I am so lucky to have such a good and caring man with me." She put her hand on Jim's leg and said, "Thank you."

Jim smiled back and said, "Nicole, I am with you in all the ups and downs, and you will never have to worry about me with anyone else. You are what I want as my life partner, and I hope someday you will say the same thing to me. I want you to know that you can always count on me to have your interests and well being first."

"That is what a woman wants and needs to hear from her guy, and you tell me that all the time," she said.

Jim asked, "We are here in Columbus so where would you like to go first?"

"I don't care. Which one is closest to where we are right now is fine by me," she said.

"Let me go to the hospital first to see if I can find some roommates posted. I will copy the list and call each one to see if we could meet before next week. I want to make sure I don't end up with someone who would not be compatible, like a party guy. That's not for me. You probably feel the same way about your new roommate. Am I right?"

"Yes, you are right," she replied.

"Well, we're here," Jim sighed. "Would you rather stay in the car or go in with me? Maybe you should come with me because I don't know how long this might take, and I don't want you sitting in the car all alone."

"Sure, I would like to go with you," Nicole answered.

Jim found a list on the bulletin board, and there were four names and phone numbers listed. He pulled his cell phone from his pocket and called the first name. "Hello, my name is Jim Martin, and I will be interning at the hospital, and I saw your name on the list for a possible roommate. Would it be possible for us to meet sometime this week?"

The man said, "Yes, I would like to interview with you. My name is Alan Hart. Your name sounds a little familiar to me. Where did you go to school?"

"I went to Southeastern High in South Charleston."

Alan said, "What a coincidence. I went to Shawnee, and we played football against one another. You were the center, weren't you?"

"Yes, and I remember you too. Well, since we know one another, maybe we would be a good fit as roommates. Do you know of a house or apartment that could be shared by several guys?"

"A matter of fact, my aunt has a house very close to the hospital, and she wants to rent it out. Would you like to come and look at it?"

"Yes, I would. Have you asked any of the other guys on the list to go in with you?"

"No, because there wasn't anyone on the list when I was there last.

When do you start?"

"I start on Monday, how about you?"

"I start the same as you."

"I have the list with me. Would you want some other guys to share the expenses?"

"Where are you right now, Jim?"

"I'm at the hospital."

"Well, I'm practically across the street from you, and I'm already here, so come on over and we'll talk."

Jim got the address and he and Nicole walked across the street to the house. They walked to the front door and pushed the doorbell.

Alan opened the door, and said, "Come on in. My name is Alan Hart."

"Alan this is my girl, Nicole, and she is a student at the university, and she is with me to check on her own roommate in the dorm."

Alan said, "It's nice to meet you Nicole and Jim. Come on in and look around. I will show you the house and the bedrooms upstairs. My aunt had the house redone to allow her to rent it out to students, so it has four bedrooms and four separate bathrooms. My room is downstairs, and I too have my own bathroom."

"Does your aunt live here too?"

"No, she has a home near my folks in Springfield. Let me show you around. As you can see the house is quite large with lots of room. The kitchen is new and has a microwave, an oven, a dishwasher, a large table and chairs. The dining area was turned into a study room. In the living room she did away with the fireplace because her insurance would be too much with tenants living here and not herself. She has excellent taste in furniture. Let's go upstairs. Since you are the first one to respond, you have the pick of the rooms. Do you see one you might like? And there is a four car garage in the back. There is a small yard, but she has a yardman take care of the outside. We would have to maintain the inside, and I expect all of us to pitch in with keeping it clean."

"Yes, I like the one in the back. It would be a lot quieter with ambulances and traffic and football fans in the front."

Nicole sat on the couch watching television while they talked about the costs involved in renting.

Jim asked Alan if he was open to a few more guys living here to help lower their costs, and Alan agreed to check the other two men on the list.

Alan asked if Jim would be available to help him interview them. "I don't want incompatible renters living here with us."

Jim agreed to help with the interviewing. "Would you like to call these other two men now?"

"Sure. Would you be available to help interview them now?" Alan asked.

"Yes."

Alan took the list and called the other two men interested in sharing a house and expenses. The men said they could be at the house within half an hour.

Jim asked Nicole if she minded waiting, and she said, "No I don't mind at all."

The interviews went well and all four of them would be living at the house and interning at the hospital. Alan said to all of them, "There will not be any overnight guests allowed. You can bring your girlfriends here, but they cannot stay overnight. Everyone understand? This is not a frat house. My aunt owns this place, and she will be checking in on us whenever she feels like it. And, when it comes time for our testing, we know that it will all be at the same time, so I would appreciate all of us spending our time studying and helping one another so we can all pass."

All three of them said, "Yes, of course."

Alan also told them about the garage. "There are four slots for cars. You may only have one car parked in the garage. If you own more than one, it will have to be stored somewhere else."

Jim told Alan that he would be moving in tomorrow and Alan said that would be fine. He paid his rent for the month and was all set to help Nicole with her mission.

Before they left Jim introduced her to David Lowell and Gary Edwards. He said, "This is my girl, Nicole. She is a student at Ohio State, and she will be in a dorm right around the corner, so I'll not only be close to her, but close to my job too."

David and Gary were very happy to meet Nicole, and David asked, "If you have any girlfriends who would like to meet two nice guys, please keep us in mind."

Nicole answered, "I'll see what I can do to find you two nice girls. I study most of the time, so I'm not really a social person when I'm at school. But, if I find some nice girls, I will introduce you to them."

Jim took her hand and led her out the door. "Do you like the house I'll be living in?"

"Yes, I really do. It sure will be convenient for us to see one another, and for you to be close to the hospital."

They were headed on campus to the Scheduling Department where Nicole got her schedule for her classes, and they both went to the book store to purchase used books. Jim said, "These are so much cheaper than the new ones."

Nicole replied. "I have a secret way of helping myself."

"How's that," Jim asked.

"I always look for the highlighted ones, and if the Dean's list is out, I check to see if a book I have in my hand belonged to one of them. Most students who buy a new book put their name in them. Sometimes it works and other times it doesn't. First semester is not a good time for that, because most of these classes weren't taught during summer session, so there won't be hardly any highlighted ones. It doesn't always work. Sometimes you find someone who highlights almost everything, plus you may not have the same professor as the person who highlighted the book."

"Nicole, that's a smart idea. I never thought of that, and I always bought new books to use as references. And you're right. When do you ever use them again? I very seldom used them, if ever.

"How do we go about finding who your roommate is going to be?" he questioned.

"Well, I can go to the dorm and put in a request for a certain type of person. I would like someone who likes to study and not socialize all the time or be on a cell phone continuously. I like it quiet when I study. I retain information better."

"Are you permitted to pick and choose?" Jim asked.

"If you are an upper classman you can. I don't really know since I am a junior, but I'm going to try."

"Well, let's go see what you can do."

They walked into Bradley Hall, and the House Mother was there, and she asked if she could be of help.

"My name is Nicole Thomas, and I will be living in Bradley Hall this semester in room 426 and I was wondering if you could tell me who might be my roommate?"

The House Mother asked, "Are you looking for someone specific?"

"Well, I'm not a social butterfly, and I study a lot. I would like someone who likes a quieter room, and one who studies in the room. I know a lot of girls just go to classes and then party in the hallways when they get through eating the evening meal. At least that is how it was last year."

"Well Nicole, I am going to change your room number to 467. You will be in the back of the dorm looking out over the terrace area. Because you will be in the quieter end, the girls will not be congregating there because the more studious students will be living in the back section of the dorm. We try to put most of the social butterflies in the front of the dorm where the floor residents can keep an eye on them. Will that be all right?"

"Do you mind if I see the room?"

"No I don't mind. I would prefer you see where you will be spending a lot of your time."

"This is my boyfriend, Jim Martin, and he will be doing his residency at University Hospital. Would it be all right for him to come with me to see the room?"

"He won't be allowed after school begins, but for right now, it would be all right."

"Thank you very much."

"Just take the elevator over there to the fourth floor, take a left off of the elevator, and follow it on around until you get to room 467 on the left side. Let me know if it will be suitable for you. I will be here when you return."

Nicole and Jim took the elevator to the fourth floor, turned left and walked forever it seemed to room 467. When Nicole opened the door she was pleasantly surprised. There were two twin beds with two large desks attached together, one facing a bed, and the other facing the other bed. The closets were large, but the community bathroom and showers were down the hall, and it was a long walk to the bathroom.

Jim asked, "Do you think you will like the room with the view?

"Yes, I do like this room. Do you?"

"It's a lot smaller than the room I'll be living in, but you can make it look a lot better if you want," Jim replied.

"Well, let's go see who my roommate will be."

When they got off the elevator the House Mother was sitting behind a counter. Nicole walked over to her, and said, "I like the room. The bathroom was a little far, but I really like the room. Could I please ask if you would know who my roommate might be?"

"Nicole, there is a bathroom right beside your room. Your room is the last room on the floor before the bathroom. The bathroom you will be using covers both sides of four rooms only. We learned a long time ago to assign bathrooms. Yes, I can tell you who your roommate will be. Her name is Virginia Turner, but she goes by Ginny. She is from London, Ohio, and she requested someone like you. I think you will be very pleased. She made the Dean's List both semesters last year, just as you did. All you have to do is fill out this form saying that you have accepted the room, and I will give you the key so you can come any time before Monday, and decorate it within reason, but no holes in the walls. Choose your bed and you will be responsible for your own bedding and pillows. We have a laundry room on each side of the elevator. They take quarters for both. You will have to learn the routine for using them, and you are not to leave clothing or towels in the washer or dryer and leave the room. Here is a pamphlet regarding the rules for the dorm. You will have an 11:00 curfew Sunday through Thursday and a 1:00 am curfew for Friday and Saturday. You must sign in and out every day, and if you are going home for a weekend, you must write that on the sheet. Breakfast is served in the Dining Hall from 6:00 to 8:00 am; lunch at 11:30 to 1:00; and dinner from 5:30 to 7:00 pm. No meals will be served on Sundays. I will be your House Mother, and anytime you need assistance, please fill free to come to me. My door is always open to my girls. I have an assistant on each floor and on each side. They will report to me of any problems, and the problem people will be dealt with. I hope you enjoy your stay here, and I also hope that you and Ginny have a wonderful time being roommates."

"Thank you so much. Are we to call you House Mother, or by your name?"

"I'm sorry. I didn't even tell you my name. My name is Jean Horne."

"Thank you Mrs. or Miss Horne."

"It is Mrs. Horne, and my husband will be living here also. He is the Head of Dentistry for the University. So if you have a dental problem just let me know. And one more thing, I don't think I need to worry about this with you, but the Dean of the University lives right across from our dorm. Everyone is to behave and not have public displays of affection in front of the dorm. I think I have touched upon everything. After everyone is settled in, we will have a meeting here in the living room area to go over everything I have mentioned and possibly some I haven't. You may move in anytime now before Monday. Okay?"

"Since I have a key to my room, I would like to move in tomorrow, if that would be all right?" Nicole asked.

"I already see that you have paid your fees and your rent for the entire semester, so yes, you may move in tomorrow if you'd like, and it is very nice to meet both of you. I hope I will be seeing you tomorrow," Mrs. Horne said.

Jim looked at Nicole and smiled, and she smiled back. "It looks like we both have picked places close to one another, and they will certainly meet our needs. I'm glad that I got to meet your House Mother. She seems to be very nice and accommodating. So, I guess you and I will be making a trip back to Columbus tomorrow to move in to our new places."

Nicole answered, "I hope I can move in tomorrow. It all depends on how my father is doing."

Jim answered, "Nicole, I really believe he is going to be all right. We got him there in time. They are going to be strict with him about taking his medication at a regular time each day, and your mother is going to have to be on him about this. You will not be able to take care of them. They have to take care of this problem."

"I want to call Mom and see if she's all right." Nicole said.

"Hi Mom, are you all right? I just wanted to check on you."

"I'm fine Sweetheart. Have you and Jim taken care of everything you needed to do?

"Yes, we have found housing for Jim, and I can move into my dorm tomorrow. When I get home, I need to pack up a few things from the boxes I put in the basement from last semester. I have a nice quiet room, and it is of ample size for me and my roommate. Our House Mother gave me the key and information about Virginia, or Ginny, as she wants to be called. We were both on the Dean's List last year. I'm looking forward to meeting her. And yes, Jim found a house to share expenses with three other guys. Alan Hart is the one who has the house. It belongs to his aunt who lives in Springfield. The downstairs is beautiful, and very large. The four bedrooms are big and they each have their own bathrooms. There is a four car garage, so each of them will be able to store their cars from the weather. It's all included in the rent. With the four of them renting, the cost won't be so high. All four of them are doing their internship at University Hospital. Jim's place and mine aren't that far apart, maybe a block away."

"That sounds very nice for both of you. Will Jim be helping you move into your dorm?" Connie asked.

"Yes, if Dad is okay we'll be moving in tomorrow, but we'll both be home until Sunday evening."

"Mom, we are on our way home now. Do you need anything?"

"No honey, I don't need anything, but thank you for thinking about me. Be careful coming home. I'll have dinner ready for both of you. Tell Jim I would like him to stay. I have some questions I would like to ask him. I love you."

"Okay Mom. I love you too.

"Jim, Mom didn't sound very chipper to me. She wants you to stay for dinner as she has some questions to ask you."

"Okay. I'll call Mom and let her know I won't be home for a while."

Jim called his mother and told her he was eating at Nicole's house because her mother wants to ask him some questions.

When they got to Nicole's home, the two of them were in such high spirits. They had accomplished almost everything they wanted to do in that day.

Nicole's mother had dinner ready, so they sat down to eat in the dining room.

"Mom, this is so fancy. Why are we eating in the dining room?"

"I just wanted everything to look nice for the both of you."

Jim added, "Mrs. Thomas, thank you so much for asking me to stay for dinner. Nicole said you have some questions to ask me."

"Yes, I do Jim, but first would you please say grace?"

After Jim prayed over the meal he looked at Connie and asked, "What questions would you like me to help you with?"

Connie had tears in her eyes and asked, "Jim, I know you love our daughter, and I want to know that if anything should happen to Dean or me, would you please take care of our Nicole?"

Nicole stared at her and said, "Mom, what is wrong? Why did you ask him that? Do you know something that you're not telling me?"

"No honey, but I just want to be prepared for when something does happen. I know that he loves you, and we couldn't ask for a better son-in-law."

Nicole looked at Jim and said, "You don't have to answer that."

"I want to answer that question so your mother will be at peace. Yes, Connie, I do want to take care of your daughter, so you will have nothing to worry about. I do love her, and I want to spend the rest of my life with her if she'll have me."

The phone rang and Nicole jumped up to answer it. "Hello, Hi Catherine."

"We're all in the dining hall and everyone is here to say goodbye to you. Okay everybody on three, "Goodbye sweet Nicole. We miss you, and hope to see you next summer."

"Catherine, please tell them I wish them the best, and I miss them so much."

Catherine repeated to them what Nicole said. "I also called to tell you we will be leaving Colorado this afternoon, and we'll try to stop on the way back if Norman's foot is not bothering him too much. I'll call you when we are in the state of Ohio. Okay?"

"I can't wait to see you, and I know my folks will be elated too. Dad is in the hospital again, but he will home by then."

"What's wrong with Dean?"

"He hasn't been taking his blood pressure medicine and other medications on a regular basis, and his blood pressure was quite high, so Jim took us all to the hospital where he had our doctor meet us there. We are going to see Dad tomorrow morning and hopefully he should be home before you even reach Ohio."

"Nicole, keep us posted. I know Norman will want to know how he's doing."

"I sure will. Love to all of you, and Mike too. I can't wait to see you. Oh hi, Mike. It's very nice to hear your voice. Are you doing okay? Oh my goodness, you aren't married yet? Well, you'll have to work on your approach. Have a wonderful time back at school and thank you for all you do for Norman and Virginia. I know they love you very much. I love all of you too. Bye now."

When Nicole got off the phone, Jim had a strange look on his face.

Nicole asked, "What's wrong?"

Jim asked, "Are you in love with this Mike guy?"

Nicole said, "Heaven's no. He was like a brother to Catherine and me. When you work at a resort like that you all get very close and become like family. Mike was always looking out for all of us, and he saved me by setting everything up to get me home quickly when we thought that Dad had a stroke. There was nothing intimate with us at all."

"Whew! I was feeling a little apprehensive about that relationship. It made me wonder where we are in ours."

"We are just fine, and I couldn't be any happier, so there," she said.

Jim looked at Connie and asked, "What other questions do you want answered?"

Connie asked, "Do you think that Dean has done damage to himself by not taking his medication on a timely basis?"

"We'll know in the morning if there is any damage. I believe we got him there in time, but they need to teach him about his medications and what happens when he decides or forgets to take them. The ball is in his court, and only he can decide if he wants to lengthen his life or shorten it. As much as I've heard him talk about how much he loves his family, I don't think he will intentionally want to shorten it."

"Well, that helps put my mind at ease. Thank you Jim for everything you've done. I know my daughter loves you. I can see it on her face every time you come near her."

He looked at Nicole and she was smiling and blushing at the same time.

Jim asked Nicole, "Well, what's your answer going to be. Will you marry me in a couple of years?"

Nicole was really blushing, but she said, "Yes, I will marry you in a couple of years when we have our education out of the way and you have your license as a doctor."

"Hey, that's not fair! I have at least four to five more years before I get my license. I don't want to wait that long."

"We'll see," she answered.

"Well, I want to do this properly." He pulled out a small box from his jacket pocket and got down on one knee. He opened the box and pulled out the ring. He looked at Nicole in front of her mother and asked, "Nicole, I know this has been a love beyond my imagination, and I don't ever want to be without you in my life. Will you accept this engagement ring with the knowledge that we will be married one day in the near future? Will you marry me?"

Nicole had tears running down her cheeks, but she smiled and said, "Yes, I will accept your engagement ring with the intent for us to be married in the future."

Jim slipped the ring on her finger and kissed her hand and then her lips. He lifted her off her chair and hugged her tightly. He looked into her beautiful blue eyes, and said, "I will love you forever and beyond."

Connie got up out of her chair and hugged them together. 'I am so happy for the both of you."

Jim gave Connie a hug and said, "I will need to ask Dean for her hand in marriage, but I'll wait until he's home and on his feet again."

Nicole said, "So I am the special person you needed to try on the ring when we were at the mall?"

Jim laughed, "It worked didn't it? I know you suspected I was up to something, but I told you it is for someone very special to me, and that could only be you."

"I need to be engaged for a longer length of time, because I can't get married until I graduate, and that's two years down the road. You will be interning for at least two or three more years, and after you pass your boards you will be interviewed to go to another hospital for your residency, and it might not be near Columbus. Is that right?"

"Possibly, but I could choose to stay at The University Hospital if I am being looked at by them, and they like my work ethic, personality, and knowledge of medicine. I will always want to go back for more training every year with newer methods and instruments being invented. Maybe I will want to work where I find cures for certain diseases. The field is wide open. I just have to find my area of interest. The field of medicine fascinates me. That's why I don't want to farm. That's not where my interests lie. I love the farm, and I love the land, but medicine is my calling."

Connie said, "Jim, I said this before, and I will say it again, you will make a very good doctor. You have a good sense of what to do, when some of us stand frozen and panicked. You told me exactly what to do for my Dean, and I know he is going to be all right."

Jim replied, "I'm glad you mentioned that because I will be here around six thirty in the morning to pick you both up to go see Dean and Dr. Roberts. I have a good feeling about this, and I am sure we will be bringing Dean home."

Connie said, "I certainly hope so. I don't like being all alone in this house without him."

"Well, just make sure you keep on him about his medications, and make sure he takes them the same time every day," Jim advised.

Connie responded, "I certainly will. I don't want him to be in the hospital away from me again."

"Well, I need to go home and collect some things I need to take to my new place of residence across from the hospital. I won't need to take a lot because I'll be wearing scrubs at work. So my trunk will hold both of our things, and we can always pack the back seat if we need to. My room is fully furnished, and there is a huge laundry room with a folding table off of the kitchen. The hospital furnishes the scrubs, and I'll have a locker assigned to me for my street clothes. I have to wear white shoes, and I have extras of them. I'll need sheets to fit a queen size bed along with two pillows, a blanket and a comforter, plus towels and wash cloths. I'll have Mom fix me up in that department. Maybe we'll go shopping this evening for that stuff. So I better get going before it gets too late. I'll see you both in the morning."

Nicole walked him to the car. He turned around facing her. He picked her up and sat her on the hood of his car. She towered over him, so he grabbed her around the waist and pulled her to him. He kissed her then hugged her and told her that he loved her very much. She responded with another kiss and hug. Jim then got in his car, blew Nicole a kiss, and left to go back to the farm.

Nicole and Connie were up and finishing their breakfast when Jim pulled into their driveway. He knocked on the front door, and Nicole let him in.

"I know I am a little early, but I wanted to make sure I was on time."

Connie asked, "Have you had any breakfast? We have leftovers. There are scrambled eggs, toast and a fruit bowl. Help yourself to whatever you want. I also made extra coffee if you'd like some."

"Thank you, Connie. I thought I would be running late so I didn't take the time to eat any breakfast this morning. Mom offered, but I told her I didn't have time. Thank you again. It's delicious Connie."

Connie said, "Nicole made breakfast this morning."

"Wow! You mean I have this to look forward to?"

"She's a very good cook, and she enjoys cooking," Connie added.

"Now there's another great quality to be admired. I know I'm going to love being married to her," Jim added.

Nicole vented, "Hold your horses, Mr. Martin. My life with you is not going to be about cooking, cleaning and taking care of you. I do these things because I love to, not because I'm expected to."

"I'm sorry if I made you feel like you will be the chief cook and bottle washer. I'm handy in the kitchen and in the house, and inside and out. I used to help my mother after Bette left for college, plus I worked on the farm. I think I'm pretty well rounded in both areas. My mom is a very good teacher. Since she worked a full-time job, I was happy to help. She taught me how to cook a complete meal, make desserts, and to clean up afterward. I will always help you Nicole."

Nicole smiled and said, "I know you will."

Connie said, "We'd better get over to the hospital. I don't want to miss seeing Dr. Roberts."

When they arrived at the hospital, Dean was sitting up and eating his breakfast. His coloring was normal, and he looked good. Jim asked him if he felt better, and he nodded.

Connie asked, "Are you all right?

Dean had his mouth full but he pointed to Dr. Roberts as he walked into the room.

Dr. Roberts looked at Dean's chart, then went over to his bed, looked at his skin tone, and said, "Are you enjoying your breakfast, Dean?"

Dean said, "It's mighty good."

Dr. Roberts replied, "Dean you can go home, but I know the nurses have told you that you have to take your medications at the same time every day, and you cannot skip a day. If you don't pay attention to what we've told you, you'll be right back in here, and the next time you may not be as lucky as you were yesterday. You have that young man to thank over there for saving your life. He did all the right things, and I suspect that he is going to make a fine doctor."

"Dean, I want to see you in my office next week. Have Connie call and make an appointment. I will be seeing you two weeks after that appointment just to make sure you are staying on your regiment of taking your medications every day at the same time, and I expect you to be diligent about this. Do you understand?"

Dean said, "Yes sir."

Jim thanked Dr. Roberts for the compliment.

After Dr. Roberts left the room, Dean asked Jim to help him get out of the bed and get dressed.

Just then Jim was feeling very much a part of the Thomas family and he liked the feeling.

Dean looked at Jim and hugged him. "Thank you for all you do for my family, and especially for loving my daughter. I couldn't think of anyone I would rather she be with. I can tell you both love one another."

Jim replied, "Yes sir, we do love one another very much, and since we are on the subject, I would like to ask you for her hand in marriage after she graduates from school. She has already accepted my proposal, but I told her I needed your approval. She is now wearing her engagement ring. I hope I am not doing this backwards, but I want you to be informed of my intentions."

"Jim, you have both mine and her mother's approval. Welcome to the family." Dean put his arm around Jim and hugged him. "You are the son I never had, and I couldn't be happier. I know you will treat my Nicole with lots of love and attention. She is a good girl with a good head on her shoulders, and I believe and trust in her decisions."

"Thank you very much for your trust in me with your daughter. I will never hurt her intentionally. I love her so much."

Connie and Nicole walked back in the room and they both noticed that both men were grinning from ear to ear.

Connie asked, "What's going on in here?"

Dean said, "We were just having a family discussion, and it was very good."

Connie smiled and Nicole looked perplexed.

Nicole asked, "What did I miss?

Dean answered, "A good and wonderful reassurance. That's all."

Connie said, "I have signed all your papers, and we are free to go home, and I couldn't be happier over that thought. These kids have to go move into their housings. Nicole will be in a dorm, and Jim will be in a house with three other guys right across from the hospital."

Dean asked, "Did you two get all this done yesterday? I am very impressed that you got that done so quickly."

"Dad, I even know my roommate's name. It is Ginny Turner and she's from London, Ohio. Maybe you and Mom could come up next Saturday to see my room and also Jim's. He will be living in a beautiful mansion. You and Mom can both come."

"I would love to do that, but I'll have to see how my stamina is by then. If I feel stronger we will definitely make the drive."

Jim said, "Let's get you home."

As they were getting in the car, Dean sat up front with Jim, and Nicole and Connie were in the back. Nicole laughed to herself when she saw Jim smiling back at her in the rear-view mirror. She looked at her left hand with the beautiful diamond on her finger and smiled back.

Once they arrived at the Thomas' home, Jim helped carry his bag, and stayed close so Dean wouldn't lose his balance.

Connie asked if they could wait for a short time while she went to the pharmacy to get Dean's prescriptions filled.

Nicole said, "Take your time Mom, as Jim and I have to load my stuff in the car. We want to get everything moved in today, so we don't have to do it while everyone else is moving in. The upper classmen get to move in first because almost all of them are on the fourth floor. The freshmen are on the first floor so they can be watched a lot easier. Because Ginny and I are were on the Dean's list for both semesters, we get to live on the fourth floor where the seniors and the more studious students will be staying. I'm very happy about that. I take my studies seriously, but some of the freshman and sophomores like to play more and study less."

When Connie returned from the pharmacy, she looked at Dean and said, "It's time for your medication."

Dean responded, "I already took my medication for the day at the hospital. They wanted to make sure I took them. The doses you have are for tomorrow. Did they give you a thirty day supply?"

"Yes dear, they did. Do you want to start you medication at breakfast or at noon tomorrow?"

"I'll let you pick for me," Dean answered.

Connie said, "I think it would be best if you took them with your lunch. Then you'll be good for the rest of the day."

"Whatever you say my dear, I'll do."

Nicole and Jim had just finished loading the car and were ready to leave. Jim walked over to Connie and gave her a hug while Nicole was hugging her father. Then Dean walked over to Jim, shook his hand and said, "Don't be a stranger now. We hope to see you soon. We will try to get up to see you both this next weekend, if you're both available. We'll call Nicole and set a time to meet and maybe go to lunch or dinner somewhere."

Jim said, "That sounds good to us."

"Mom, I'll call you tonight after I get all settled in, okay?"

"Sure. You be careful driving there. We love you both. Bye."

Nicole stopped and ran back to them saying, "I almost forgot that Catherine called and said they would probably be stopping in to see us. I forgot all about it. Maybe we'll drive home tomorrow to see them if they're here. Mom, call me if Catherine calls here at the house. She said she would call when they reached the state line of Ohio. I really want to see all of them, so please call me. Okay?"

"Who's all of them?" Connie asked.

"She said she would be driving Norman's big van because he hurt his ankle or foot, and it's not healing right so he can't drive. Virginia and Catherine are the rest."

Connie answered, "I'll be sure and let you know so you'll have plenty of time to get here. Love you both. Bye."

Jim said, "I need to stop by the farm to pick up a few things I forgot, so I'll hurry."

When they arrived at the farm, Nancy and Dan were sitting on the front porch drinking their coffee. When they saw Jim drive in with Nicole, they stood up and walked to the car. Nicole got out and gave Nancy and Dan a hug.

Nancy said, "I hear you are going to be our daughter-in-law one of these days? I would like to see your ring."

Nicole lifted her hand and showed Nancy and Dan the ring that Jim had bought for her.

"It is very beautiful. Have you set a date yet?"

Nicole answered, "No, it will be awhile until I graduate from college, and he is done with his internship and residency. Then we will make definite plans."

Dan responded, "We'll all be happy when you will legally be a part of our family. We already feel that you are family now, but we will be very happy to have an upcoming wedding. Maybe you might want to consider having it at the farm?"

Nicole responded, "That is a beautiful thought, but we are not even ready to be thinking about a wedding. We just want to get through school and his internship right now, but I cherish your thoughtfulness."

Just then Jim came back to the car with some more items for his room along with more clothes.

He looked at Nicole and said, "You think we might have a little more room for these?"

Nicole laughed and replied, "We'll make room," and they did.

They each hugged his mom and dad goodbye, and drove off toward their new adventure.

Jim asked Nicole, "Would you want to help me take my stuff up to my room first since I don't have as much, or do you want to take your things to your room first?"

Nicole answered, "Let's take your things in first because you definitely don't have as much to haul as I do. Where do you want to start, in the trunk or the backseat?"

"It doesn't matter. Wherever you want to start is okay with me."

Nicole said, "Well, let's clean out the backseat first then it will look like we've accomplished something."

"Okay, I'll pull the stuff out and fill up your arms with what you are able to carry then I'll get the rest. Okay?" Jim asked.

"Sure. Where I am taking what's in my arms?" she asked.

"We'll go in the back door and up the stairs to the back room over the kitchen. That's my room."

As they walked in the kitchen, Alan was sitting there reading and asked if they needed any help. Jim answered, "If you would like to help, it would be greatly appreciated."

Alan took the load of clothes that Nicole had in her arms and walked up the back stairs.

It took them three trips to get everything in. Nicole then organized and hung his clothes in the closet, put his folded clothes in the drawers of the dresser, and placed his shoes on the floor of the closet. Everything was neatly put away in its proper place. Then she made his bed.

Jim thanked Alan for his help, and said, "I will be back later this evening or maybe in the morning. I don't know yet if we are going back to Springfield this evening."

Jim grabbed Nicole in his arms and gave her a whirl. "Nicole, I don't know how to thank you. Your organization skills are fantastic. This looks better than it did at home, not because my mother wasn't neat, but because I wasn't. Thank you again. Now are you ready to tackle your move?"

Nicole told Jim that the dorms have elevators plus rolling carts to help carry everything. "It won't take us very long even though I have a lot of stuff."

Jim parked up against the curb right in front of the steps to the front door of the dorm. He could only park there while unloading then he would have to park the car somewhere else. He raised his eyebrows while he was looking at all that was left in his car. Nicole went into the dorm and retrieved two carts and started placing things on them. The way she packed everything made it so they only had to make two trips with two carts. She organized her closet first then she made her bed. She placed her books on her desk with a lamp and two pictures, one of her parents, and the other with Jim and his parents. She looked at Jim and said, "I'm tired, aren't you?"

Jim, sat on her roommate's chair, and said, "Yes, I am a little tired, but I'm glad we finished placing everything where it needed to be. I'm going to try and keep my room looking as nice as you made it. So now that we're done, would you like to get something to eat? I'm really hungry."

Nicole looked at Jim and smiled, "I'm a little hungry too."

As they were riding the elevator down to the first floor, Nicole's cell phone went off.

Nicole answered it, and it was Catherine. "Nicole, we are in Ohio right now, and I think it will be another couple of hours before we get to Springfield. I just wanted to give you a heads up. We are eating lunch at a restaurant right now but we'll be back on the road shortly."

"Catherine, how are Norman and Virginia doing?"

"They are doing fine. I think they're a little tired of riding, but they're anxious to see you and your parents."

"I'm at the dorm where I'll be living, but Jim and I will be heading home very soon. I think we'll beat you there, but I will call

Mom and Dad and tell them that you are on your way. Please be careful, and we'll see you soon."

"Hello, Mom. I just got a call from Catherine and they are about two hours from reaching Springfield. They stopped to get something to eat near the Ohio line. Jim and I will be on our way as soon as we get something to eat. We got both of us moved in and set up. Jim's place is beautiful. Well, I'll tell you more when we get home. I love you. Bye."

"Jim, where is the car?"

"Oh, I drove it back to my place because it is closer than me finding somewhere to park around here. It's a very short walk."

"Okay. That was a good idea. I have no idea where there is open parking except at the stadium."

"Would you like to eat at that restaurant your Mom took us to?" Jim asked.

"That would be really good right now. I am so hungry," she replied.

"So am I."

After they ate their lunch, they got in the car and drove back to Springfield.

Jim said, "I'll go on out to the farm so you can visit with all of them."

Nicole said, "Please don't leave until you have met them. Catherine has heard so much about you that I want her and the Parkers to meet you. Please say you'll stay? And besides, my mother wants to show you off."

"Okay. I'll stay. Do you want to spend the night in Springfield or do you want to go back to your dorm?"

"Since we'll be home, why don't we just spend the night at home?"

"Well, I should probably go to the farm. It wouldn't look right with me staying all night at your house."

"We have a spare room and bathroom. It would not be an imposition for me or my family. As far as they're concerned, you are already family."

"We'll see how it goes. I may want to go home and see my folks. I don't know when my schedule will allow me to see them again."

"I understand, but you are more than welcome to stay at my parent's house."

"I appreciate the invitation, but I still think I should go back to the farm. Later today we can plan on a time for me to pick you up tomorrow to head back to Columbus. I know I will need a good night's sleep to start Monday off on the right foot."

"That's the same for me. I would like a little time to get to know my roommate since we'll be living together until next June."

After they ate lunch, they headed for Springfield, but the traffic was heavy near the campus entrance as there were cars everywhere trying to get students unpacked and into their dorms. After an hour's drive they reached Springfield. When they pulled into her parents' driveway, Catherine pulled up in front of the house with Norman and Virginia.

When they all got out of their vehicles, Nicole ran to Catherine to give her a hug. Catherine was stretching when Nicole reached her, and she immediately hugged her.

"Wow! It sure is good to see you," Catherine said.

Nicole responded, "I am so glad to see you see. How have you been?"

"We've been fine, but it seems like this trip back gets longer and longer, but I guess age makes it seem that way. Let me help Norman and Virginia get out of the van."

Catherine opened the door and Virginia got out, and then both Catherine and Virginia helped Norman get out of the vehicle.

Nicole gave them a moment to stretch then she hugged them both. Norman was on crutches, and Virginia helped him along.

Virginia hugged Nicole and said, "Norman isn't stable on these crutches, so I need to help him."

Just then Jim came over to help them, and Nicole said, "I'd like you all to meet my guy, Jim Martin. He is Bill's brother. You know Bill, the forest ranger at Estes Park."

Virginia and Catherine both said at the same time, "We've been so anxious to meet you." And then they laughed.

Jim hugged them both and shook Norman's hand.

Norman said, "We have been looking forward to meeting this special guy of our Nicole. She's like a daughter to us, and we only want the very best for her, and she has told us that you are the one."

Nicole responded, "He is very special, and I know you are going to love him as much as I do."

When Connie looked out the window she saw everyone outside, so she and Dean walked out on the porch and down the steps to greet everyone.

Connie hugged each of them, and Dean did the same. "It's so good to see all of you again. It's been such a long time. Please come on in so you can be comfortable."

Jim looked at Norman and said, "Let me help you." Even with his arm in a cast, he picked Norman up and carried him up the steps and into the house where he placed him in a very comfortable chair.

Norman said, "Wow! Jim, you sure do have muscles. I'm not a light weight any more, and I thank you for helping me get into the house."

"That's quite all right. There's no sense in you hurting yourself any worse than you already are. After you have had time to relax with your friends, I would like to take a look at your foot, if it's all right with you?"

"That's right. You are almost a doctor aren't you?

"Norman, I have two years of internship plus two to three years of residency to go before I'm a certified doctor, but I've learned a lot by going to Louisiana during the hurricane catastrophe, and in Haiti during their last earthquake where I was working with the medical teams. If you don't mind me looking at your foot, I might be able to help you."

Dean spoke up, "Norman, he's good. He got me to the hospital this last time before I had a stroke."

"Sure. I would very much like your prognosis," Norman said.

Virginia and Catherine watched as Jim removed Norman's shoe and sock. Jim held his foot in his hand and gently rubbed over the ankle bone and the rest of his foot. He massaged his entire foot and said, "Norman I can't feel where it could be broken, but in my opinion, you have sprained your ankle and that's the reason for all the swelling. You should stay off of it as much as possible, at least for two weeks anyway. If Virginia or Catherine could get you an elastic one piece ankle wrap, it would help if you wore it for a couple hours at a time, especially if you are going to walk on it, but take it off before going to bed. The swelling should go down. You can also let it soak in cooler water if you can stand the temperature for an hour every day. The main thing is to stay off of it as much as possible. I would tell you to continue using your crutches and try not to put hardly any weight on your bad foot. Do you have a recliner at home?"

Norman said, "Yes, I do, and I can't wait to sit in it."

Jim continued, "Don't sit in it all day or else the rest of your body will be stiff. Having the recliner in the reclined position will also help the swelling go down."

"Nicole, you have a real winner here. I really like this young man of yours," Norman said.

Nicole smiled and replied, "Thank you Norman. I think you're right. He is a real jewel to me."

Virginia said, "I like him too. How about you Catherine? Do you feel the same way?"

Catherine responded, "If he makes her happy, then I think the world of him."

Connie got Norman two ice packs and a couple of towels to put under and over Norman's ankle. Then she responded to their conversation about Jim. "He's the best thing since ice cream. Dean and I love him dearly. He's so good to and for Nicole, and we feel very blessed to have him in our family."

Nicole put her arm through Jim's and said. "I'm very happy with my guy."

Catherine said, "I got a call from Todd before we left the restaurant, and he said that Scott left the rangers to take a job with Emily's father's firm. Emily and Scott are getting married. He seems to be very happy now that he has Emily back in his life."

Nicole smiled. "I just hope he treats her right, and I hope they will be as happy as I am with Jim. I can trust Jim with anything, but I couldn't with Scott. After I got to know him, there was always an uneasy feeling about our relationship. I don't have those doubts with Jim, and I am so happy."

Catherine asked Jim, "Do you any doubts about Nicole, and are you as happy as she is about you?"

Jim replied, "With her in my life, I have no doubts, and I am happier than I've ever been."

Virginia said, "We can't stay long. I am very anxious to get home and get Norman in his recliner."

Jim offered, "Would you like me to follow you to help get him into the house?"

Norman said, "Oh no. Thank you for the offer, but I can make it into the house, but I really appreciate you offering."

Catherine and Nicole went into the kitchen, and Catherine hugged her. She said, "Nicole, I wish you and Jim the very best. You look so happy, and he's quite nice looking and a very good hearted man. I couldn't ask for anything else for you. Your happiness means the world to me. I love you little sister. I wish we could spend more time with you, but I've got to get them home. They are very tired, and so am I."

"Will you be spending the night with them?"

Catherine said, "Yes, but I will be heading home in a day or two. I will get him the ankle wrap that Jim suggested and get them all settled in before I head home. I'm tired, and I'm glad the season is over at the resort. Mike told me to tell you he loves you like a sister, and he hopes to see you again someday soon."

"Maybe he can come to my wedding in a few years, as well as you, Virginia and Norman?"

Catherine responded, "You know I will be there for sure as long as the good Lord allows me to live that long."

Nicole said, "It's going to be a very long engagement, Catherine. You will be there, you'll see, because I am going to need you to stand up with me."

Catherine asked, "Let me look at that rock on your finger. Oh, Nicole, that is such a beautiful ring, and I think he has very good taste all the way around."

"I know it's quick, but I already love him so much. His family has accepted me with open arms, and my parents love him dearly. I know God's hand has been involved in us meeting on the plane. Who would have ever thought things would turn out like this? I will let you know when we make plans for our wedding, and who knows where we'll be after he is finished with his internship and residency. It's all in the future, but one thing I can truly say is that this is a summer to remember, and now we are in a new season and there will be more adventures to come."